THE
TICKET

CHRISTIAN H. WECKER

The Ticket
©Christian Wecker

Print ISBN 978-1-66785-782-4
eBook ISBN 978-1-66785-783-1

This book is dedicated to every LAPD Officer who does the thankless job of patrol. Also, to the Los Angeles Police Department, the organization I love, and which has given me so much. May it one day be led to its former glory.

AUTHOR'S NOTE

THE FOLLOWING IS A WORK OF FICTION AND A PRODUCT OF the author's imagination. Any semblance to actual events, persons (living or dead), business establishments, or locales is entirely coincidental.

PROLOGUE

HE GOT A SURPRISINGLY GOOD LOOK AT THE GUY. HE WAS black, about 5'10", 175 lbs., with an orange T-shirt, black Dickies shorts and white shoes. He was probably about 28 years old, which would make him an OG by ghetto standards. The thing that stuck out the most was his 5" natural...you couldn't miss it...but if he got bedded down in a friendly house, he could shave that fucker off and look like a new man in about 15 minutes. The other thing Friedman got a good look at was that cut-down tube. It had the stock cut to pistol-grip and the barrel cut to just in front of the fore grip. Obviously 12 gauge...no question. It looked like Satan's asshole belching fire when it went off about 10 feet from the passenger-side window of their shop. That cowardly motherfucker must have been lying off to cover his homie...

Breathe. Breathe. Breathe. If you don't catch this asshole soon, it'll be too late. He'll be in the fucking wind, and you'll have failed. You'll have to broadcast, and he'll just get captured...that would break the promise. Do you think The Brass will consider this splitting up? Jesus...focus! Who gives a fuck what they *think? The things you think of when the shit hits the fan. Where the fuck am I? Figueroa's to the east...we were rolling northbound on Hoover* *from Manchester when it all went down…long blocks…an east/west alley… feels like north of about 82nd…Breathe.*

They had sworn to conduct no more police work. They didn't have to anymore. Everything had changed, and they were only biding their time. Getting revenge, in the way that only ghetto patrol coppers dream of, for many years of getting fucked-off by everyone…The Brass, the citizens… anyone who could shit on an average Blue Suiter. They were slowly amassing a string of bizarre complaints, generated from inside and outside the Organization, which would elevate them to mythical status when they finally went southbound through the houses. Fuck that urban legend of a motor cop who rode his Kawi up the elevator of old Parker Center and left it for the bewildered pogue Sergeant, claiming he was "returning all city equipment upon retirement as required." Even if that story *were* true, he was a fucking piker. They had planned everything, done all the necessary research, checked with their own high-priced legal vultures. They were having the time of their lives, exacting payback on a baffled command staff and slowly getting labeled as suicidal (career-wise) by their peers. It was fucking magical. It was just about time for them to retire In-Lieu-of-Termination and let the cat out of the bag at the Desert Room during the 77th Street Unofficial Christmas Party. How could everything have gone *so* wrong, *so* quick?

CONTENTS

CHAPTER 1

REDBONE AND FRIEDMAN

IF THIS BITCH MOVED ANY SLOWER SHE'D BE STOPPED. I'M pretty sure she's asleep. How is it that a person who types for a living can only type 15 words per minute? Fucking city workers. I swear she punches a key, and then checks to see if the letter appears on the screen...is that possible? I will not stoop to her level. Two can play at this game. I'm going to kill this slacker-ass with kindness. Fuck it...I'm on overtime anyway...

The 77th Street Jail used to be legendary department-wide for its slowness. Friedman had been booking bodies there long enough to know that much of that was undeserved criticism from high-speed, low-drag, uptight young cops. He used to be one after all, and he'd had his battles. With time he learned that you get more flies with honey than vinegar, but he was still driven periodically insane by some of the LAPD civilian staff. In fact, the jail was much better and faster than it ever had been since some of the older civilian supervision had retired. It was rapidly becoming the go-to jail in the city.

While he waited for the Slowest Human on Earth, he recalled the time he verbally thrashed an older female civilian jail supervisor several years ago in front of her subordinates. He had been down in the jail (beneath 77th Street Station) to book a whore and had a female police officer strip-search her while she waited to book her own body. When his turn came up, the jailer behind the glass told him he needed to have someone conduct a pat-down search on his arrestee.

Friedman had never seen this jailer before and assumed he was new, so he scanned his nameplate and explained patiently, "Mr. Rodriguez, this young lady has just been strip-searched because of her narcotics priors. So no pat-down search is necessary."

Jailer Rodriguez was having none of it though. He insisted the search be conducted at the window in his presence, telling Friedman, "It's protocol."

Thinking he must be confused, Friedman tried to educate him, "A strip-search is much more in-depth than a pat-down search. There's no need to search her again."

After more insistence, it finally became apparent this new jailer had been coached. Friedman asked the same female police officer to come over and conduct a pat-down search to satisfy the jailer, which she did with knowing looks.

Mr. Rodriguez then began to revel in his new role as police dominator.

"You need to put your name and serial number on the yellow medical screening form," he demanded.

Friedman told the now-smug jailer, "I already have," and pointed through the glass to the back of the sheet.

Rodriguez flipped the form back through the hole with panache, and informed Friedman with an air of superiority, "You need to sign in the box on the front too."

This was almost too much.

Resisting the urge to reach in and drag jailer Rodriguez through the 4 by 6 inch opening at the bottom of the inch-thick safety glass, Friedman pointed out the section of the form and read out loud for his benefit,

"If this is your Department's primary medical screening form, do not fill out this box."

Rodriguez the jailer shrugged and told him, "I've been told to make you guys sign both front and back."

In a masterful display of composure, Friedman complied.

Upon completing the booking process, Friedman sought out the jail supervisor and attempted to explain to her what had just unfolded at booking window five.

He pointed out, "It was slightly unreasonable to insist on the pat-down search requirement in light of the fact that a strip-search had just been conducted."

The supervisor practically shouted, "If officers weren't so inept in their searches, then jail staff wouldn't have to insist the pat-down be conducted in their presence!"

Friedman maintained his poise, realizing that she wanted him to lose control in front of the now attentive jail staff so she could beef him. He calmly changed the subject to the medical screening form.

"I also think we should be following the directions as indicated on the Los Angeles Sheriff Department forms."

She bluntly informed him, "The LASD demands it be that way, so you should just do what you're told."

The gauntlet had been thrown down, and Friedman accepted... professionally.

"Supervisor Acosta," he addressed her formally. "Are you aware the 77th Street Jail has a city-wide reputation for laziness? In my view this is a supervisory issue. Your behavior is the exact reason there is friction between officers and certain jailers."

"How dare you call my whole staff lazy!" she shouted.

He countered with a roll call of dependable, hardworking jail staff that he knew personally, but questioned her ability to motivate certain jailers.

"We were just commended by South Traffic Division for our work ethic!" she bellowed.

Seeing an opening to verbally disembowel her, Friedman paused briefly to mentally compose his response to that gift.

"With all due respect, Ma'am, being commended by South Traffic for your work ethic is like being commended by the French for your military," Friedman retorted.

Unbeknownst to Friedman, Supervisor Acosta's son worked South Traffic Division and she exploded with indignant malevolence.

"How dare you! Officers like you want to be put on a pedestal and want the detention officers to be subservient!" She screamed.

"Madam. I was raised to believe that officers *should* be put on a pedestal," he countered. "And I'm not interested in you being *subservient*; I want you to be *subordinate*. The most senior civilian detention officer is subordinate to the newest probationary police officer. Without us, you don't have a job. You need to understand your role as *support services*."

To say the least, this ended the discussion.

The next day, jail supervisor Acosta and one of her minions attended 77th Street morning watch roll call with a long list of grievances—everything from A to Z that officers regularly did wrong. Friedman was off, but some of his friends called to let him know the morning watch crew had given her both barrels, but his name was being bandied about as a rabble-rouser. Apparently, she left roll call beaten and angry, then went straight to the watch commander.

Realizing she would file a complaint against him and that some self-defense was in order, Friedman drafted a "To Whom It May Concern" letter, written from the perspective of a fictitious female jailer who had witnessed the entire exchange in the jail. The letter backed up Friedman's point of view and stressed his professionalism while decrying the behavior of the supervisor. He came in on his day off and posted it in a place where it was sure to be read and dispersed.

When the inevitable meeting with Captain Cox came, Friedman was ready. The Captain, like nearly all LAPD Captains, believed he was omniscient and began their little chat with an earnestly stated desire to right any wrongs.

Friedman knew better though, and told him, "I know it's easier to order *me* to leave the jailers alone than it is to fix the problem…so I'll be sure to suck jail dick in the future."

The Captain was incredulous at having his thunder stolen so quickly…he was eventually going to tell Friedman to suck jail dick…but he'd be damned if he wasn't going to get the privilege of ordering him to. He insisted that if there were problems, he'd like to hear what they were. Unfortunately, being a member of the elite LAPD command staff, Captain Cox was not accustomed to hearing the truth. Friedman told the stunned Captain the problem was systemic with civilian employees and spanned beyond the jail to include the records section, the Police Service Representatives and the property clerks.

"What do you think the biggest issue is, Officer?" the Captain asked.

"Basically, we hire shitty people from within the local community, Sir," Friedman replied.

"Whoa, whoa, whoa…now that sounds racist!" Cox said. "I was raised-up down there in Watts, and when I hear something like that, I just don't know what to say…"

"My point exactly Sir! *You* are my argument! Anyone who has worked in the South End for more than 5 minutes knows that 85 percent of the people here are good, hard-working, blue collar folks…what the fuck are we hiring the 15 percent for?" Friedman asked.

Stunned into silence by the logical truth, Captain Cox was sure Friedman was fucking with him. He recovered quickly though, and fell back on negative discipline, the mainstay of the LAPD staff officer.

"Detention supervisor Acosta wants to file a formal complaint against you for your behavior."

Friedman smiled inwardly and told him, "I understand there is a letter circulating which backs my version of events, Sir..."

The Captain had seen the letter...his sneaky adjutant Sergeant had secured a copy for him...and he knew it was too well written to have come from any jailer, but could never say *that* out loud. He just sighed and wondered how close he was to pulling the pin so he'd never have to look at another veteran Police Officer II like Friedman. They were a command officer's worst nightmare...no aspirations, working patrol in the shittiest Divisions, on the shittiest shifts, content to actually be patrol officers and generally too smart for their own good...and practically untouchable unless they made a big mistake.

Friedman finally finished getting his body booked, and after profusely thanking the Slowest Human on Earth for the overtime cash, he headed back upstairs to meet his partner to complete their arrest.

"What took so long?" asked Redbone. "I've been done here for almost an hour."

"I got down there about half an hour before their watch change and couldn't get anyone to make eye contact with me. Then I got porked by the jail gods and drew that ignorant fuck Clark...I thought she died there for a second, but it turned out she was just hibernating." Friedman replied disgustedly.

He passed the jail paperwork over to Redbone, who began to quickly and efficiently fill out the proper boxes before getting the report signed by the watch commander. He was anal about checking boxes and putting all the appropriate titles in the right places. Friedman had long since quit caring about such things.

The Ticket

"You want me to take it in there? That wise-ass Sgt. Garcia is sitting in the seat."

"Nah," replied Redbone, "I'll take my chances…we're over anyway… it doesn't matter if he makes me write the whole thing again."

Timothy Patrick Obrador had five years on the job. He was 32 years old but looked about 20. Everyone thought he was a rookie because he worked with Friedman, and the sergeants continually scrutinized his work as if he were fresh out of the Academy. He was thin and lithe, about 5'10" and covered with red fur. His hair was copper-red, and his arms and face were thick with the stuff. (When he grew an impressive moustache people on the street quit fucking with him so much.) His folks were from the East Coast, but he was born and raised in Riverside, California; aka Rivertucky; aka, The I.E.; aka, The Desert. From his Irish mother he inherited his ginger-ness, his temper and his drinking ability. When the last two came together (and they often did) it could (and often did) create a shit-storm of problems. His father was a Sephardic Jew, whose only tie to Judaism was the festivals. From him he inherited his Spanish last name. He had recently decided to receive Confirmation in the Catholic Church, which made his maternal grandmother ecstatic and Friedman nervous. Friedman was born and raised Catholic but was like Redbone's dad…connected by funerals and weddings. He had tried to explain that Catholics were born, not made. Joining a religion as an adult smacked of Mormonism or Scientology or some other cult, but Redbone would have none of it. He was now officially completely Irish. He was also semi-miserable in that he had just been fucked over by the CHP with a drunk driving arrest and had been forced to move back into his parents' house. It was a crushing blow financially but earned him some street cred at 77th Street, where it was once famously said, "You're not a real cop until you've been booked."

He also had the distinction of being the first cop anyone had ever seen wearing an ankle bracelet monitor in uniform. The DA in Riverside County was a dick and insisted that as part of his probation he would have to be monitored electronically for two months. He couldn't even zip up his boot because the thing was so big. It made him kind of a hero to the younger cops and earned him respect from the older ones. It made him an instant asshole to the command staff. He had the misfortune of arriving at 77th Street Division at a time when there was another Obrador, and to differentiate between the two he got nicknamed Redbone. The other guy left, but the name stuck, and that's what most people still called him. Redbone is an old Southern term for a red-haired, copper-skinned, freckled black person. Red Fox was a redbone. Malcolm X was a redbone. Timothy Patrick Obrador was a redbone. In a division like 77th Street, it caused a lot of amusement among the black population to overhear officers calling him Redbone. The officers never thought twice because it was his name to nearly everyone…including the supervision. A large percentage of the white and Hispanic officers had no idea what a redbone was, unless they had spent time working the southern end of Los Angeles, but it made him distinct…and an accepted part of the morning watch crew.

Christoph Lewis Friedman was a different story. He was 42 years old, about 6 feet tall and roughly 195 pounds. He had a full head of dark brown hair and bluish/greenish eyes that made him an object of desire for nearly every black woman (over 250 pounds) that he ever encountered. "Hey, Green Eyes" was as common a greeting as "Good evening, Officer" for Friedman while working in The Hood. He'd been a cop for 18 years and had spent the last 13 or so working morning watch at 77th Street. He liked working the 6 p.m. to 6 a.m. shift and was always pissed when the command staff bumped him to day watch for three deployment periods. They did that periodically because one of the Hollywood Burglars (that group of cops that got busted for committing burglaries in the '80s up in Hollywood Division) told the investigators he did it because he was "too close to the guys." Bullshit, of course, but they bought it hook, line and sinker, and the bump policy was the command staff answer. So, every once in a while, he had to break out the sunblock and sweat because he inevitably got moved for those three months during summer. Friedman had a silver tongue

The Ticket

and could motherfuck someone one second and the next be thanked for being so professional. He rarely received citizen complaints, was generally respected by his peers and could be relied upon by the field sergeants to handle his shit. In short, he was a professional Patrol Officer. Friedman was stubborn when it came to his personal honor and despised Office pogues, Climbers, Ass-Kissers, Politicians, Lawyers and most LAPD civilians.

He detested almost everyone over the rank of Lieutenant and, in turn, was detested *by* almost everyone over the rank of Lieutenant. He never cared. He felt it was the responsibility of senior patrol officers to stand up for what was right and against what was wrong...politics be damned. Friedman also labored under the belief that those who sought and accepted the privilege of command had an obligation to protect those they proposed to lead. He was regularly disappointed by LAPD's version of leadership.

Redbone and Friedman worked well together. Neither were elephant hunters...they didn't care whether their arrests were felonies or misdemeanors. They only worried about trying to do what was right when it came to enforcement. Some of their most satisfying capers were misdemeanors, and they knew from experience that if you "got the stink off early" with a chicken-shit misdemeanor arrest, oftentimes a kick-ass felony would fall in your lap later in the shift.

CHAPTER 2

PROVIDENCE

THEIR NEXT SHIFT WAS FRIDAY NIGHT, AND FRIEDMAN WAS walking into the underground parking structure after roll call to get their car loaded.

"What shop did you get?"

"87230," Friedman replied, "Why?"

"I thought so...I'm pretty sure that's the one that smells like piss," said Redbone. "Better change it before we load it up. I can't handle driving around in that thing for 12 hours again."

"Good call," Friedman said as he flipped around and headed back to the kit room to exchange the keys for a less ripe vehicle.

Fiscal times being what they were in the City of Los Angeles, the LAPD was cutting corners everywhere they could. Officers qualified with their side arms only a few times a year, and most of their cars were beat down and had nearly 100,000 miles on them. That doesn't seem like much until you consider how they got driven, and with 24-hour coverage they got used and abused practically nonstop. There were countless other "cost-saving" measures in place...all while the Department continued to hire new officers to keep the workforce at 10,000. The mayor had hitched his political wagon to the LAPD star, and one of his big posturing points was that magic number, even though only about a third of LAPD cops were actually working as field police officers or table detectives. The rest performed "administrative functions" or worked secret squirrel jobs, which was a constant source of torment to Friedman.

The LAPD was famously understaffed when compared to other major metropolitan police departments. But the reality, as Friedman saw it, was they had more than enough people to do the job. What they really needed was about 8,500 working police officers and detectives, with a sizeable staff of civilians working support. His view was that every time a cop retired they should replace him with a civilian until they got to that number. That would eliminate cops doing office pogue jobs and get them in the field where they belong. The unfortunate rule at LAPD was, "Give us two years on patrol, and we'll give you a lifetime of stories." The cops working inside jobs thought anyone working the field was either a fool or lacked ambition. Friedman always thought the pogues were disingenuous at best and outright cowards at worst. No one ever told their oral board when they were applying, "I'd like to work patrol until probation is over, then I never want to wear a uniform again. I think I'd like to work some kind of audit detail or maybe be a secretary for some captain until I can be promoted through favoritism."

Friedman became an officer to make a difference, and while he had done a two-year vice tour at 77th Street, he thought working patrol was where the game was played. Like many south-end cops, he also thought if you hadn't worked the ghetto then you shouldn't claim to be an LAPD officer. As the saying went, "If you haven't had a 12 (77th Street Division) or an 18 (Southeast Division) on the trunk of your shop, you haven't been the Po-lice".

"I take it we didn't win on Tuesday," said Friedman as he drove up to the gas pumps to fill up before starting the shift.

"Negative. But tonight is the big one...nobody won...it's up to like 330 Million. I'm pretty sure I could live with that." Redbone replied.

They played the lottery religiously and had a theory that the only people who ever won were illegal immigrants, old people and slacker-assed ghetto crack heads. Their practice was to buy their five-dollar ticket at the nastiest liquor store they could, thereby tricking the lottery gods. It was their fondest dream to rob South Central of millions of dollars in Lotto money as payback for years of being taken for granted.

"We better hurry over and get our fiver ticket before the shit hits the fan and we miss the 7:45cut-off." advised Redbone.

"Done and done," replied Friedman as he adjusted the seat, still warm from the last driver. "Christ in a sidecar! Who the fuck was driving this thing last!? We gotta quit hiring dwarves...I'm telling you Redbone, the days of the six-foot-tall cop are over. But you never know...they could be poised for a comeback...I think we've hired all the 4'11" humans in the country...we're running out of options."

They drove south on Broadway from 77th to westbound Manchester to hit their favorite liquor store over on 92nd and Western Avenue. That store had a constant stream of losers, baseheads and drunks loitering in the parking lot, drinking cheap booze and smoking crack. Friedman had assured Redbone that if they were ever going to trick the gods, that would be the place to make it happen.

"Officer Fryed-man!" shouted an improbably named basehead called Smokey. "Where the fuck you been? I ain't seen you since you ate shit cha- sin' that mothafucker in the G-Ride down the alley ahind the bungalows!"

This amused the other dregs standing around, and they all high- fived and backslapped each other.

"I told you before, it's 'Freed-man,' Smokey," admonished Friedman with a smile, as he hopped out of the driver's seat, "and I would've had that bitch-made '90s motherfucker if I didn't fall...and you know we caught him in the perimeter anyway...that's how we roll in 77th Street..."

This also amused the crowd, who all knew Friedman from multiple contacts over the years.

Friedman and Redbone had chased a stolen car about a month prior, and the Rollin' 90's Crip who was driving had crashed into one of the big green alley gates that South Central has at the end of most alleys. The gates were designed to keep crackheads out, but they basically created cages that kept the crackheads in and the *cops* out. The gate had fallen on the car, pinning the driver's side door shut, and they thought they had the guy dead to rights, but he had other plans. While they were holding the car at gunpoint, waiting for back-up to arrive, he elbow-smashed the driver's window, jumped out and ran southbound through the alley from 92nd Street. Friedman approached the car, cleared it for additional suspects and then attempted to jump over the downed gate to go in foot pursuit. Unfortunately, he caught the toe of his Danner boot and fell hard. His Glock 45 went flying, and he gouged the shit out of his right knee and both hands. Redbone forgot everything, pointed at him and started laughing.

"You ate shit!" he screamed, barely able to stand as he convulsed.

The liquor store parking lot vermin witnessed the whole thing and joined in with Redbone, amazed at their good luck to have had a front row seat to watch an LAPD cop crash and burn. Friedman reeled in Redbone and told him to chase the motherfucker while he'd set up a perimeter. One of the responding units captured him almost immediately, and Friedman drove over to where they had him, anxious for some payback.

When he got there, the suspect took one look at his bloody hands and torn pants and began to apologize.

"I'm so sorry Officer! Man! You a-ight? I'm on parole for a G-ride, so I had to run...you know...you gotta job...I gotta job. I'm real sorry you got hurt…you gonna be a-ight? You need a amberlamps…you bleedin' bad. Damn!"

Friedman was extremely pissed about his $150 pants being torn and none too happy about his Glock getting scratched up. He would have liked nothing more than for the guy to struggle (even a bit) so he could waffle-stomp his ass, but he was so cooperative, and so genuinely sorry he'd been hurt, that there was nothing for it but to be professional.

"You got those warrants taken care of, Smokey?" asked Redbone, "Cause if you want to, we can get that handled for you right now…just a quick trip to 77th, and you'll be good to go. It'll be a burrito and a little apple for dinner…"

"Officer *Freed*-man say I was cool wit those," replied a suddenly nervous Smokey, who sidled up to them and spoke with a hushed tone so the other crackheads couldn't hear. "He say I was cool for helpin' him out wit that *thang*"

Friedman and Redbone had jammed up Smokey a while back for drinking in the liquor store parking lot, and when they found out he had about $65,000 in misdemeanor warrants, they asked for his "help." They were having a Burglary From Motor Vehicle problem west of Western and south of 92nd Street. The neighborhood was clean and relatively crime free and was filled with older, retired black folks that couldn't afford to be replacing their car windows and stereos twice a month. Smokey gladly told them who to look for, what time the individual was conducting his malfeasance and where he was disposing of his ill-gotten gains. The information resulted in the suspect's capture and fixed the BFMV problem for the time being. Friedman gave him a six-month pass on his warrants and told him to take care of them on his own during that time. He wouldn't, of course, but when his time was up there would probably be another problem he could "help" with.

"He's cool for a while yet, Redbone," said Friedman, "But I think you might be mistakin' my kindness for weakness, Smokey…"

"You right. You right. My bad…I'm straight."

They walked in the liquor store and gave a head's up to the Korean owner. He was kind of standoffish with the police for fear of getting a reputation of being on the wrong team. He knew where his bread was buttered for sure. His employees were cool though and knew Friedman and Redbone by name. They were older black men, who had nothing to fear from the parking lot crowd because they had the power to ban them from the store.

"You want the usual fellas? Sure you don't want to double up?" said the huge black man behind the counter, "It's gettin' big…"

"Nah…you know we're not gonna win anyway," replied Redbone as he tossed a five-dollar bill under the inch-thick protective glass. "We just keep givin' the state our money every week."

The big man laughed and passed their ticket through the glass. Redbone pocketed it, and they walked back out to their shop. The baseheads had all wandered off because they knew that the mobile crack dealer would never enter the parking lot with a black-and-white there. They'd be back within 30 minutes, but for now the place was deserted.

CHAPTER 3
PATROL

"ANYTHING YOU NEED TO DO? YOU GOT YOUR GAME FACE on?" asked Friedman.

"Not a thing…brought my lunch, no need to eat…we're in business," Redbone said as he hit the button on their shop's Mobile Data Computer that logged them on.

He then hit the button that showed them clear, but because they were assigned to work 12Z4 and weren't subject to regular radio calls they knew they still had a little time to chill.

LAPD patrol generally ran a couple types of radio cars. The "A" car was the most common and represented the main day-watch and morning-watch cars assigned to handle radio calls. The "X" cars represented mid-watch cars. The "Z" cars supplemented the "A" and "X" cars, but were generally assigned to handle special problems or special areas and handle radio calls only when the others got overwhelmed. In 77th Street Division, the regular patrol units got overwhelmed every Friday and Saturday night for sure and often other nights, too.

There were myriad letter designations for the radio-call signs of the specialized units within the department, ranging from the guy who did the random piss testing to the Big Chief. Everyone had a call sign on the radio, and the longer and more complicated, the more important you felt you were.

Friedman preferred to work an "A" car, but for some reason they had been assigned to a "Z" car for almost a year. This was good and bad. Some officers thought it meant they could pick and choose their calls or just focus on observation arrests, but in reality it meant that you did what you wanted until the division exploded...then you got activated by the watch commander and assigned everyone else's shit calls.

The night was warm, and Friedman knew things would jump off later because everyone had been drinking all day. They drove around the division and checked out all the local trouble spots and chatted with several people they knew...both citizens and criminals. In an area where many of the residents had never seen the ocean (even though it was only about a 20-minute drive) the police and police activity represented a diversion from daily life.

As Friedman had told Captain Cox several years ago, 85 percent of the people who lived in South Central Los Angeles were good blue-collar people. They worked for the DMV, the County or City, in construction or many other normal, hard-working jobs. Redbone and Friedman viewed their job as the protectors of the 85 percent. The 15 percent were well protected by politicians, the ACLU, pro-bono lawyers and activists of all kinds. None of those people had to live in 77th Street Division and fear for their kids, their property or their lives on a daily basis. They loved to give sound-bites to the news and quotable quotes to the *Los Angeles Times* rag about police abuse and unequal enforcement in "South Los Angeles" as they had re-named the area after the '92 Riots. They must have forgotten about Watts, the Strip and San Pedro...all of which are south of South Central.

Friedman always called it South Central, because that's what everyone who lived there called it.

They got activated to handle calls early and spent the majority of the night going from house party to house party. Most of the calls were for family parties that had ridiculously loud DJs. Seventy-Seventh Street Division was experiencing the same demographic changes that most of South Central was experiencing. It was traditionally a black area, but starting in the east and marching west, the population was becoming increasingly Hispanic.

By some estimates, the Division was now 50-50, with most of the Hispanics being Mexican, with a smattering of Salvadorians and Guatemalans. Tension was always high between the blacks, who saw the Hispanics as invaders, and the Hispanics, who saw the blacks as predators. Friedman spoke Spanish (one of his ex-wives was from South America) and had a lot of family from southern states, so he could identify with both groups pretty readily. One of the upshots of the racial tension in South Central was that nearly every call they went to they were alternately told, "If we were black, you wouldn't be doing this," or, "If we were Hispanic, you wouldn't be doing this." Redbone and Friedman always tried to hit the parties early and tone them down if they were family gigs, or end them if they were gangster parties or house raves. The key was to get them handled early before everyone got drunk and emboldened…because that's when the rocks and bottles would start flying.

By about 3 a.m., things had mostly settled down and 12Z4 had some time to relax and do a little snoop and poop.

"Let's roll up Fig," said Redbone. "See if anything's going on…the whores were deep yesterday, and I bet they're out like flies right now since it's payday and all."

They say that "Once a Vice cop, always a Vice cop," and Friedman was no different. He had taught Redbone that the whores were a wealth of knowledge and, if treated with respect and a firm hand, would always help out when needed. The Figueroa corridor was home to the largest prostitution problem in the City of Los Angeles. The Hollywood of *Pretty Woman* fame was a thing of the past…most of the hookers up there did Internet work, out-call to hotels or had regulars that they dealt with exclusively. The LAPD still considered Hollywood Vice to be the cream of the Vice crop, and they over-staffed the unit with a Lieutenant, two Sergeants and a ton of officers…it was ridiculous. The 77th Street Vice unit was seriously understaffed, with two Sergeants (usually), and maybe 10 officers at any given time…equally ridiculous, but for the opposite reason. Some nights the corners of Figueroa north of Florence Avenue were like a circus…four girls on each corner and traffic backed up around the block. Redbone and Friedman always cruised Fig and shooed the girls off in their own strange language, admonishing them to get off "The Track." They knew Vice was overwhelmed and tried to help out, even though Friedman had been told by an old timer that "There was whores on Fig when I started 30 years ago, and there'll be whores on Fig when you retire in 30 years."

"Hey Jackie," called Friedman as he hit the curb at 69th Street and Figueroa. He jumped out of the black-and-white. "What's been going on?"

Jackie was one of the few Hispanic prostitutes who worked the Figueroa Track. She had a regular partner named Showanna, who was always nearby, and they looked out for each other. Friedman suspected that they might be two of the only renegades on the track, but it was always hard to tell because Rule No. 1 was never admitting to the police that you have a pimp. A renegade was a pimp-less whore who basically ran a sole proprietorship and kept all the profits. Both Showanna and Jackie were young and pretty…real moneymakers…so he always found it hard to believe that they hadn't been turned out by some greedy criminal.

"Hey Green Eyes," said Showanna, emerging from a shadow nearby. "Where you been, Redbone? You guys been on days off?"

"You know it. How's business been?"

"Good. Always good," replied Showanna "How's business with you boys?"

Showanna was funny. Friedman had jammed her up once when he knew she had a felony warrant. She had kicked off her heels, slipped the grip from a rookie he had been working with and was off like the wind. Freidman had never seen anyone run so fast. She hitched her dress up around her waist (sans underwear) and took off like a track star. She was short and stout…didn't even look like a runner, but with her arms pumping and knees high she simply ran away from the rookie, who was no slouch. Friedman had hopped in the car and driven after them to get the rookie after he gave up. He caught her several days later, and she was unapologetic. "That rookie was slow. Ya'll need to train more." Turned out she ran track in high school and was scouted by some of the best schools in the United States before she changed career paths.

12A15 drove up while they were working the girls for information. Most of the Figueroa prostitutes tried to flirt with the cops to let them stay on the Track, and it worked regularly with the younger guys. These two, Robinson and Williams, knew Jackie and Showanna from multiple flirtatious contacts and couldn't resist stopping to hang out.

They got out of their black-and-white to chat, and after a while the conversation turned to the two girls. Friedman told them the story of Showanna running away from the rookie, and they all laughed, but Redbone wasn't buying it. He knew he was fast, and swore up and down he could never be outdone in a street race by some hooker.

"I don't know about you guys, but I'd put my money on Redbone," said Williams, laughing.

Friedman countered, "Listen, bro…I've seen Redbone in action and he's fast, but I'm telling you this chick is dynamite. You remember that rookie Del Pinto? He was stick thin and built for speed. She made him look like he was standing still. She shot across Fig…fuck traffic…and was half a block away before Del Pinto even knew what was happening."

"Maybe if we were racing across traffic she might get the upper hand because of adrenaline, but in a one-on-one street race I could take her," proclaimed Redbone.

"I beaten girls twice my size…I bet I could take you, Redbone," Showanna boasted.

Friedman thought about it for a second and came to a decision.

"Tell you what we're gonna do. You guys can use 69th Street. I'll block Fig with my black-and-white, and you guys use your shop to block Denver. I'll call it. Make sure you got your camera on…this'll be sweet to show the guys in roll call," declared Friedman.

LAPD had recently installed a Digital In Car Video system in all the South Bureau shops for testing. South-end cops believed their bureau was picked because they were always perceived as dirty by the command staff and activists alike.

The DICV system had a camera facing front and another in the back seat of every black-and-white on patrol. The officers also wore synced microphones that captured their conversations when the system was activated. It automatically activated itself when they turned on the car's overhead lights, and they were required to self-activate it on all pedestrian stops.

Friedman and Redbone both liked the DICV because they generally handled their shit correctly and it squashed a lot of beefs, but most of the cops felt it was just another game of "Gotcha" being played by the Department. Like always, it was a great tool if command staff didn't abuse it, but the general consensus was that the Brass could never be trusted to do the right thing if there was a second option. The other point of contention was the cost. LAPD was spending millions of dollars on the system when they were starving other vital areas. Friedman always felt DICV was a good idea, but thought it was a fiscally horrible time to be spending money to satisfy the LAPD haters of the world. He intended to put it to good use, though.

"What if Showanna wins? What's in it for us?" asked Jackie.

"What do you want?"

"You guys can never mess with us again. We get to stay on the Track as long as we want."

"Come on Jackie," Friedman said. "You know how we feel about your business, but we gotta job to do. Be realistic. What if Redbone wins? You guys plan to stay off the Track forever?"

"Six months then," negotiated Showanna.

"Tell you what…three months…and only from me, Redbone, Robinson and Williams…to everyone else, you're fair game. Fair enough? But if she loses, then you guys gotta stay off Fig for three."

"I'm gonna whoop your ass, Redbone," Showanna said.

"Bring it," Redbone taunted.

After negotiating a few minor conditions—Showanna didn't have to wear shoes or carry her purse, and Redbone didn't have to have his PR-24 side-handle baton in the ring on his Sam Browne belt—they set up the cars. Running east and west between Figueroa St. and Denver Ave., 69th was only one short city block long and traffic free, especially at three in the morning. Perfect for a clandestine foot race. Friedman moved his shop to the middle of the street just west of Fig, facing Denver so the camera in the front window got a clean shot. Williams and Robinson moved theirs over just east of Denver facing Figueroa for the same clear view. Friedman keyed up the mic on the Public Address system in his black-and-white.

"Welcome one and all to the Figueroa Derby! Ladies of the Evening versus the Gallant Defenders of Justice! Redbone representing the Thin Blue Line and Showanna Johnson representing the No Panties Line. Right in front of my car…line it up you two! I'll call 'ready, set, go,' and you're off. The finish line is the front bumper of the other shop. Good luck to you both, and may the best man win!" Friedman called in his best circus barker voice.

"Ready…set…False start! Goddammit Showanna!"

She was already halfway down the block with Redbone in hot pursuit before he could get them to come back. They walked back with Showanna talking shit.

"You fuckin' slow, Redbone! I'm gonna own you! You weak!"

Freidman lined them up again and called them off. Once again there was a false start, and once again he called them back and made them line up.

"Jesus Christ! Last chance, Showanna! One more and Redbone wins by default! This is gonna be fair!" shouted Friedman as Williams and Robinson jeered and cheered from their end.

"Ready!...Set!...Go!" Friedman shouted. Showanna left a bit early, but not enough to have called it completely unfair, so he let it ride. She ran a little strange, sort of off-balanced with her arms pumping slightly off-kilter, but there was no doubt she was fast. Redbone was fast too...especially considering he was in full uniform with a bulletproof vest, boots and the heavy utility belt...but not fast enough. To the sounds of Williams backing the cop and Robinson clearly cheering for the prostitute, they crossed the finish line with Redbone the obvious loser.

Jackie was beside herself with glee, and Showanna was very gracious in her victory, as she danced around with her arms in the air then gave the vanquished Redbone a big consolation hug. He attempted a protest, but Friedman told Redbone the time to protest a false start was at the beginning of a race, not the end, and he reluctantly let it go. They all gathered around the two shops and played back the videos several times on the screen in the cars. It was roundly agreed that the DICV system was a brilliant success. They promised the two prostitutes the three-month pass, and while driving away to conduct police work of major importance, Redbone told Friedman that he could have had her if she hadn't jumped the gun.

"Jesus, Redbone, what the fuck do you expect? She sucks dick for a living. I'm pretty sure a little false start isn't a violation of her moral code. Deal with it. You got smoked by a whore."

CHAPTER 4

THE CLINIC

IT WAS NEARING END OF WATCH WHEN THEY GOT THE CALL. Actually, they had been holding the call in their stack on their Mobile Digital Computer for over an hour while they ran foot races with whores, but since it was only a Code 30 Ringer they figured it could wait. The Code 30 Ringer was LAPD-ese for a burglary alarm, and 99 percent of them were bullshit. Most of the houses and businesses in the ghetto had alarms, and they went off all the time, usually by operator error or an ordinary Act of God. Friedman directed their shop to the intersection of Cimarron Street and Manchester Avenue. The call came from a two-story strip mall on the northwest corner, and the business in question was on the second floor in the middle. The comments stated it was a medical clinic of some kind. Usually cops would do a drive-by and if there was no outside evidence of burglary they would broadcast a Code 12 (false alarm) and drive away. Redbone and Freidman liked to get out and at least check the doors and windows to see if there was actually anything going on.

Friedman parked their shop on Cimarron just north of Manchester, where it couldn't be seen from the strip mall. They walked to the front of the business, but the parking lot gate was locked and they didn't really want to jump over the six-foot fence if they didn't have to.

"Let's check out the back, Redbone," said Friedman.

They walked around to the rear of the property into the east/west alley west of Cimarron.

"Hey, bro...look at this gate."

Friedman walked over to where Redbone was standing. There was a ten-foot-tall fence that enclosed a trash and storage area and three or four parking spaces behind the building. Redbone was pointing to the sliding gate that allowed the big trash bin to be removed for pickup. The gate was closed, but there was no lock. In South Central, anything that could be locked usually was, so it deserved a second look. Freidman walked over and quietly slid the gate open, cupped his flashlight and looked around to see if there was anything else unusual.

"Check it out, Bone...there's no lock on this, either."

Friedman was pointing to the lockable metal cover that was supposed to secure the roof access ladder. It was about six feet tall and was designed to keep unauthorized people from climbing up.

"Friedman!" whispered Redbone, "This thing's been cut for sure! It was up here on the ledge..."

He was holding two pieces of a padlock, and when Friedman checked it out under his light he could see the tool marks on both sides of the U-shaped locking shank.

"We might have a roof-job, Redbone...I'm gonna call for another unit to cover the front...they're probably gone...this call's pretty old...but just in case."

He called communications via his Remote Out of Vehicle Emergency Radio and requested an additional unit and an Airship. 12A73 and 12L20 acknowledged over the air and put themselves en route. Communications raised him just a few seconds later, saying Airships were down due to weather.

"Fuck. No helicopter *and* a supervisor is coming. Who's working L20 tonight?" asked Friedman.

"Pretty sure it's Leinen," said Redbone. "Just be glad we aren't wearing beanies."

Most field supervisors in 77th Street Division were fairly decent. The south-end divisions were not places that timid supervisors worked unless they were unlucky enough to have been sent there on probation when they first made rank.

LAPD was famous for promoting people who had never worked in the field and then the first place they were assigned was patrol. Friedman could always tell on that first day in roll call if they were going to last. During their "One minute, one second" introduction to the watch, the insecure office pogue types would regale the officers with their extensive experience. They would always place emphasis on how much time they had on The Job and would try to explain how their last six years working Internal Affairs could be used by the officers to help them if they were being interviewed on a complaint. Inevitably, they would end with something along the lines of, "All I ask is that you are professional and conduct constitutionally sound police work." The rookie Sergeants who knew patrol, had never worked an inside job and never planned on promoting any higher would always just say, "Hi. I'm Sergeant So-and-So. Excited to be here." Those guys would usually turn out to be good field supervisors, while the pogue types would get found out quickly and be moved to an inside job before they could fuck up morale.

Sgt. Leinen was definitely a cop's cop. He was fair and only asked that his officers work hard. He, like all Sergeants, had his pet peeves, though. If he thought you were lollygagging, he would clear your status through the computer in the watch commander's office. Many an unsuspecting slacker was stunned to hear communications assign them a child abuse radio call when they thought they were safely "out to station" and therefore unavailable for calls. He also hated to see a patrol cop wearing a beanie. He thought it looked unprofessional and would jump a guy's shit over it. All in all, he was pretty easy to get along with and simple to work for: Do your job, and don't wear a beanie. Check.

Sgt. Leinen and 12A73 arrived at the same time. Redbone broke down the situation and had Ponich and Kazan take positions on the front of the property while Sgt. Leinen covered the rear alley. Since there was no Airship, there was only one way to see if there had been a roof-job burglary…climb the ladder and check it out. The plan was for Freidman to go up first and Redbone to climb to the landing halfway up and cover him with his Glock as he went over the ledge onto the roof. Not exactly super safe, but as an old timer at 77th liked to say, "Sometimes you just gotta be the police."

Friedman hung his PR-24 on the fence and began to climb up the ladder, with Redbone right behind him. He was trying to be as quiet as possible, but he kept catching his Sam Browne on the circular cage that surrounded the ladder. They got to the small landing at the halfway point, and Redbone took up his cover position while Friedman kept going up. When he got near the top, he felt the ladder shudder, and for a horrifying second he thought it was going to pull away from the wall and he was going to die in some shit alley in South Central. He looked down and saw Redbone shifting position for a better angle on the lip of the roof. Friedman unholstered his Glock, and with as much stealth as he could manage in the cramped space of the ladder/cage he peered cautiously over the edge.

He couldn't believe what he saw, and it took his brain a second to process the scene. There was a guy dressed in all black, like a ninja, with a face mask and gloves and everything, standing six feet away from him, holding a big yellow pry-bar in his hands. He was looking down into a four-foot by eight-foot hole in the roof from the side opposite Friedman.

He obviously hadn't seen or heard the cops outside and had no idea he was being ogled at that very instant.

"If you move one fucking inch I will shoot you," advised Friedman by way of introduction, standing fully upright on the ladder to show himself.

"LAPD 77th Street. Drop the bar and lie down on the ground. You're done. My boys are all around the building, and you got nowhere to go."

The guy looked at Friedman, and he could see The Ninja's eyes get big. He seemed to be frozen in place, as Friedman climbed over the lip of the roof while holding him at gunpoint. Then he suddenly came back to life. With the bar still in his hands, he turned and ran to the western edge of the roof. As Friedman gave chase, he could hear Redbone clambering up the ladder to help. The guy ran to the edge, looked over, then spun around and raised the bar up over his head menacingly, apparently ready to bring his pry-bar to a gunfight. Friedman pulled up short and leveled his 45 at the eye-gap in his ninja mask.

"You must be one dumb motherfucker if you think I won't shoot you right off this fucking roof. You're caught. Give up now, and you'll live to steal another day."

Perhaps hearing the ring of truth in those words, The Ninja threw down the bar and turned back to the edge of the roof. He glanced back at Friedman, then put one leg up on the lip.

"Dude. If you jump off this roof, you are going to get seriously fucking hurt. Badly. Don't do it. I promise you'll regret it," implored Friedman as he lowered his gun.

And then he jumped. Friedman holstered up as he ran toward the edge, figuring there must have been a house next door or something else tall that would make someone think they would land a 30-plus-foot drop.

If that stupid motherfucker can make it, then so can I. I'll be damned if he's gonna get away after we did some serious detective shit to discover his ass. He must be some kind of super-genius to be doing roof jobs when the Airship is down for weather. At least he thinks he is. I'm gonna ruin his fucking day...

It turned out he didn't have to. Friedman prudently ran and looked over the edge about 10 feet to the right of where the burglar jumped, in case he was lying in wait, and all he could see was a crumpled ninja 30 feet below in the parking lot next door. He was screaming that his back was broken, as Ponich ran up and cuffed him for the easiest capture of his career.

Redbone made the top of the roof and came running over.

"You crazy motherfucker! Did you throw him off the roof? This is classic! I'm gonna tell everyone you're guilty! Tell me he jumped... Please...I can't handle another big beef right now."

"He jumped. Shit-for-brains actually thought he was going to fly away. Jesus H. Christ, Redbone, let's get focused. These guys work in teams...there's got to be at least one more around here somewhere. You cover that hole, and I'll take a look around."

Redbone moved quickly to a position of cover and concealment behind a large air conditioner, where he had his back to the ledge and could cover the four-by-eight-foot hole with his service pistol. Friedman moved behind him and scanned the roof with his flashlight.

The new hand-held LAPD flashlights were badass for lighting things up for sure. They had about a million-candle-power white light and would illuminate anything in a 15-foot radius. Friedman was torn about them, because he remembered the good ol' days of having a three D-cell battery flashlight to use as a close-quarter combat tool when needed. It was nice to be able to see anything and everything, but when push came to shove (and it sometimes did) patrol officers didn't have anything to fight with now but their fists. You always get hurt in a fistfight, and people seem to think that if a cop gets punched it's his job, but if he punches a suspect he's an asshole.

A couple of years ago, under a different Big Chief, there was a filmed incident at the end of a vehicle pursuit where it looked as if one of the cops gave the suspect a flashlight shampoo. The activists were outraged, the command staff was outraged, the politicians were outraged…everyone but the suspect. It turned out the view from a news helicopter didn't provide an accurate depiction of events, because the suspect was never hit on the head with the flashlight. He was hit on the shoulders and the use of force was legal, within policy, and documented by the officer involved. The Big Chief was a political creature though, and he boldly announced that "Flashlights were for illumination, not for beating people" and immediately banned the old flashlights. He let all the patrol cops know their heads would be on a platter if they used them. Friedman always figured that even if the copper *had* hit the suspect on the head, then he should be dealt with—not everyone else. There were approved strike zones on the body for the baton, and the flashlight was the same. Why take *his* flashlight because someone else didn't play by the rules? The Brass threw the baby out with the bath water, though…just like always…and the result was working cops getting hurt. But that sort of thing never mattered to people that had "done their time" on patrol then ran inside as fast as possible.

Friedman assumed the other suspect (or suspects) was still inside the clinic below because the Flying Ninja had been looking down inside when he got ram-shackled by the po-lice, but he wasn't going to take any chances. Just as he was preparing to move from his position of cover, he caught a glimpse of white reflecting off his beam. He swung the light back and saw a pair of legs sticking out from behind another air conditioner about fifteen feet away. The white was a small piece of exposed sock. Friedman moved the light away and whispered to Redbone.

"Bro. We got another one over there behind the other air conditioner. You want to have some fun? Let's slide around to the other side of this hole…keep it covered and follow my lead."

"Hey, partner," Friedman announced loudly, "I'm thinking that if we find anyone else up here we should beat the ever-living shit out of them. There's nobody up here but us. We can write whatever we want on the report…it'll be our word against his."

"Fuck that, bro…let's just shoot the first one we find. I haven't killed anyone in at least a year. I'm due," chimed in Redbone, "Who'll ever know?"

"Good call. If you want, we can both shoot him at the same time. That way we can keep our stats equal. What would that make it? Five kills apiece?

There was a soft whimpering moan coming from behind the air conditioner, but the suspect was trying to stay game. He was lying face down, covering his face with his hands, employing the Ostrich Defense: If I can't see them, they can't see me. It was completely ridiculous, since about a third of his body was exposed, but he figured he wasn't about to stand up and make himself a statistic.

Friedman crept over, and as he switched on his über-light he practically whispered to the suspect, "Listen here, my man…put your hands directly out in front of you where I can see them. If you move anything but your hands, you're dust. You need to tell me how many of your partners are still inside. If there are any surprises at all, or one of my boys gets hurt, you come off this roof in a fucking body bag."

The suspect, who was 17 years old and had wanted nothing to do with the burglary in the first place, slowly slid his hands forward and wailed, "Please, please, please don't shoot me, Officer! There's no one inside…I promise…it was just me and Ta'quan…and now he dead cause you threw him off the roof. I don't wanna die! Please! They made me do this! Fuck Inglewood Family! I'm just puttin' in work! I wanna live! We coulda just buy the weed! We don't have to steal it! It's legal!

Friedman suddenly realized what he guessed Redbone had known all along. The "clinic" was a marijuana dispensary. For some reason, Friedman was thinking of drugstore cowboys stealing prescription drugs. Redbone just assumed it was a weed shop from the start.

"Hey Redbone, this a weed clinic!" called Friedman.

"No shit, bro…what did you think it was?"

Definite generation gap between me and Redbone...am I getting old? Why are Inglewood Family Blood gangsters doing rooftop burglaries for weed? They usually just buy it big from the Mexican gangsters and sell it small on the street...must be getting greedy...more profit in stealing it, I guess. How did they get sophisticated enough to do it on a night with cloud cover and no moon? Fuck it...who cares? Back to the business at hand...

"If we find anyone else inside, you are gonna be one dead Slob. You hear me?

"I promise, Officer! Ta'quan made me do all the hard work...I just got done opening the roof...took me like an hour while he just sat and smoked," answered The Ostrich.

Friedman could hear the sirens of additional units coming Code 3 to the back-up that Sgt. Leinen must have put out, so he decided to just sit tight until he had some more resources with him. He switched his ROVER over to simplex and told Leinen to send two more guys up because they had an open roof and one suspect at gunpoint. He told Redbone and The Ostrich to just sit tight for a second.

They ended up having to call out the fire department to cut the front doors off the dispensary so they could clear it for additional suspects. They also had to ask the firefighters to take The Ostrich off the roof in a basket. It turned out that not only was he still shaken from surviving his brush with death by the police, but he was also terminally afraid of heights. Several of the firefighters commented on the odd choice of occupation for someone with acrophobia. They were also collectively pissed at having been woken up at 4:30 in the morning.

After strapping The Ostrich into a basket, they raised him about 50 feet above the roof with their truck-mounted extension ladder. Then they swung him out over Cimarron, and as payback the guys holding the guide lines on the street started swinging the basket around in large circles. Friedman had never heard anyone scream so high-pitched...or for so long. It was embarrassing.

CHAPTER 5

INTEGRITY

THEY WERE OVERTIME FOR EIGHT HOURS ON THE CLINIC arrest. The Flying Ninja did indeed have a broken back, and so Ponich and Kazan had to babysit him at the hospital while he received tens of thousands of dollar's worth of medical care courtesy of the taxpayers. The Ostrich, being a juvenile, brought a whole different set of time-delaying problems to the table. By the time they were done writing reports, handling evidence and booking the two suspects, they were exhausted. The watch commander from day watch ordered them to take a TO for the next shift, and considering it started in just three hours Freidman and Redbone didn't complain. Thanks to the 3-12 work schedule, they were only on for two nights, anyway, and were off for the next two. So they went home to sleep with no thought of the Lotto ticket in Redbone's uniform shirt pocket.

Friedman was sitting on his couch at home watching the news before work when he saw a quick blip about someone in Los Angeles being a solo winner of one of the biggest lotteries in history. The talking head giddily informed the audience that the ticket had been sold in South Los Angeles and as of that moment had gone unclaimed.

He knew it was still one in a million, but that was better than the one-in-gazillion odds of winning in the first place. His logical mind told him that there was still no way, but he called Redbone, anyway, just to hear the bad news. He had to leave a message, as usual, since Redbone never answered his cell.

"Hey, bro. I assume that since you didn't call me that either we won and you took the ticket and left town or we still gotta handle radio calls. Don't know if you heard or not, but the solo winning ticket was bought somewhere in South Central…ain't that a bitch? I'll see you in roll call."

Friedman pulled into the back gate of 77th Street Division and drove up to his regular spot on the second floor of the parking structure. He saw Redbone standing by the elevator, and as Friedman parked he came rushing over. He was pale and fidgety.

"Dude. I just checked my messages. I don't know if we won. I can't find the ticket. It's not in my wallet, and I'm pretty sure I didn't take it home. Fuck. Fuck. Fuck. What are we gonna do?"

"Relax, Bone…you know we didn't win. Even if it *was* bought down here, it's still gonna be like one in a million. Probably some basehead bought one with his EBT card and used it for toilet paper in a crack-induced stupor. Check your locker. We'll find it, but don't get caught up in this, dude…"

Friedman was changing at his locker when he heard a stifled scream from across the locker room. Redbone appeared a few seconds later.

"I left it in my shirt!" he practically cried, "I took two uniforms to the dry cleaners on 84th and Vermont on my way home after end of watch on Friday! It must have been in the pocket!

"Redbone. Get a hold of yourself, bro. I told you, we didn't win. The odds are ridiculously against it…even now. You gotta slow your roll, or you're gonna stroke out," said Friedman. "We'll swing over there right after roll call...they're open till eight."

"You're right. I know in my mind we didn't win. I'd just hate to have lost the winning ticket and think on it for the rest of my life. I'll feel better when we find it and confirm we're still just cops."

Roll call was the usual arduous exercise in Departmental bullshit. The new Lieutenant was a typical office pogue, and he took the information from the daily rotator as gospel. Some dipshit officer had been braced up by his Sergeant about having a soul patch under his lower lip, and he started a whole mess by pointing out how everyone else had exposed tattoos and smoked and used chewing tobacco. He figured that if some of the rules weren't enforced, he shouldn't have to shave. This put the command staff in a tizzy, and so the Lieutenant was all excited to remind everyone about the Department's tobacco policy. At least half of the guys in the roll call room had tobacco in their lips as he lectured them about it, but he was either too dense or too afraid to say anything. There never seemed to be good news in roll call anymore. No discussions about crime trends or tactics...only what was being done wrong by the officers in the Department's eyes.

Redbone and Friedman were especially anxious to get out of there and over to the dry cleaners...if only to confirm how close they had come to sticking it to South Central. When they had their assignments for the night and the watch commander was done with his tobacco lecture, they practically ran to the kit room and grabbed their gear.

The drycleaner on the corner of 84th Place and Vermont Avenue was a 77th Street institution. It was owned by an older black man whose brother had been an LAPD officer in the late sixties. He'd been killed off-duty while attempting to take a bank robbery suspect into custody. The owner was forever grateful to the LAPD for having tracked down the suspect—and for shooting and killing him rather than taking him into custody for trial. Things were done differently in those days. LAPD took care of their own, and even the media understood back then. If that kind of shit went on today, there would be a national outcry for justice for the "as yet inno-cent" asshole. He cleaned all police uniforms for just a couple of bucks and always provided tailoring service for free. It was a small store and it seemed as if he barely got by, but he was always friendly and would have done any-thing for the people he believed had delivered justice to his parents.

They pulled in the parking lot just a little after 7 p.m., but the sign outside was off and the business seemed to be closed.

"That's weird," said Friedman. "I've never known Mr. Davis to close early. This place has been like clockwork for as long as I can remember."

They got out and checked the door, but it was locked. Redbone noticed a light coming from under the back office door and told Friedman to call and see if anyone answered. Friedman whipped out his cell and dialed the number. It rang. Someone picked up, then immediately hung up. He tried again, and it rang several times before going to the store answer-ing machine.

"Strange. I hope there's not a takeover robbery going on…someone answered and then hung up…then it went to the machine," said Friedman.

Just then they saw the back office door open and Mr. Davis walk out. He was alone but looked worn and older for some reason. He walked slowly to the front of the shop, lifted up the pass-through counter and approached the front door. He stopped just short of the door and stood staring at Redbone and Friedman. They looked at each other and then half-waved at the glass door. Mr. Davis sighed visibly, moved forward and unlocked the door.

"I figured it would be you. I closed the shop today at three. I've been sitting in my office looking at it since I found it," said Mr. Davis.

Then he staggered back into one of the chairs in the front of the store and began to cry.

"Mr. Davis, are you OK? What did you find? What do you mean you 'figured it would be us'? You're making me nervous," said Friedman while scanning the store.

"I thought all day about keeping it. But I knew it wasn't mine. I knew I could never cash it in without getting caught. Mostly I knew that I didn't have a right to it. God blessed you boys, and I'm grateful it was you and not someone that didn't deserve it," sobbed Mr. Davis.

He reached up and pulled The Ticket from his chest pocket. He held it like it was on fire, between the thumb and index finger of his right hand. He sort of directed it toward the two befuddled Blue Suiters.

"Please take it…it's yours. God bless you. People dream of such things their whole lives, and you boys have had your dreams come true."

Friedman took the ticket from his shaking fingers and pocketed it. He told Redbone to run to the back and get Mr. Davis something to drink.

"Get the bottle of Maker's Mark from the desk drawer, Officer Obrador. I could use a drink," said Mr. Davis.

When Redbone came back with the bottle, Mr. Davis popped the top and took an amazingly long pull from the bottle and handed it to Friedman.

"Have a drink, Officer Friedman. Your life has changed. You don't need that badge anymore."

Friedman thought about taking a gulp just to calm his nerves, but figured he needed to sort out his brain first. Redbone grabbed the bottle from him, put it to his lips and turned it straight up and down. Friedman glared and snatched it back…it wasn't even in his hand for a second when Mr. Davis snatched it from *him* and up-ended it again. Friedman took the bottle from him and stepped back.

"Mr. Davis, I've known you for 15 years and never seen you like this. What the fuck is going on? What are you saying? We won? How much? Talk to me, please," said Friedman.

"I was doing catch-up this morning, when I came across Officer Obrador's uniforms. They were marked for pick-up tonight but somehow got put in the wrong stack and hadn't been cleaned yet. I stopped doing what I was doing and prepped them before they got handled. I always check you boys' uniform pockets before I clean them. About half the time there's something in the pockets…I know you're usually in a hurry to get out and work or go home to your families. I always put what I find into a little plastic bag and attach it to the coat hanger after they are cleaned. Well, I come across that ticket in the chest pocket of one of his shirts. I listen to talk radio all day long, and I'd heard someone in South Central had bought the winning ticket, so just for fun I went to my office and checked the numbers on the computer. I closed the store and sat in the office staring at it until you boys showed up."

Friedman uncorked the Maker's and took a long, deep drink. His head was spinning, and he didn't even notice Redbone take the bottle from his hand and take his own long, deep drink. Mr. Davis took it from Redbone and had *himself* a long, deep drink. Finally, Friedman came around and he began to think clearly. He pulled out his smartphone and clicked on the Internet. He surfed over to the Lotto website and pulled up the winning numbers from Friday's drawing. He pulled out The Ticket and checked.

"Redbone? We. Fucking. Won. The whole thing. We really fucking won," declared Friedman as he slumped onto a chair next to Mr. Davis.

Redbone started to dance in a little circle. Friedman figured they needed to get the fuck out of the store and away from Mr. Davis. Talk about counting money in front of the poor. He told Redbone to go and get in the shop and put them Code 6 on the MDC at 84th Place and Vermont. That would give them some time to think through their next move. He was overwhelmed, and the reality of what had just happened was beyond understanding. He knew they needed a plan.

"Mr. Davis, there is nothing I could ever say to express what I feel about you right now. You are a man of honor and a good friend to us at

77th Street…always have been. I'd like to ask that you don't tell anyone what happened here tonight. I'll make sure you are rewarded for your honesty and friendship. Please keep this between us until I've figured out how we are going to handle this," said Friedman.

"You don't have to worry about me, Officer Friedman. I've seen some strange things in my life, but nothing like this. You can count on me. I'm happy for you boys. This is between us until you say otherwise."

Friedman walked numbly out of the store and sat down in the driver's seat of their black-and-white. Redbone was quietly doing math on his cell phone. They watched Mr. Davis lock the door and walk slowly back to his office with the bottle of Maker's dangling from his right hand. Friedman pulled out of the parking lot and drove straight over to the roof of the parking structure at 77th Station. He put them on a follow-up to the station on the MDC and then got out of the car.

"We need to get the fuck out of here," said Friedman as Redbone hopped out.

"Let's take the black-and-white to Vegas and just leave it on the Strip," suggested Redbone. "They can come and get it. We don't need this place anymore. Fuck 'em."

"Bro. We need to be smart. What if there's some kind of a mistake? What if we do need our jobs? We can't fuck anything off until we are completely sure and we've got the money in our hands. Neither one of us trusts the government…you know how things can get fucked up," said Friedman. "I'll go tell Lieutenant Dumbass that we both just got food poisoning from a roach coach and are shitting and puking. We'll go to my house and try to re-group and form some sort of a plan. Whatever we do, we can't mention this to anyone, Redbone. This could be a total and complete life changer… everyone we've ever known is gonna come out of the fucking woodwork and want something. We gotta be smart."

"You're right, dude. This is gonna be a tough ride. We definitely need a plan. I'll take the shop down and unload it, then go in and get changed and head straight over to your pad. We'll relax and have a beer and decide what our next step is. I hope this is the real deal. We deserve it," replied Redbone.

CHAPTER 6

THE VULTURES

WITHIN THE HOUR THEY WERE SITTING ON FRIEDMAN'S BACK porch drinking cold Pabst in cans and staring at The Ticket. They had checked several times on his home computer and had confirmed they were, in fact, holding the only winning ticket. It was listed at over $350 million. They had a lot of questions about their next move. They had no idea what to do or how to go about cashing in while remaining as anonymous as possible. They knew if they just showed up and let the Lotto officials have their way with them, it would start a circus that they might never recover from. They decided to keep The Ticket in Friedman's wall safe until morning and then head over to the Farmer's and Merchant's bank near his house in Long Beach and open a safe deposit box. They sat and drank and dreamed out loud until midnight, and then Friedman set up the guest room for Redbone. They both went to bed and fell into fitful sleep punctuated by nightmares of lost lottery tickets and lives ruined.

Friedman had a classmate and friend whose father, Richard, had earned huge at the peak of the dot-com boom by selling off his software company. He now dabbled in big real estate and various keep-busy projects but had basically been retired since about 1999. He was the closest thing that either Friedman or Redbone knew to a person who could keep quiet *and* put them in touch with the kind of high-powered legal help they needed. They called him in the morning, and at his suggestion they took a copy of The Ticket and went to meet his personal attorney and childhood friend, Henry Dexter Smith, Esq., over near Palos Verdes Estates in the small bedroom community of Malaga Cove.

They parked in the driveway at the address Richard gave them and knocked on the door of what appeared to be a rather unassuming Spanish-style bungalow.

"Good morning, gentlemen! Henry Smith. Richard said to be expecting you," said the man who answered as he extended his arm and provided each of them a confident handshake.

Henry was high-speed, low-drag for sure. His exquisitely tailored suit must have run him 5 grand easy. He ushered them in and both Friedman and Redbone both felt like Oliver Twist standing in front of the headmaster asking for more soup. They looked around in awe at the impressive display of wealth as they walked through the home. His antique collection was staggering and multi-disciplined.

The house was deceptive. It cascaded down the Palos Verdes cliff from the first floor entry and was about 10,000 square feet with a view from Redondo Beach all the way to Malibu. Henry walked them down into his library and Redbone thought the room looked like something out of an old Humphrey Bogart movie. It had twenty a twenty-foot ceiling and a balcony half way up with gleaming mahogany bookshelves and rolling ladders all around. He offered them seats and plopped down behind a desk that belonged in the Oval Office. Being a bit of an amateur art aficionado himself, Friedman was shocked. He was pretty sure the painting mounted under glass on the wall behind Henry was an original Caravaggio.

If that thing's legit, I wonder what it set him back, thought Friedman.

"So, Richard explained your situation," said Henry, seemingly without a hint of interest or the typical predatory leer they had come to expect from attorneys. "Tell me about your concerns."

"Well," started Friedman. "We're holding one of the biggest winning lotto tickets in the history of California. We're afraid if we just walk in and collect, we'll never get our lives back. We want to recover the loot and not have anyone know about it. We don't want any media. Being LAPD cops in South Central, we're afraid we'll end up as targets for lawsuits."

"That sounds reasonable to me," replied Henry. "So your main concerns are remaining anonymous and avoiding lawsuits? I'm pretty sure we can help with the first issue, simply by being creative, and that should, in turn, help with the second."

"This is out of our league," said Friedman. "Money can be lost so easily, especially money that wasn't earned. We'd also like to have some kind of long-term help in place to make sure we don't go broke."

"I think I can point you in the right direction with that too," said Henry.

"There's something else…something specific," said Friedman. "We have a law suit pending right now. It's going to trial in a couple of months and the City Attorney handling it has already told us to expect a loss. It wasn't our fault; the guys we backed-up were the ones that fucked up, but the CA said we could expect to get hit with punitive damages. That's usually no big deal, because the city takes care of the officers if they were acting in good faith. The problem is how they calculate the punitive damages. If a jury looks at our bottom line and sees what our winnings have made us worth, they could award millions to those assholes. There's no way the City Council will vote to pick up that kind of a tab. You probably know more about that kind of thing than us."

"Well, I think a plan for your anonymity and wealth preservation should attempt to cover all contingencies," said Henry. "Since you are friends of Richard's I'll be more than willing to assist you...even if your future net worth is somewhat less than I'm accustomed to dealing with."

Friedman and Redbone stared at him openmouthed.

"You have no idea how much that reassures us," said Friedman, who recovered first.

Henry showed them to the foyer and stated, "Tell no one about your situation. Head home for a while and I'll be in touch. I'm going to make some phone calls to some people who can be trusted and know how to handle such things."

"Bro," said Redbone as they walked up the driveway. "Who the fuck thinks 350 million dollars is chicken feed? We came to the right store."

"I was just gonna say the same fucking thing." replied Friedman.

Henry called later that same morning and arranged a meeting with their new "legal team." By two o'clock, they were back at the lawyer's crib sitting down with Richard and Henry, and two guys they could tell were crafty. Henry introduced the two as Tony and Brian Batts and claimed they were the best legal and financial minds he'd ever known. The brothers were in their early 40s and oozed brains and confidence. They looked like they were cut from the same mold as Henry: $5000 suits, $300 haircuts, subtle (but expensive) shoes, watches and jewelry. The whole group looked like something out of a movie.

Everyone in the room was a millionaire, but Redbone and Friedman couldn't think like millionaires yet, so Henry immediately began laying out the scenario. No bullshit—all business.

"First things first," said Henry. "An actual individual will need to present the ticket, according to California law and Lotto rules. They have up to a year, so we've determined it would be best to wait until some of the hoopla died down, and your pending lawsuit is settled, before you claim the prize."

The team had decided to legally change Friedman's name, so after he claimed their winnings he'd be harder to trace. It was decided to set up two trusts (one for Redbone and one for Friedman) to handle the money once it had been redeemed. His name would be changed back after a sufficient amount of time and his trust modified accordingly. Richard was able to provide a "permanent" mailing address for Friedman, using one of his many real estate investment properties. It was a small studio apartment in a 100-unit building with tight security.

Apparently, certain amounts of money created certain types of rules, which Redbone and Friedman had a hard time understanding. If you had enough cash, you could make anything happen. Everything would be done on the lawyer's end to ensure anonymity, and the rest was up to The Winners, as they came to be known during the course of the meeting.

Contracts and confidentiality agreements were signed.

"I will be your primary contact for all things legal, and Tony and Brian will be in charge of your investments and trusts," advised Henry. "Tell me about Mr. Davis, the drycleaner from 84th and Vermont."

When he ascertained the nature of their relationship, he assured Friedman and Redbone he would have someone contact him and secure his cooperation in maintaining their secret.

"Once you have the money, it's yours to spend as you see fit, of course. Tony and Brian will facilitate expenditures, provide solid investment advice to help ensure you don't end up broke, and manage your trusts." finished Henry.

After several hours of strategizing, he congratulated them on their winnings. Then shortly after, he dropped the bomb. They knew it was coming, but it brought a jolt of reality to the otherwise dreamy day of planning their wealthy futures.

"Now…you won't have the money in the trust accounts for at least six months, if we stick to the plan we've formulated here today," cautioned Henry. "In order to protect your privacy and your winnings, you'll need to make some sacrifices up front. But in the long run, you'll appreciate the control you'll have over your lives, and the control you'll have over your money."

"What should we do until then?" asked Redbone, as if waking from some kind of daydream. "I understand what you've laid out for us and I agree with everything. Your advice is super solid and makes complete sense. We appreciate your help more than you know. It's just that we're filthy rich…and it seems impossible that we should just go about our business as if nothing happened."

"That's a decision you'll have to make. It will require both of you to work with us to make this anonymity plan work. If one of you changes his mind or lets the cat out of the bag too soon, then everything you're asking us to do is for nothing. It will surely take discipline. My recommendation is to attempt to forget. Pretend you didn't win," suggested Henry. "You'll need to continue your routine. For example, keep buying your weekly Lotto tickets at the same store. Remember that they'll know someone from their store held the winning ticket. If you never show up again or change your pattern, they could become suspicious. All it will take for the whole plan to implode is the media getting involved. Two street cops in South Los Angeles winning one of the biggest Lotto drawings in California history would be a big story. The L.A. Times reporter who received that tip would go after it."

"We still have to eat. We live pay check to paycheck, and we've both got bills to pay. Friedman's got alimony and child support, I've got legal bills and DMV fines from my deuce," lamented Redbone.

"You both have good jobs with good benefits. Keep working for six more months. Live within your current means. We will facilitate loans for you in the meantime to pay all outstanding bills and to provide relief from immediate day-to-day expenses, but you *must not* exhibit questionable expenditures. Remember, it's not just about the people you work with, it's about friends, family, old high school acquaintances…pretty much anyone you've ever met, as well as the regular vultures that prey on people like you," advised Henry. "I'll be doing some research into your 'special' problem stemming from your current lawsuit. That's about the only issue that gives me any concern. I'll feel much better when I find out who their attorney is."

"What if we get sued for something new that we get into at work?" asked Friedman.

"The likelihood of that occurring is no different today than it was last week. You are generally sheltered from punitive damages through your employer, but even in the event a plaintiff was awarded any damages by a court decision, we'll have your winnings hidden by then. They'll only see what we want them to see, and they can only have what we let them have. Your lawyers are much better than theirs now," replied Henry with a smile.

"That being said, I would avoid becoming involved in potentially litigious behavior for the next six months or so, just to ease your minds," offered up Brian. "To the extent that such a thing is possible, of course. I'm fascinated by what you do for a living. I've heard that private citizens can go on a ride-along with officers. Is it possible that you could arrange something like that for us?"

This motherfucker's insane. He might be a genius millionaire lawyer, but he's like a little kid in the presence of a couple of ghetto cops. He wants to go on a fucking ride-along because he's 'fascinated by what we do for a living?' Jesus. I've got bad news for you, buddy. It'll be one boring fucking ride-along if you come out on a night I'm working. I'm not doing another bit of police work as long as I live. I can't believe squares like this guy get excited by what we do. Fucking Hollywood…

"Yeah, I'm pretty sure I can make that happen," replied Friedman.

CHAPTER 7
LET THE GAMES BEGIN

"YOU KNOW, FRIEDMAN…I'VE BEEN THINKING," SAID REDBONE while driving to work on their first day back after the Vulture Meeting.

They had decided that Redbone should move into Friedman's house. He had two extra bedrooms, and his place in Long beach was only about 25 minutes away from 77th Street Station. They reasoned that since their days off matched, they could carpool, and they would be less likely to slip up in conversation with others if they were both around. They could take care of each other and stick to the plan—especially when drinking—which they both liked to do.

"No shit!? Watcha been thinking about Redbone? I bet you've been figuring out ways to get laid using a shit load of money as bait…," laughed Friedman.

"Nah, man…for real, bro…I was thinking that since we have to go to work anyway, we might as well have some fun while we're there. Think about it…how many times did you want to tell someone to fuck off, but didn't because you were worried about the 1.28?"

Every single piece of paper in the LAPD had a form number. Many of the frequently used forms came to be known by that form number. It was common for someone to "fill out a 15.7," which was the form number of an Employee Report used for passing along any type of information up the chain of command. The "1.28.0" was the form number of the face sheet of an employee complaint. The first supervisor conducting the investigation filled it out, and the result of any complaint was called a "1.28." The 1.28 struck fear in the hearts of all rookies, office pogues, climbers and anyone else with any kind of aspirations in the Department. Sustained complaints stayed in an officer's package, and during all interviews they were used as reasons to deny advancement. The supervisors who had run away from patrol as quickly as possible were the ones who conducted the interviews. They, of course, had no complaints and could never trust someone with the package acquired through years of working the field. Friedman had long since quit fearing complaints because he knew he was never going to promote. Redbone had his complaint cherry popped with an arrest by an outside agency, so he wasn't all that afraid of them, either. But, unfortunately, the fear of a 1.28 kept the modern LAPD officer from expressing his true feelings to his supervisors, and many times from doing what needed to be done in the field. Too many officers were afraid to use the appropriate amount of force against a combative suspect because they didn't want a blemish in their package, or had too many recent 1.28's and were afraid of getting taken out of the field and assigned desk duty. Many stupid-visors within the Department liked to use the threat of 1.28 to gain compliance from officers. That had backfired once too often when used against Friedman, so it rarely happened to him anymore, but it was still the favorite tool of those who had promoted beyond their ability to lead.

"Redbone...we've talked about this...we need to fly low to keep from getting sued. Let's just drive around and wave for six months. I did it for years when Lord Voldemort was Big Chief. It's easy. Bro...you've got to promise me we just do our time and get the fuck out of here."

"Look…I hear what you're saying. I'm not talking about committing crimes or shooting gangsters for fun. I'm talking about doing stuff that every Blue Suiter always wished they could, but would never dare because they needed the money," reasoned Redbone. "I'm talking about our debt to everyone on the job…about making some things right before we leave. You've always told me the way to be the best cop possible is to not have to rely on the paycheck to feed your children. We are in a unique position to right some wrongs. To make some assholes pay. To get some revenge for everyone like us who never could. Think about it, bro…most guys wait 30 years to have the power to tell the truth around here, and then they only have it for a second before they retire. Like Mr. Davis said, we were given a gift. If we don't use it, I think we'll regret it."

Friedman thought about it as he transitioned from the northbound 405 Freeway to the northbound 110. He could hear himself in Redbone's voice. He had always believed in speaking the truth, and he'd paid for it plenty. He had never let political considerations get in the way of doing what was right.

Is he right? Have I become like the others that quickly? The cowards who just don't give a fuck what happens to the rest of us because they're going to retire soon? How many times have I seen senior officers fail to stand up against some sort of injustice committed against my friends? What did I always say… 'When will that guy have enough time on the job to do what's really right instead of what the Department says is right'?

"You know what, Redbone?" said Friedman as they pulled into the big yellow gates at the rear of the station. "You're right. We've already decided we're not doing any more police work, but we can certainly have some fun and maybe get the voice of the Blue Suiter heard before we leave. We don't have to do illegal shit that'll get us sued or indicted…but why not do everything that we always dreamed of doing? Why not stand up against that asshole right there?"

Walking into the station, directly in front of their car, was their archenemy. Captain I Patrick Fiacla Capall was the divisional Patrol Captain for 77th Street. He was hated by nearly everyone, with the possible exception of a couple of office pogues who had attached themselves to him and were counting on him to be a shooting star. He was a super-religious Catholic and came down unreasonably hard on CUBO complaints. Conduct Unbecoming an Officer beefs encompassed a lot. They were sort of a catch-all but were usually related to women. Most often they were allegations of converting an on-duty contact into an off-duty relationship. This usually only became an issue when the cop was married, and the contact became what was known as "on-duty booty." He was famous department-wide for hammering guys for beefs that other captains would have thought nothing about. If you had a CUBO complaint go across his desk, you needed to worry. Captain Capall was as Irish as he could be without an accent, but in spite of that he was also famous for stomping on officers who got involved in alcohol-related incidents. He had given Redbone a two-hour lecture on how he disgraced himself, the Department, and the Irish, hit him with a 10-day suspension and then put him on the desk for three DPs for his deuce. The shame and ignominy of the ankle bracelet coupled with Redbone's newly discovered Catholicism was almost more than he could stand. He never forgave or forgot. Since he promoted early and often, he had no frame of reference for patrol. He was one of the many command staff who firmly believed that everyone working patrol was some sort of a miscreant. It was typical. He was both intimidated by those who did what he never dared to and embarrassed that he didn't know how. No matter the reasons, he was collectively despised by the men and women of 77th Street Division, and he despised them right back. He particularly hated Friedman because he was always pointing out the hypocrisy of the command staff... in public.

They were sitting in roll call when Captain Capall walked in. The Watch Commander giving roll call immediately stopped and began to fawn all over him. Friedman wondered what he was doing in the station so late on a Friday, and Capall being in roll call explained it. There was never good news when a Captain showed up in roll call.

"Is there anything I can do for you, Sir?" asked the new Lieutenant Jim Short, one of the worst ass-kissing climbers in the history of LAPD. "To what do we owe this honor? Would you like to address the troops?"

"Yes, I would, Lieutenant...but go ahead and finish roll call first," replied the Captain. He stood and eye-fucked the morning watch crew while Lieutenant Short finished handing out the assignments and went through the rotator with a fervor seldom seen by his officers.

"There needs to be extra patrol provided to 10th Avenue between Hyde Park and 63rd Street. It's due to the recent shooting death of a member of the Rollin 60's Crips by someone the gang unit suspects was from the Van Ness Gangster Bloods," intoned Lieutenant Ass Kisser. "I want to see it logged by 12A51, and I had better see it documented or I'll have you standing tall to answer why."

The Lieutenant looked over to the Captain, who beamed approval at his talking down to the two 25-year veterans that worked A51. Both their faces dropped when one of the old-timers chimed in with, "Why don't we just let them sort it out themselves, Lt.? I knew the asshole that got smoked from back when I worked CRASH in the mid-'90s. He was a stone OG criminal. We were looking at him for two homicides even back then. Those VNG Slobs did us a favor on that one."

The Lieutenant panicked slightly then turned red in the face at the audacity of having his authority questioned in front of the Captain.

"These are human beings, Plazola! They have families and loved ones just like you and me. They need your protection and you *will* provide it," admonished Lieutenant Short.

"They're more like you than me," Plazola muttered, "but we'll be over there VNG hunting all night for you...at least the log will say we were..." under his breath just loud enough for those around him to hear. Everyone in the back of the room laughed, and the Lieutenant turned red all over again.

"That's enough!" barked the Lieutenant. "Let's just listen up to what the Captain has to say…"

"It seems that someone on this watch thinks they're funny," sneered Captain Capall as he walked to the middle of the room, thinking to himself how weak Lieutenant Short was. "I arrived here the other morning to discover a private vehicle in my personal parking space with all four of its tires missing. This vehicle happened to belong to my adjutant, and she'd left it in the parking lot while she was on vacation abroad."

Every head in the room turned to look at Plazola and his partner Horst. They were attempting to look innocent, but it wasn't going very well. Luckily, someone walked into roll call late through the front door and drew the Captain's attention away.

"We have been conducting a thorough 1.28 investigation and will shortly determine the culprits. It would be in everyone's best interest if the guilty party would step forward right now and ease their conscience. There was severe damage to the Sergeant's vehicle, and I will not go lightly when I discover the criminals responsible," said the Captain.

No one in the room moved. You could have heard a pin drop.

Suddenly Redbone spoke up, "Sir, I remember seeing Lieutenant Short walking around in the parking lot the other night at about three in the morning. I think it was last Wednesday…"

The Lieutenant practically shrieked, "You insolent red-haired little…!"

"Sir," protested Redbone to the Captain, "I was simply suggesting he might have observed something out of the ordinary that could assist you with the investigation."

"Control yourself, Lieutenant," said Captain Capall, "Officer Obrador, I assume he would have already made public any knowledge he had that could help the investigation."

"Just trying to help, Sir," said Redbone.

"So. There is no integrity in this room. I assure you, when I discover who you are, I will not only make you pay for the damage to my adjutant's car, I'll send you to a Board of Rights for insubordination and the crime of felony vandalism. I will ensure you are punished to the fullest extent of my ability," said Captain Capall as he stalked out of the room.

After roll call, Friedman hit up Sgt. Leinen in the hallway by the kit room. "Hey Sarge, was his adjutant's car really fucked up?"

"Nah...I heard her crying about it to the day-watch Watch Commander...she was saying that it pulled to the left a bit. Thought she needed to get it aligned or something. When he asked her if it did that before the gag, she said she wasn't sure. Basically, Captain Capall doesn't have shit for suspects and was trying to scare someone into copping out. He made the whole thing up," replied Sgt. Leinen.

"Go fucking figure," said Friedman

"You just don't understand the burden of command, Friedman," laughed Sgt. Leinen. "You better tell Horst and Plazola to lay low for a bit. That Lieutenant Short would love to catch him some veteran fish. It'd make him look like a hero to the Captain."

Redbone and Friedman were walking out to the parking structure with their gear when Redbone suddenly looked at his shop keys and groaned, "Dude, we got 87230! Fuck! It stinks, and now we're stuck with it! There aren't any cars left, and there won't be until mid-watch goes EOW..."

"Tell you what, bro, I'll go and fill it up and wash it. You run back in and grab a TASER. I forgot to get one, and you never know when it'll come in handy. I'll be right back down," said Friedman, an idea brewing in his head.

Friedman drove the nasty, piss-stenched shop up the ramp, and as he made the turn at the top he saw Captain Capall's shiny new Chrysler 300 parked in his private spot. Since 77th Street was South Bureau headquarters, there were many command staff assigned to the building. Each got a brand-new city car every year, and all were assigned the very best parking spaces in the building.

Captain Capall had just received his new city car and was absurdly vain about it. He made sure his adjutant washed and cleaned it almost daily. It being Friday night, all the other office pogues were home with their families and the Captain's was the only car there. It was at the very end parking stall with about 30 yards of open space right next to the car wash. Friedman drove past it and continued past the entrance to the car wash, where he stopped and put the shop in reverse.

"Pride comes before a fall," whispered Friedman to himself as he looked over his right shoulder.

Redbone was carrying his war bag and the Remington 870 shotgun as he entered the underground parking structure where all the black-and-whites were parked. He set his stuff on the ground and leaned the tube up against one of the big yellow poles to wait for Friedman. He was playing with the laser sight on the TASER when the whole building seemed to jump. He heard a loud boom and saw the yellow pole in front of him shift as the shotgun clattered to the ground. He thought it was an earthquake, but it was just the one impact so he ran to the stairwell to the main floor of the parking structure. On his way up, he heard someone broadcast a help call to the rear of 77th Street Station behind the carwash. He made it to the top of the stairwell, and when he looked left he couldn't believe his eyes.

Friedman had managed to get the Piss-Mobile up to about 50 mph when it hit the Captain's car. He struck the left front quarter panel of the 300 with the middle of the trunk of shop 87230 at a near exact 45-degree angle. The impact shattered the front axle of the Captain's car, broke the engine loose from its mounting bolts and rammed it backwards into a vertical structural beam with absolutely zero give. That put the 300's trunk into its own backseat. The momentum it had built catapulted the rear end of the black-and-white up and over the hood of the Chrysler and left its rear bumper nearly sitting on the roof. Friedman's car was literally on top of the Captain's.

Officers were helping Friedman out of the driver's window of the black-and-white as the door had been jammed shut. He was stoned faced, but Redbone could see his eyes smiling. Redbone had to turn away to keep from laughing out loud and was desperately trying not to piss his pants. His whole world seemed out of control from their life changing winnings, but it dawned on him that the next six months of his life were likely to be the most fun he'd ever had. He couldn't believe that Friedman had kept him in the dark about what he was going to do, though, and the thought was oddly hurtful. He caught Friedman's eyes as he approached, and they both shook their heads slightly—Redbone in disappointment at having been left out of the loop and Friedman in a silent reminder of their pact.

"You are fucking crazy," whispered Redbone.

"My Danner got stuck between the bottom of the brake pedal and the gas…I'm pretty fucking lucky to be alive, partner. Thank God you weren't in the car. You could've been hurt bad. What's the new Department policy regarding TC's, Sarge?" said Friedman

"I think you get three before you're subject to discipline," replied Sgt. Leinen, "but I'm not too sure that Captain Capall is gonna take this fuck-up lying down. This thing is totaled. You stirred up a hornet's nest with this one, Friedman. He was in love with this 300. You hurt? Someone call this fucking idiot an RA just in case."

Friedman sat down on the ground to wait for the Rescue Ambulance while all the other coppers busted out their cell phones and took pictures. An event of this magnitude would undoubtedly make social media in record time.

"WHAT DID YOU DO TO MY CAR?!?!?!?!," screamed Captain Capall stopping short as he ran into the parking structure. For a few brief seconds, he couldn't pull his eyes away from the carnage that used to be his beloved Chrysler 300. He marched over to where Friedman was seated on a curb and loomed over him. There were about 30 officers standing around… all of Morning Watch obviously, but several off-duty people from the prior watch, and a few Detectives, as well as people from outside Divisions who were there to book bodies. There were even a couple of crackheads craning their necks from the back seat of a black-and-white that had stopped to watch the show before going to book in the jail. His adjutant was in-tow as usual and tried discretely to get his attention.

"I am going to make sure you get done up for this, Friedman," said Captain Capall with such vitriol in his voice that everyone stopped and stared.

"Um, Sir?" whispered Sgt. Borjorquez, "Everyone is listening, Sir. Is Officer Friedman hurt? Did someone call an RA?"

"You had better have a good fucking reason for what happened here!" shrieked Captain Capall, completely ignoring his adjutant.

"Sir, I'm pretty banged up from this unfortunate accident…but I think I'll be OK. Thanks for your concern. You know, I find it pretty hard to believe that you're more worried about your car than the well-being of one of your officers. Pride is one of the seven deadly sins, Sir, and I'm not entirely sure that Jesus appreciates your language," said Friedman with a sideways glance at Redbone, who was convulsing behind the Captain's back.

It had begun.

CHAPTER 8
FRONT DESK FUN

FRIEDMAN WAS ASSIGNED HOME BY THE CITY DOCTOR FOR back and neck pain stemming from the violent nature of the "accident." He and Redbone laughed all night long about the look on Captain Capall's face when he ran into the parking structure. They decided he would have to be a specific target for future adventures because his reaction was so noteworthy. He would be a lot of fun to torture.

True to form, the Captain did his best to punish Redbone and Friedman in any way he could because he knew that, absent proof, the destruction of his city car was just another traffic accident. They were both bumped to Day Watch and assigned to work the front desk, but because Friedman was out for a while due to his Injured On Duty status in conjunction with his Regular Days Off, Redbone had to go it alone. He caught his first beef within two days.

The LAPD did certain things that no other Police Department did. Much of this was due to tradition, but much of it was due to the command staff being out of touch with reality. One absurd policy was to staff every

Division's front desk with uniformed police officers whose job was to take walk-in reports and basically kiss public ass. Most other municipal police departments used civilians during the day and closed their front desk at night. LAPD staffed theirs with sworn personnel 24/7 and damned the waste of resources. Because 77th Street was South Bureau headquarters, its front desk personnel had to suffer the additional humiliation of being subjected to all things political. It was on the front steps of 77th Street Regional Police Headquarters that Assistant Chief Sterling Anderson used a large black flashlight to crush symbolic heads (cantaloupe) for the media while his South Central activist friends looked on appreciatively. This was the very next day after the aforementioned televised flashlight shampooing, prior to the investigation of the incident, which later revealed no wrongdoing by the officer involved. The 77th Street desk officers had to stand by with no recourse and witness their leadership throw one of their brothers to the media wolves. They also had witnessed the same Command Staff officer hug and dap with the Nation of Islam parolees after their leader started a street brawl with uniformed officers. Friedman had been there for both indignities and especially despised Anderson for his betrayal. The humiliations were many and varied for those privileged few who were assigned to the desk at 77th Street, but the hardest part was dealing with the various assholes that demanded to be treated like "clients." Among these were the 290's.

A "290" was a registered sex offender that was mandated by California Penal Code 290 to register with the police department that had jurisdiction over their place of residence. South Central being South Central, there was a shit-load of halfway houses that facilitated parolees' transition back (however temporarily) into society. There were also a huge number of criminals who lived in the area with their families that were assigned home by their parole officers. This caused quite a bottleneck at the 77th Street front desk every Thursday between 0900 and 1200, when the 290's came to register for the first time or to do the confirmation of their address. The problem with the Sex Registrant system was that almost any sex crime required the convict to register for life as a sex offender. It didn't matter if an 18-year-old was convicted of indecent exposure while urinating in an alley or a grown man was convicted of raping a child. In the eyes of the sex registrant system, they were all 290's. This caused an understandable bitterness among the 290's that were not really sexual deviants, but many of the truly twisted sexual predators tried to play off this injustice and the anonymity that the flaw in the system provided.

It was the unwritten policy of the 77th Street Desk and Sex Detectives (those lucky individuals responsible for maintaining the 290 registrant files) not to make the 290's reveal their convictions publicly, but to just sign in under their names at the front desk. They would then get called by name to meet with detectives for registration.

While he sympathized with the one-time ass-grabber, Redbone felt that the Rape-by-Force assholes should be called out on their heinous criminality. They shouldn't profit from LAPD's politically correct bullshit. So his plan was to wait until the lobby was full of both 290's and inmate family visitors (usually angry females with children) and then start having some fun. When the first 290's of the day began to arrive, he had them first sign in and then asked them for their dates of birth. Since in the past they only had to provide their name, a few of them looked at him slightly askance and one of the most shifty-looking deviants openly questioned him.

"New policy, fuck-knuckle. You don't provide a valid ID that I can verify, I'll violate you right now. You make the call," said Redbone.

Mr. Shifty tried to hem and haw around a bit, but Redbone stood his ground and he finally provided the information. He took their names and dates of birth and ran them in the NECS computer to find out their primary conviction charge. Then he made a list.

When the lobby was crowded and the sex dicks began registration, Redbone grabbed the list at the desk and shouted, "Johnson, James! 288 (A) PC! Unlawful sex with a minor! You're up! Was that with a boy or a girl minor?" The 60-year-old man that walked up seemed unfazed and responded, "Oh, that was with a girl, Officer. I'm no queer."

The old-timer sex detective laughed out loud and walked him back into the interview room as the lobby started buzzing. Redbone could see some of the 290's starting to fidget and look around.

The next two were bullshit sexual battery capers, but Redbone announced them to the lobby in the same loud authoritative voice. "Zaby, David! Tello, Steven! 243.4 (E)(1)! Sexual battery! Are you guys ass-grabbers or tit-grabbers!?"

Both men approached at the same time—apparently, they had gotten to know each other after meeting several times in the lobby for registration.

Tello proclaimed for the whole lobby to hear, "Man, this is bullshit! All we done was grab a little ass at the night club, and next thing we know we fucked for life!

"I agree with you there, partner," replied Redbone. "Doesn't seem too fair."

"Does that seem fair to ya'll?!" Zaby challenged his audience, as he turned to follow the rookie female detective, whose mouth was agape.

The lobby was now abuzz with people debating the merits of the sex registrant system. The Hood could be an infinitely fair place and with street-justice often dispensed at the point of a gun, the people waiting to visit their own accused criminals were very introspective. It seemed the consensus was that being a 290 was OK if you were accused of a simple ill-timed and/or unauthorized dalliance.

The attention they were getting was making many of the more criminal 290's very nervous, and one or two got up and walked out, apparently preferring to be violated and have a warrant issued rather than face the mob. When Redbone again grabbed the clipboard, you could have heard a pin drop in the lobby as everyone waited with baited breath for his next announcement.

"Hernandez, Miguel! 288 (A) PC! Lewd and lascivious acts with a child under 14!" called out Redbone. "You look the type," he said as the little 50-year-old Mexican cowboy 290 approached.

Mr. Hernandez spoke almost no English and was generally confused about the entire legal process into which he had been immersed. He never really understood the charges against him since the legal age of consent in Mexico was 12. Sure, the girl's father was upset, but fathers were always upset. He didn't blame the man. It was his misfortune to have sired girls. Mr. Hernandez had 12 boys (that he knew of) with three different women. All he knew was that in this strange land it was (apparently) against the law to be a man. But he figured he needed to follow the rules for at least another five years until he had enough money to retire back to Zacatecas. Then he could leave all this strange Gringo business behind.

The lobby audience was too busy debating the terms "lewd" and "lascivious" to get a real handle on the criminal nature of Mr. Hernandez's deeds. Most of the ladies in the lobby were black, and it was generally agreed that Mesicans (the generic term used for all Hispanics – applied near correctly in this case) could not be trusted around children at all. Except the women, who were by all accounts decent mothers and good cooks. The debate devolved into which was better, Soul Food or Mexican Food, with Mexican food (specifically Taco Bell burritos) coming out the winner by a hair.

No one was interested in going down to the jail to visit inmates by now, so the other desk officer quit calling out names from the visitor list. All eyes were on Redbone, as the old-timer detective came out for another registrant.

"Adams, Justin! 286(B) PC! Sodomy by force with a child under 14!" shouted Redbone. For a brief second, there was no movement in the lobby as everyone absorbed the nature of the charges. In the calm before the storm (as Redbone later recalled it to Friedman), the super-deviant Shifty Fuck-Knuckle practically ran to where Redbone was standing with the old sex dick and whispered fiercely, "Who the fuck do you think you are? Making me out to be some kind of criminal! What I do in my bedroom is my business…"

"Oh, hell no!" bellowed a six-foot-two, 325 lb. black woman with two 9-year-olds at her knee. "Why the fuck ain't he in prison!?! Dirty motherfucker!"

"You watch your mouth, you fat bitch," sneered Mr. Shifty

Redbone saw the look on the alleged bitch's face and could see the disbelief in her eyes. He looked back at her accuser and noticed that the guy was preparing to resume his argument with the police and clearly had no idea what he had just done.

"You just made a colossal mistake, kid-fucker," advised Redbone, who was well aware of the penalty for calling a black woman a bitch in public.

"Oooooooo…he just called you out yo name!"

"You gonna let him get away with that shit!?!?!"

"I would fuck that muthafucka up!"

The large woman with two small kids had been given no choice by Mr. Shifty Adams. With the crowd egging her on, she told her twin babies to sit down on the green benches in the lobby and then she attacked. Adams weighed about a buck-fifty soaking wet and was only five-foot-six. He never stood a chance. When she smashed him against the chest-high 77th Street front desk using only her body weight, he seemed to fold in Half as he collapsed to the floor.

The other desk officer grabbed his ROVER and broadcast a help call at the front lobby, as the old detective and Redbone moved around to safety behind the long curved desk. The crowd was in a fury. It was pandemonium. Babies were screaming, women were mobbing Shifty Kid-Fucker trying to get their licks in, and the other 290's were doing the mad scramble trying to escape through the front lobby doors. The primary aggressor was knee-dropping all 325 of her pounds on the child molester's head and upper body. She had been to state prison a time or two and was in no way shy about fighting like a man when she wanted to. The helpless deviant was crying and screaming for mercy, but there was none to be had. The way she saw it, this was a rare opportunity to punish someone who really and truly deserved it. By the time additional resources began pouring into the front desk area, Mr. Justin Adams had been reduced to a quivering bloody mess. His attacker was unrepentant. As she was led back into the station to be booked for ADW, she politely asked officers if one of her play-cousins could be allowed to take her babies home to her auntie's house. She was aglow with pride at having done the right thing.

"This shit'll be a DA reject!" she proclaimed to her supporters in the lobby, as she was led away. "It'll get kicked down to misdemeanor battery, and I'll do six months in the County! With good time, I'll be out in three…I can do that shit standing on my head!"

Redbone was impressed with her grasp of the Los Angeles legal system and knew she was right. Even the DA would have no sympathy for a child molester with a record like Adams'. She'd probably be out of custody before her victim would get out of the hospital.

"I have to tell you, bud," said the old sex detective to Redbone as the firefighters from 57's wheeled the semi-conscious Shifty Adams out to the waiting RA. "You know you're gonna catch some heat over what just happened. But think on this for a second: That bastard Adams has been molesting little kids for more than 20 years, and the State just keeps letting him get away with it. He might forget every one of his victims, but I bet he never forgets today. Good work, young man…I can't think of a better way to get a 1.28"

CHAPTER 9

LIFE GOES ON

"OFFICER FEEMAN! OFFICER OOBADOO! I THOUGHT YOU gone for ever and ever!" shouted the Korean owner at the 92nd and Western liquor store. "Someone win biiiiig Lotto…at MY store! We no see you for long time! Thought it was you…too bad…you still have to work…I'm gonna never work again."

He was as animated as they had ever seen him. Friedman noticed that he was now sporting frosted tips in his suspiciously dark hair. He wondered how much cash the guy got. It had to be a big chunk of change if it was based on percentages. Whatever it was, it had the effect of making him weird and his employees surly.

"That cheap-ass motherfucka gonna get over a million dollars for me selling someone their winning lottery ticket," grumbled one of the big guys behind the counter, as the Korean sashayed his way to the back room of the store. "I bet he don't give us shit. Heard him telling his son that we should each get a bottle of Courvoisier…racist motherfucker…I don't even like Courvoisier…tastes like cat piss."

"Man, when the fuck you ever drank cat piss?" laughed another worker, "You just mad 'cause you didn't win. Leave Mr. Kim alone...he been down here puttin' up with people's shit for years. How many times he been robbed? Eight? Ten times? Remember when those gangsters shot his old lady in the leg? How about the riots in '92? Lost everything and no insurance. He earned every dollar of that money."

"Courvoisier tastes like cat piss *smells,* ya stupid motherfucka," replied Big Man. "What you need, Friedman? The usual? We thought for sure you guys hit it big. Where you been?

"Just regular days off, bud. I can't believe we came so close. This place is used up. We're gonna have to find another store to buy ours at now," said Friedman. "What are the odds of lightening striking twice? Just gimmie two bucks for tonight's, bro..."

The big man passed him the ticket under the glass, and Friedman and Redbone walked back out to their black-and-white.

It only took a quick call to The League to have them put back on morning watch and re-assigned to the field. The Los Angeles Police Protective League was the police officers' union for the LAPD. It wasn't really a union in the truest sense of the word, since they didn't have the lawful power to strike, but it did provide them with legal protection against the Big Blue Machine and did all their contract negotiations. The LAPPL was a much sought-after endorsement by politicians of all ilk and that was where their true strength lay. It was staffed by member-elected sworn officers who were graciously assigned to The League office by the Department—full time. Friedman always thought that was weird of the Department to do—pay for their enemies to gather together and plot against them. Most of the Directors of the League were non-cops who used their position to further their career goals, or their post-career goals, depending on their aspirations. Friedman was sorely unimpressed with their performance. Instead of hiring professional contract negotiators to deal with the City every three or four years, they would all sit around and try to figure out what would be in everyone's best interest. Then the City's sharks would bowl them over, and the membership would generally get screwed.

Friedman always thought the cops should align themselves with the International Longshore and Warehouse Union down on the docks in San Pedro. The ILWU knew how to negotiate. Since the officers couldn't strike, the ILWU could do it for them. They were the only union in the country that wielded any real power, because when they had a work action it cost millions of dollars per day for idle shipping. Friedman figured they could name their price at the table and the City would buckle right away under pressure from the Pacific Maritime Association, the organization that represented the shippers.

Friedman had called them from home and spoke with the League president while Redbone was reorganizing the 290 issue at the front desk. The president called the 77th Street divisional captain III, Reggie Yasuke, and since he and the captain used to work an "A" car together, back in the day when both were lowly P2s, the problem was quickly resolved. The League pointed out that both Officer Obrador and Officer Friedman had only just recently returned to morning watch after having been bumped the summer prior. Since they were nowhere near the top of the bump list, this made their watch transfer smack of retaliation. The League president also pointed out that the "accident" in question was the first traffic accident of Officer Friedman's long and storied career — it was only an administrative issue and not disciplinary in nature. It was brought to the captain's attention that Officer Obrador was, in fact, not involved in the accident, which made his transfer obvious retaliation.

Finally, it was noted that Captain I Capall had only just recently cost the citizens of Los Angeles $6.2 million via a verdict handed down by a jury of his peers stemming from a hostile work environment lawsuit. Two P2s (now wealthy P2s) had found themselves in Captain Capall's crosshairs in another division for the egregious act of not only dating, but of daring to both be men while dating. He had transferred them around and made their lives miserable using his prerogative as patrol captain to keep dating couples from working the same watch. He let slip that he would do whatever was necessary to keep "those two fags" from disgracing the uniform. Unfortunately for Captain Capall, he had let that slip to a female sergeant named Pat with unusually short hair and life partner named Chris. "Who would have guessed?" was all he could say to the Big Chief as he shrugged his shoulders and graciously accepted his own transfer to 77th Street Division as the new patrol captain.

Friedman cruised eastbound on Manchester then to northbound Vermont. As they passed 84th Place, he almost wrecked the car.

"Jesus fucking Christ, Redbone!" shouted Friedman, "Check out that shit!"

The small strip mall on the southwest corner of 84th Place and Vermont Avenue was in the process of being completely remodeled. The original building was in an "L" shape. Mr. Davis' dry-cleaning shop occupied the southern half of the lot, and there were two small commercial rentals that occupied the western half. Both of the commercial rentals on the western half had been torn completely down, and the house directly behind the property to the west had been leveled. There was foundation framing laid out, and it appeared that the drycleaner would be extended to the west and the commercial rentals would be in the same place facing east, but back along the new property line. That would retain the original "L" shape configuration, but would make the parking lot and the commercial rentals much bigger. A six-foot chain-link construction fence had been erected around the property, with just a small portion of the parking lot left open for the dry-cleaner customers to use. It was open for business during the construction process.

Friedman flipped a U-turn and pulled up to park on the wide commercial sidewalk, leaving the few parking lot spaces for the real customers. They got out and walked into the lot, and Redbone pointed out the new 5-series BMW parked in the space where Mr. Davis always parked his 10-year-old piece of shit Ford Taurus.

"That car's 50 grand if it's a dollar, bro…" said Redbone.

There were only two customers in the store, and Mr. Davis was in the back getting one of their orders from the rack. Friedman and Redbone sat down in the lobby chairs — the same chairs they'd sat in just a short time ago when their lives had changed forever — and waited for their turn. Redbone had two uniforms with him that he had grabbed out of the trunk of their shop. Mr. Davis walked up with the customer's order, took the man's money and made change. He looked over and offered a friendly hello to Friedman and Redbone and then helped the lady who was next. There was no change in his demeanor, and when the pretty young professional inquired about all the construction, he didn't bat an eye.

"Well, Miss, I've owned this building for many, many years, and it has quite a bit of equity built up. I decided that with interest rates so low, it was the right time to do some upgrades. When I found out the property behind me was in foreclosure, I arranged with the bank to buy it on a short sale. I've hired a contractor to expand the building and upgrade the plumbing and electrical. It will leave a nice little something to my daughter and her husband when I'm gone."

He glanced at Friedman and Redbone as he moved to the back of the store to retrieve the lady's order.

When she left it was right at closing time, so Mr. Davis locked the door behind her, flipped the sign over, and picked up Redbone's uniforms from the counter.

"Same as usual, Officer Obrador?" he asked.

"Uh…yes. Please."

"How is everything with you boys?" asked Mr. Davis "Things looking up?"

"I suppose you could say that, Mr. Davis." said Friedman. "Things seem to be looking up around here, too. I didn't know you owned this building. I always assumed you rented this space for your shop."

"Well, you wouldn't believe it. I was recently contacted by a gentleman I haven't seen in quite some time. We were Marines together. Became fast friends in basic training down in Lejeune and then helped each other live through that death trap Viet Nam, but we kind of drifted apart after the war. Those things happen. But war tends to make men close, and it creates a bond that's hard to shake. Did I ever tell you boys I was in The Corps?"

"No, I don't believe you ever mentioned it," said Redbone.

"Huh. Well, my old friend just walked in here out of the blue a couple of weeks ago, and it seems he's done pretty well for himself. Used the G.I. Bill to go to college at UCLA and then to law school at USC. Now he owns his own law firm up on the Miracle Mile. Getting ready to retire and leave it to his son. He told me that he'd been entrusted by some associates to handle a small piece of business for them, so we went back to the office and had a couple of Maker's while we did a little paperwork.

My friend handed me the deed to this property and to my own house over on Gramercy Place, down there below Manchester. Can you believe that? Although, I've been paying on that house for quite a while...wasn't much left on the note...maybe $50,000," said Mr. Davis "He told me the only conditions was that I play along with the story he concocted about me always owning this property and deciding the time was right to remodel, if anyone ever asked."

"You know what else? It appears I'm the proud owner of the property behind this business on 84th Place as well. It also seems he knew a young contractor that was looking to establish himself in the commercial construction industry who would be willing to remodel this property for a fraction of his normal fee."

"What was his normal fee?" asked Friedman.

"Well, I'm not quite sure. We never discussed that. He's a smart boy, though. Showed up last week with approved building plans and a demolition crew. My new tenants both came to me and told me they would be just tickled with my offer to pay their monthly incomes during the construction in exchange for suspending their leases. Said thank you for the generous cash advances. The contractor told me the construction would be finished in two months. Mentioned having a friend at Building and Safety who could expedite the process."

"Hmm." said Redbone.

"That seems like a just reward for a man who has lived an honorable life," said Friedman.

"Well, Officer Friedman, I've worked my whole life and never expected to be given anything. I'm not like these kids today that want everything right now and want the government to buy it for them. I've always believed that if you worked hard and did the right thing that good things would happen.

"I remember when my brother became an officer with your LAPD, my parents were beside themselves with pride. They felt it was *their* reward for having always done the right thing. When he was killed, it just about broke them. I remember seeing the captain from over there where my brother worked in the 77th Precinct come to the house. I was hiding in the bathroom, listening to what they were saying while they talked in the living room. They hadn't told me anything yet. He told my daddy and momma that my brother was a hero, died with honor defending strangers. I remember the night about two or three days later when he came back. My momma had gone home to Alabama to stay with her sisters cause she was so hurt. He told my daddy and me that a special group of officers — they was called SIS — had found my brother's killer and had shot him dead. There wasn't gonna be no trial and that cowardly sonofabitch wasn't gonna live on forever and haunt our lives from prison. Told us that my brother would never be forgotten by *his* brothers at the LAPD. That kind of saved my daddy.

They were never really the same, but it gave them hope knowing that there were people out there that believed in doing the right thing…like they did.

"This thing that happened to you is what it is. Now you have to decide how to live the rest of your lives. I thank you kindly for everything you've done for me, but it wasn't necessary. We believe in the same things. I would stand by you all no matter what. But thank you just the same. It'll be nice to never have to worry about money again," said Mr. Davis.

"That's quite a car you've bought for yourself too," said Redbone. "You need to be careful driving around here with a brand-new BMW. Lots of gangsters wouldn't mind jacking you for it."

"Officer Obrador, they'll be in for a little more than they bargained for if they have a go at me. I may be old, but I can still take care of myself," replied Mr. Davis as he lifted his shirttail and exposed a stainless steel Rossi 357 magnum revolver in a black leather holster. "And that car…I always wanted a BMW, but I'll be damned if I'm *ever* gonna buy a brand-new car. You lose $10,000 as you drive off the dealer's lot. That there is a low mileage lease return. It's a year and a half old, but I got a great deal," laughed Mr. Davis, "New car? Shoot, my momma didn't raise a fool."

CHAPTER 10
FIGUEROA

THEY DROVE AROUND FOR THE REST OF THE SHIFT, AIMING to lay low and get to end of watch. Friedman was still trying to suppress several years of developed work ethic, and Redbone was just trying to curb the natural tendencies of street cops everywhere to get involved in capers. At about 0100 hours, they were rolling up Figueroa Street just north of 66th Street when they saw Showanna standing on the southwest corner of 65th. They knew that she was still within the grace period for winning the foot race against Redbone, but there was something about her body language that made them stop and hit her up. When Friedman stepped out of the car and threw out a friendly greeting, she seemed to panic.

She immediately looked across Figueroa and then yelled at Friedman, "Why you fucking with me?! I ain't done nothin' wrong but standin' here on the corner!"

She was way too loud and obviously forcing her anger. Friedman stepped closer and saw that her left eye was swollen practically shut. He glanced across Fig and saw a black male with cornrows standing next to the open passenger-side door of a black Chrysler 300 rental with Nevada plates. He was facing southbound, away from the disruption Showanna was making with Friedman and Redbone, which only served to make him more conspicuous.

"Hey Bone, be discreet but watch that asshole in the blue Pendleton across the street next to the black 300," said Friedman.

He walked over to where Showanna, looking super nervous, was standing on the corner. As he approached, she stage-whispered, "Please, Green-Eyes, you gotta get the fuck away from me...please."

Friedman pulled a field interview card and mechanical pencil out of his chest pocket and assumed the classic interview stance. He already knew everything about Showanna, but if his guess was right he needed to put on a show for the gangster across the street.

"Where is Jackie, Showanna?"

"She's at Centinela, Friedman," replied the shaking young prostitute. "I think she got fucked up bad. I can't talk to you anymore...please. Just let me be. I'll get off the track, I promise."

"That motherfucker across the street turn you both out?" asked Friedman.

"Friedman..." Showanna's eyes were begging now. "Please leave me alone. You can't help. No one can. You know the rules..."

The life of a street-walking prostitute in South Central Los Angeles was as strictly regulated as any corporate service-industry job. The rules were clear and concise, and any violation had consequences. But unlike corporate America, however, a violation could be deadly.

The rules for the non-crack-whore pimp girls went something like this:

Once the girls had been turned out (declared to be under the protection of a pimp), they were the property of the pimp. Everything they made went to him, and woe to the girl that dared to hold out. In exchange, the pimp provided booze, weed (rarely cocaine — addicts weren't trustworthy), hotel rooms in which to sleep and turn tricks, and occasional shopping sprees at the Slauson Super Mall at Western Avenue and Slauson. The pimp also provided theoretical protection from other pimps and bad johns.

Rule No. 1 when contacted by the police was never, never, ever admit to having a Daddy (street vernacular for a pimp). Pimping and pandering held vicious punishments, according to the California Penal Code, and there were horror stories among gangsters about pimps getting 10 to 15 years for a single charge. The girls had to memorize the information of another prostitute who was roughly their height, weight and age and who had recently been to jail and therefore had no warrants. Any clean-record individual would do, but one with a prostitution record was more convincing if the officers ran her criminal history. She should stick to the story to the bitter end. If arrest was imminent, she should try to get booked under that name to confuse the system. The girls should flirt with the police and try to get them to let them stay on the track. Tell them they needed the money for their babies, their auntie with cancer, their student loans or anything else they could so they were allowed to stay. If the cops were rookies, they should try to make a fuss and claim racism for being stopped. A girl must attempt to avoid jail (and thereby costing her Daddy money) at all costs. If a pimp felt that a girl didn't work hard enough to avoid jail, or failed to comply with any of the rules, she would be "regulated" when she got out. "Regulated" could mean a simple ass kicking, a "lesson" rape, or anything else Daddy could devise.

Rule No. 1 when it came to *working the street* was beware of dating black men (most Figueroa pimps were black men and social rules against stereotyping did not exist on Figueroa. The black john *might* or *might not* be a rival pimp, so why take the chance?). Girls should never even make eye contact with a black male if they thought he could be a pimp. They should turn their backs to all questionable black male customers to show their Daddy that they were following the rules. And Daddy (or one of his surrogates) was always watching.

According to the established ways of pimping, if a girl made eye contact with another pimp, she was "out of pocket" and looking for a new Daddy. She was fair game. This is where the "break yourself" line originated. If a girl was out of pocket, her old pimp would approach her, determine she wanted to leave his custody, and the new pimp would order her to "break yourself." She would turn out her pockets and give all the proceeds from her previous transactions to the old pimp, and all further earnings would be the property of the new pimp. The deal was done.

That was the courteous manner in which a girl exchanged protectors. The other, more sinister, method was "gorilla pimping." If a girl got gorilla pimped, it was an unpleasant experience she was not likely to forget. It essentially consisted of a pimp running up and beating the fuck out of a girl while she worked the street. It was a vicious man's method, which was usually practiced by hard-core OG gangsters. Most pimps were cowardly by nature — they usually cried when hemmed up by Vice — but the guys that gorilla pimped the girls were hard. Rather than having a girl give the old pimp his fair due, the gorilla-pimp method kept all the proceeds and struck fear in the hearts of the other pimps in the area. It was psychological as much as physical, but inevitably the gorilla pimp would lose out, because his stable of girls would eventually turn on him due to his violent nature. That was when the LAPD Vice units got the good pimping cases — when the girls turned vindictive.

"I know the rules," replied Friedman. "Do me a favor and sit tight for a second. I'm gonna pretend to run you on the computer in the car. When I come back, you are gonna need to do what I tell you to do, even if it sounds crazy. Now scream at me a bit, just for show, OK?"

While Showanna mother-fucked him at the top of her lungs, he walked over and dropped into the driver's seat of their shop. He called Redbone over to the car and told him what had happened to the girls, what was about to happen in the next 60 seconds, and what he was going to need to do to keep them all safe.

What the fuck is wrong with me? This chick chose her path. Why should I give a shit if she got gorilla pimped? She knew the rules when she started, and she knows the rules now. That asshole across the street is just another predator. There's a hundred in line behind him ready to take advantage. This isn't gonna solve anything, and I know it. She'll be back on the track in a couple of weeks, and I'll have only delayed things...not changed them. Fuck it. Beschütze die Schwachen, *just like Opa used to say...*

Friedman popped out of the car and walked over to Showanna. He reached back and pulled out one of his sets of Peerless cuffs, and when she looked at him with wild eyes he spoke smooth and calm.

"When I put my hands on you to hook you up, you spin around and slap me hard with your right hand. Make sure it's loud enough for Shit-Bird across the street to hear. Struggle around a bit, and Redbone'll put out a back-up. That'll bring the troops. It'll be a good-enough show for that prick to go easy on you later, and it'll give us time to get Jackie from the hospital."

"I can't hit you," she practically cried.

"Showanna, do what I fucking tell you. It'll be fine. We just need some time to breathe and a little distraction. Do it now," said Friedman as he reached out and grabbed her left arm to spin her around.

She slapped him so hard Friedman was pretty sure they heard it at Parker Center up in downtown. He was momentarily stunned by the force of the blow, but luckily Showanna was motivated by fear of her new Daddy and remembered to do her part. She screamed and began to writhe around while Friedman recovered his composure. His leg swept her gently to the ground and began to wrestle her around, pretending to try to cuff her while Redbone broadcast a back-up.

Redbone was supposed to watch the pimp across the street to make sure he didn't try to defend his property, but he was also supposed to protect Friedman and Showanna from the incoming cops. LAPD officers who arrived at the scene of a back-up usually had no idea what they were going to find upon arrival and were always amped up and ready for conflict. In the south-end divisions of the city, a back-up meant that things had gone fuck-wrong and the officers that put out the call needed people there now. It summoned the force of an entire division and anyone else that happened to be nearby from neighboring divisions.

Unfortunately, in this case, there happened to be another unit one block west of their location, and they were on the scene within 15 seconds. Before Redbone could react, they were out of their car and coming to "help" Friedman. They were new to 77th Street and were classmate rookies. It was on like Donkey Kong. The first one drew his side-handle baton and struck Friedman on both legs with a vicious power stroke, missing his thrashing prostitute target by a mile. The second copper was attempting to help get the still-struggling prostitute into cuffs as Redbone inserted himself discreetly between The Stick Master and his prey to keep him from killing Friedman. When Redbone looked up, the pimp across the street and the 300 were both gone, so he broadcast a Code 4 and cancelled the other responding units. Showanna quit struggling, and they cuffed her easily.

"Shouldn't you guys get a supervisor here?" asked The Stick Master. "We had a 'Use of Force.'"

"*You* had a 'Use of Force,' bro. There's no *we* in this shit. What do you want to tell 'em? Friedman was taking a misdemeanor prostitute into custody, and you ran up and beat the fuck out of him with your stick? You gotta actually make contact with a suspect for there to be a 'Use of Force,'" laughed Redbone.

While they were talking, additional units continued driving by, which was how things always were. Cops were curious creatures by nature, and even after they were cancelled off a back-up or a help call they still came over to check things out. Redbone waved them off with four fingers, while Friedman limped with Showanna over to their shop and put her in the back seat.

A mid-watch boot Sergeant pulled up, hopped out of her shop and walked over to where Redbone was talking to the two rookies.

"Was there a 'Use of Force'? Is the suspect injured?"

Redbone must have looked at her funny because she immediately became defensive.

"What's the problem, Officer? Didn't you understand what I asked you?"

"No, Ma'am," replied Redbone. "I understood. There was no 'Use of Force.' If there had been, wouldn't you think a more appropriate first question from a supervisor would have been 'Were there any *officers* injured?'"

She was obviously new to both her rank and to 77th Street, and her lack of field time was reflected in her demeanor. She probably hadn't worked patrol since probation several years ago and was intimidated by her new assignment. Since she had no frame of reference for patrol, she fell back on what they taught in LAPD Sergeant School, which was basically to lead by fiat. There was a phenomenon at LAPD among the supervision that Friedman had seen developing over the years as the Department struggled to achieve parity with the community it served. This week's protected classes were actively recruited and promoted regardless of their leadership capabilities. The result was insecure supervision extremely prone to what the military guys called "leading from the sleeve." There were two kinds of leaders — those that led by example, and those that pointed to their stripes and said, "You do what I tell you because of these." The latter is leading from the sleeve. Friedman had been ordered to do something by LAPD supervision only twice in his career…both times by female (a perennial protected class) sergeants…once to make copies, and once to send a fax. That alone spoke volumes about what passed for leadership in the new LAPD.

The rookies stood open-mouthed. They couldn't fathom anyone talking to a sergeant-god as if that sergeant had made a mistake. Apparently, she couldn't either.

"You are dangerously close to insubordination, Officer … Obrador" the boot Sergeant informed Redbone as she leaned in and scanned the nameplate on his chest.

"Insubordination is the willful disobedience to a direct order, Ma'am. It's an automatic Board of Rights issue and a firing offense," interjected Friedman as he walked up. "Any supervisor making a career-damaging accusation like that should be real careful they aren't confusing insubordination with their own inability to lead."

Friedman was never the type to bully or be bullied. Throughout his career he'd gotten himself in trouble by his unwillingness to stand down. One of the things that irked him the most about the para-military nature of the LAPD was how the rank structure was consistently abused by weak individuals. The comfort that the Ticket provided never entered his thought process as he put Redbone's bully in check. It was just who he was.

She stared at Friedman as if he'd just told her to fuck off. She looked down at his left arm and saw that he had two more hash-marks on his sleeve than she did and decided it was probably safer to keep her mouth shut. Instead, she stalked over to where Showanna was sitting in the back seat of their shop.

It was obvious that she was hoping to drag a "Use of Force" out of her so that she could pencil-fuck both Friedman and Redbone, but the wily prostitute had been well prepped by Friedman and probably knew department policy better than Sergeant She-Pogue. After getting nothing she could use against the officers, the rookie sergeant practically ran to her shop and drove off in the direction of the station with the engine roaring and tires screeching.

"She's on her way to cry to Lt. Short about how you just hurt her feelings, Friedman," said Redbone.

"Fuck it, bro. Who cares? Let's get over to Centinela and see if we can spring Jackie before that asshole gets his fucking claws into her."

Friedman turned to The Stick Master and laughed, "You've got a mean swing, brother. I'm gonna have fucking bruises on both my legs for weeks. You owe me *big* time. Do me a favor and keep this whole thing on the down-low. No locker-room chit-chat over this one. It needs to stay between us."

"You got it, Sir. I'm real sorry about my boy putting it on you. We ain't saying nothing. It's kind of embarrassing, anyway" replied his partner, as he shot a dirty look at The Master.

The rookies just stared as Redbone and Friedman flipped a U-turn and drove down Fig with the hooker in the back seat.

"Hey fool," one rookie said, "my last training officer up in West Valley warned me about the kind of shit that goes on down here. He was wrong about the cops, though. He kept telling me they were all gunfighters and they thought they were too cool for the rest of the Department. That's bullshit. These motherfuckers are crazy for sure, but laid-back crazy. I'm never leaving the south end — this is where I belong. What the fuck did you stick the Veterano for, asshole? Way to build us a rep."

CHAPTER II
CENTINELA

LIKE ALL OTHER LOS ANGELES COUNTY HOSPITALS, CENTINELA Hospital was a clusterfuck of inefficiency. Since the downsizing and closing of Daniel Friedman and Martin Luther King, all ambulance issues from South Central were sent to California Hospital in downtown Los Angeles, Harbor General Hospital on the Strip, or to Centinela in Inglewood. That meant anyone with a head cold or fever who felt a free ambulance trip to the emergency room would result in their instant magical cure would be clogging the hallways. Because the hospital administration was terminally afraid of being sued, and the government was paying the bills, everyone who showed got a full-blown work-up. This created a huge bottleneck in the emergency room because in addition to the non-emergency ambulance traffic and regular walk-in patients, Centinela was also one of the only trauma centers. This meant that the staff had to drop everything when patients with gunshot wounds and cuttings came through the door. Having South Central as a trauma patient source guaranteed a shit-load of cuttings and GSW's.

The hospital staff also operated under the illusion that everyone brought in by the police was a "patient" — not a criminal. It was hospital policy for the cops and their charges to get in line behind all the sniffles and cramps and wait their turn to see a doctor unless they qualified as trauma. This usually resulted in a six-to-eight-hour trip, removing the officers from the field for nearly the entire shift. Friedman could never understand that mentality. The reality was that a majority of the county hospital employees lived in low-income, high-crime areas. It seemed to him that they would want to get the cops in and out so the officers could get back to protecting their neighborhoods, but logic seldom prevailed. Whenever Friedman had a body to book that needed medical clearance, he always drove the extra 20 minutes down the Harbor Freeway to the hospital in San Pedro. It was a private, for-profit hospital that contracted with the city. The staff appreciated the officers, took zero shit from the suspects and put them in front of everybody except trauma to get the officers back out on the street as soon as possible.

Friedman pulled their black-and-white into the back parking lot of Centinela, but had to back out again because there were three L.A. City, two L.A. County and two private R.A.'s taking up all the emergency vehicle parking spaces.

"I hate this fucking hospital," sighed Redbone.

"No shit, brother," replied Friedman. "But don't sweat it...we're just here to see if we can spring Jackie and get the fuck on. It shouldn't take too long."

"Famous last words, dude. We'll see what happens. I bet they won't even tell us where she is. These nurses with their HIPAA fascination love to tell us to fuck off. We'd stand a better chance if we weren't in uniform and told them we were family."

The HIPAA regulations were basically designed to protect patient confidentiality with regard to their medical records, and the hospital staff had been threatened with everything from firing to jail time for any unlawful disclosure. The result was that officers couldn't even get a patient number or treating doctor over the phone anymore. Several of the County hospital LVN's and clerical staff also hated the police, so it gave them great pleasure to tell cops to pound sand.

"You're probably right. You know where she's at, Showanna?" Friedman asked the hooker, who was waiting patiently in the backseat.

"I ain't got a idea Friedman. The last time I seen her she was gettin' in the ambulance over on Flower. All I know was they said they was takin' her here." She replied through the window in the backseat. Showanna was still shaken up from the whole ordeal over on Figueroa. She apologized to Friedman all the way to Inglewood and only stopped when he finally told her he'd slap her back if it would make her feel better.

Friedman figured Jackie had been admitted since Showanna told him that she was pretty bloody and only semi-conscious when she got in the R.A. He told her to walk through to the front lobby and see what she could find out. They watched her walk in the entrance of the ER just as one of the ambulances pulled out and created a space for them to park. Friedman backed in, and they got out and sat on the hood of their shop to wait for Showanna to come out with some info.

Redbone heard it first. He could hear a car screeching its tires around several nearby corners, and it appeared to be getting closer.

"Man. Someone is either running from the cops or they're drunk and driving like an asshole," opined Redbone.

"It sounds like they're heading this way...it's definitely getting closer," said Friedman.

Suddenly an early '90s tan Toyota Camry came into view going southbound on Myrtle Avenue. It was hauling ass and barely made the turn into the emergency room parking lot. It skidded to a stop directly in front of Friedman and Redbone, as they moved to the rear of their shop for cover.

A young black male in a Seattle Mariners jersey jumped out of the driver's seat and started to run toward the emergency room entrance when he suddenly noticed the two cops and the black-and-white. He scrunched up his brow as if trying to decide whether he needed legal or medical help, and then suddenly blurted out:

"Officer! My friend's been shot, and this car is stolen!"

Friedman calmly walked over and turned the guy around, then pulled out his cuffs.

"Man, what the fuck you doin', Cuz?! I told you my boy's been shot! Why you puttin' handcuffs on me?!"

"You just told me you were driving a stolen car. I'm no doctor, but I am a cop. G-ride's a felony," replied Friedman as he hooked him up.

"Ain't that some shit."

Redbone had walked over to the passenger side of the vehicle while Friedman dealt with the now bitching self-proclaimed felon. Several hospital staff came running out to see what was going on after having been summoned by a janitor who had been smoking a cigarette by the ER doors.

"This guy's brains are all over the headrest and there're 12-gauge shells on the floor in the back seat, Friedman…what the fuck happened, Holmes?"

The Felon suddenly forgot about the injustice of being handcuffed for G-Ride and began to stammer about having been the victim of a crime somewhere over on Western Avenue.

Smelling bullshit, Friedman grabbed his ROVER off his Sam Browne intending to check if there had been any shootings involving a mid-'90s Toyota Camry, either in Inglewood or on Western.

Before he could key the mike, he heard communications broadcast additional information to 12A73 for their shooting on Western at 62nd Street. He hadn't heard the original call, but he asked communications to have A73 switch to an available tactical frequency so he could determine if there was any connection to their Camry at Centinela.

Communications advised them to switch to South Bureau Tach 1, Channel 38 and he raised Kazan.

"Hey, bro…we're over at Centinela and we got a tan mid-'90s Toyota Camry here with a bunch of holes in the passenger door and at least one in the passenger's head. Is it possibly related to what you got going on over there?" asked Friedman into his radio.

"Really?!" replied Kazan, "You get the driver, too? Wits are saying an old tan Toyota or Nissan with a male black driver with a blue sports jersey. Got one victim DRT and one who is saying that the passenger was a male black who claimed Rollin' 60's right before he opened up on him with a tube…there was return fire, too…"

"I think we got your suspects…they drove right up to us…looks like a Ghetto Ambulance caper, but we happened to be sitting at the entrance to the ER and caught the driver off guard. I'll get this held down for the Homicide Dicks. Call my cell if you need me for anything…we'll be here until further."

It turned out The Felon driver and his passenger, Head-Shot, were members of the notorious Fronthood Set of the Rolling 60's Neighborhood Crip gang. They were out looking for some Six-Deuce Brim enemies to kill with their 12-gauge shotgun when they observed a group they believed to be rival gang members near the intersection of Western Ave and 62ndStreet. Unfortunately for The Felon and Head-Shot, one of the individuals they mistook for a rival turned out to be a Gulf War Veteran (1st edition) who was not only a conservative Republican recently moved to Los Angeles from Michigan, but also the proud possessor of a lawfully issued Concealed Carry Weapons permit from the County of San Bernardino. He was a California Bureau of Security and Investigative Services licensed security guard who spent his spare time in his new city at the shooting range honing his skills with his 40-caliber Glock handgun.

The Felon pulled up alongside Mr. CCW and a couple of his co-workers, who were standing curbside on 62nd just east of Western. Head-Shot shouted out, "Neighborhood 60's, muthafucka!" and blasted one of the innocent off-duty security guards directly in the chest with nine 32-caliber pellets of double-aught buck, making him Dead Right There. While he furiously worked the action and fired for effect against the now fleeing crowd, he got tattooed by Mr. CCW, who was most definitely locked on target. In a rookie maneuver, Head-Shot emptied the tube and could only stare back as CCW aligned his front sights and popped one good one to his forehead just above his right eye. He fired several more at the fleeing Toyota as it raced away southbound on Western. The Felon panicked when he realized his homeboy had been hit. He *thought* it was bad but couldn't see where all the blood was coming from because Head-Shot was slumped over in the passenger seat. He *knew* it was bad that they had just dumped a Brim and still had the shotgun in the car with them. He raced down Western to westbound Gage and passed a black-and-white police car rolling Code 3 eastbound on Gage at Cimarron, responding to the crime scene they just created.

He called his play cousin and told him what had happened, and that Head-Shot didn't look too good. His play cousin had him swing by his crib on Hyde Park and 4th Avenue to drop off the gauge, and then told him to drop Head-Shot off at the entrance to the emergency room at Daniel Friedman. He passed off the shotgun and tried to get all the shells but missed two on the floor in the back seat. Unfortunately, the play cousin just got back from a six-year stint at Corcoran for robbery and had no idea that Daniel Friedman was closed. Neither did The Felon. It took about 20 minutes and several stops for directions before he managed to arrive at his destination at the rear of Centinela Hospital…only to have LAPD 77th Street waiting for him. Ain't that some shit?

They spent the next several hours standing by at the crime scene they had set up in the ER parking lot of Centinela Hospital. Turned out that Head-Shot was not only *not* dead, he was listed in stable condition. That was good and bad. Good for The Felon, because now he was facing only one count of homicide. According to the Felony Murder Rule, he would have been charged for both the security guard's death and for Head-Shot's death because it happened during the commission of a felony crime. Bad for Head-Shot, because as soon as he got out of the hospital he was going to be done up on a murder charge for the death of the security guard. It was just bad all around for the security guard.

"I can't believe that guy wasn't dead. He got hit in the forehead for God's sake. There was brain matter on the headrest. How is that fucking possible?" asked Redbone.

"I don't know, bro. Bullets do weird things. I heard of a motor cop who got shot in the head one time — from dead straight in front of him — the bullet hit the left side of his head just above the ear and ricocheted around in his helmet and came out the right side just about his right ear. Word was he only got scalped. Weird shit happens," replied Friedman.

They were debating the nature of strange shootings that they had seen over the years when Showanna came outside with Jackie in tow. She had her entire head wrapped up in a bandage in what the old-school LAPD cops used to call a "Newton Turban."

"Daaamn, Friedman...did ya'll shoot someone right here in the parking lot of the hospital?" asked Showanna.

She was clearly impressed with all the hoopla surrounding the crime scene. She had been inside for nearly an hour looking for Jackie because she had checked in under a different name. Then she had to stand around for another two hours before they would confirm the results of a shitload of tests. Turned out that Jackie had been punched in the face and fell on the ground and hit her head. That was exactly what Jackie had told the ER doctor who treated her within the first 20 minutes of her arrival but he felt that a CAT-SCAN and blood work and X-rays were needed to properly diagnose her cut head and black eye. It was a good thing she gave a fake name and social security number, or she would have been on the hook for about $40,000 worth of medical bills.

"Nah…it's a long story, but basically these two 60's shot someone, one of *them* got shot in the head, they drove themselves here, and we snatched them up," said Friedman.

"Daaaaamn," was all Showanna could think of to say.

Friedman and Redbone had them wait in a coffee shop around the corner on Prairie Avenue until the Homicide Detectives were finished and they impounded the car to Al's Tow for evidence. Another unit had already come by and swooped up The Felon, and the Dicks had someone sitting on Head-Shot in the hospital. They went by and picked up Jackie and Showanna as soon as they cleared the scene and drove them down to a semi-nice hotel on Vermont and 190th Street down below the 405 where they could hole up and not have to worry about being found by their new Daddy.

Friedman paid for five nights in advance, and when he asked them if they had a plan neither had a clue.

"I'm not gonna give you guys a lecture or try to tell you to stay off the Track, but if that asshole gets a hold of you again, sooner or later you're gonna end up dead or permanently fucked up. I know you guys are skipping right now without giving him his money. That's gonna be a problem. At the very least you should try to get another Daddy, but what the fuck do I know?" said Friedman.

"Friedman…you and Redbone a-ight," said Showanna. "I wish all the po-lice was like you two. I know you trying to help…but we only know one thing, so that's what we'll do. What you want us to do? Get jobs at McDonald's?"

"Thanks a lot, Friedman. I owe you for sure," said Jackie.

CHAPTER 12
THE BONDSMEN

A WEEK OR SO LATER, REDBONE AND FRIEDMAN WERE assigned to work carnival security on Broadway. That was just fine with them because it meant that they could basically sleep in the parking structure and then drive a loop around Broadway from Florence down to 79th Street every hour or so to make sure the carnies were all still alive and none of the equipment had disappeared.

Like most LAPD Divisions, 77th Street held a carnival every summer where they closed off the streets and contracted with a roving carnival company. The Division would split the profits with the carnival management, and everyone was happy. It was pretty much the only time that many of the local kids ever saw anything like Disneyland, because at the price of tickets it was highly unlikely that any more than a handful of them had ever been to the Happiest Place on Earth. It was always a boon to the Divisional coffers and as a bonus the command staff could stroke each other's egos in the media and to the Community Police Advisory Boards, showing how much they cared. Everyone was happy except the businesses on Broadway, which were basically told to shut the fuck up and get with the program by the Senior Lead Officers. The multiple bail bondsmen on Broadway were always particularly pissed off because there was serious competition to begin with, and the loss of a good weekend's earnings could really put a hurt on them.

Freidman and Redbone never liked bail bondsmen because the way they saw things, the bondsmen were predators just like the criminals. They made their living off the misfortune of others. They also liked to pretend they were providing a service and would get butt-hurt if questioned about the morality of their usurious interest rates or the fact that they assisted a criminal's ability to re-plague society. They essentially took advantage of good, honest, family members who couldn't bear the thought of their accused baby boy criminal spending another night in a cold, dark cell.

Redbone, in particular, despised the bail bondsmen because one of them had beefed him for false arrest the year prior when a sergeant ordered him to book the agent for soliciting in front of a jail facility—a crime that was laid out in Title 10 of the California Code of Regulations.

For some reason, the Command Staff of 77th Street had one day decided that they were no longer going to enforce that code. The result was almost instantaneous. With nearly a dozen bail bond companies in the immediate vicinity of 77th Street Jail, competition was fierce. They all began to employ people to stand on the front steps of the station and solicit business from unfortunate family members of the incarcerated. It got so bad that they had guys dress up as Abe Lincoln and Uncle Sam and pass out flyers with their rates. It caused the exact problems envisioned when the regulations were devised.

There were fist fights among the bail agents, and families complained to the police about the "bait and switch" of low interest rates that proved too good to be true with the real cost always coming out after the paperwork had been signed. It caused no end of problems for the front desk personnel.

The south end of the city was not a place for timid supervision. Sgt. Peter Brothers was anything but timid. He actually was thought by many at 77th Street to be bat-shit crazy. He was a former Marine who liked to call officers "Fuck-head" and "ShitBird."

He came off so rough around the edges that some people were just plain afraid of him, but the majority of the field cops respected him. He was openly gay and didn't give a flying fuck who knew about it.

There were several supremely funny stories whirling around 77th Street about him, but one of the best was when he cornered a young male officer, gave him a banana and made him eat it in front of him while he watched. The copper later told a riveted crowd of Blue Suiters how dirty he felt after the last bite. The coppers all convulsed with laughter and couldn't hear the story often enough to satisfy their twisted senses of humor.

He didn't care what the people above or below thought about him and brooked no excuses from his subordinates. He had been a high-speed, low-drag field cop and expected the same level of dedication from the officers in his den. Friedman knew he would never last, but figured the south end would be the only place he might stand a chance. He would have been fired long ago if he had tried his sexual-harassment shenanigans in the Central or West Bureaus or, God forbid, the Valley.

He was finally undone by his "get it done" mentality after being tasked by the captain to ensure his den had 100 percent compliance for online training. He knew cops hated online training and would never get it done on time, so he got their information, logged on in their names and did the work for them. Bam. One hundred percent compliance. He was the only supervisor to achieve the goal laid out by the captain. As a reward, he was given an administrative transfer (a career death sentence) for his efficiency. No one thought he gave a fuck—he went right back to being a hard-charging street cop without missing a beat.

Prior to his supervisory Waterloo, Sgt. Brothers was sitting in as watch commander one evening, eyeing the live video feed from the front of the station. He saw a bail bondsman harassing a little old Hispanic lady as she tried to enter the station. He ran up to the front desk where Redbone was working that night and inquired about the confrontation. The lady, who was practically crying, told him (through a translator) that the bondsman had told her that her grandson would never get out of jail unless she went with him and signed the necessary paperwork. Brothers flipped out. He started to run outside, probably to kick the bondsman's ass in front of his peers as a life lesson to them all, but remembered at the last minute that he had to man the inside phone lines in the watch commander's office. He ordered Redbone to go outside and arrest the asshole bondsman. Redbone started to remind him that the captains had decided it was OK for the bail bondsmen to solicit in front of the station, but Sgt. Brothers only had to look at him to make Redbone's blood run cold. He did as he was told, and went outside and snatched the guy up. The bondsman was pissed. There were at least five other bail bondsmen on the steps soliciting business, and he tried to make it a race beef until, much to his chagrin, Brothers told him to fuck off because Redbone was Hispanic, too. He then tried a different tactic and ultimately a false arrest complaint was taken and investigated by IA. All bail bondsmen were forever tainted as far as Redbone was concerned.

The main job of the officers assigned to the carnival detail was to protect and serve the carnies. They kept the baseheads from stealing the copper-wire electrical cords used to power the machines, kept the teenagers off the equipment after closing time, and ensured that no one sneaked their cars into the perimeter. That way, the carnies could move their equipment around freely in the morning.

Friedman and Redbone were making a lap up Broadway at about 2330 hours when Redbone spotted a car parked on northbound Broadway directly in front of his arch-enemy's bail bond storefront. The guy who had beefed him was one of their employees, and they were a known and confirmed anti-cop outfit. The car was a PT Cruiser with one of those advertising wraps for that bail bond company.

"Hey Friedman, was that PT Cruiser there when we drove by earlier?" asked Redbone.

"Negative. They must have just put it there within the last hour. This whole thing is barricaded up tight with crime-scene tape everywhere. They had to have moved a bunch of shit to get in the perimeter."

"I'm gonna pull over there and tell them to move it. If they get to park inside, then everyone is gonna want to and we'll be dealing with the 'How come he got to do it?' crowd all night," said Redbone.

Redbone pulled to the curb behind the Cruiser, and before he got out Friedman said, "Let me handle these guys. They already hate you. One more thing, bro. They have video *and* audio surveillance inside and outside of this place. Don't let them bait you."

Friedman had conducted door-knocks there for a homicide investigation that had occurred just around the corner on 76th Street a couple of years back. The suspect vehicle had fled northbound on Broadway, and the bail bond shop's video had captured the escape. They made the homicide dicks get a warrant to get the tape, which was a further demonstration of their asshole quotient.

"I'm good, bro. Fuck these people. Let them lead their miserable lives. They're nothing to me anymore," said Redbone.

Friedman walked over to the front of the business and looked inside. All the lights were on and it appeared they were open, but the front door was locked. He pushed the bell and saw a little Hispanic man peer around the corner in the back and then disappear. He waited for another five minutes or so and then rang the bell again. He saw the same guy peek around the corner and mouth "What!?" at him as he threw his hands up in the air in apparent disgust. Friedman motioned for him to come to the front door, and he saw the guy sigh dramatically then disappear again.

"This guy is gonna be a piece of work. I can tell. Let me handle him, cool?"

"I'm cover, you're contact. You don't need me." replied Redbone as he walked back to the open driver's door of their shop and sat down in the driver's seat. He rolled up the windows and whipped out his phone to check his Facebook and practice Sudoku.

"I'm gonna turn on the DICV when this guy comes out just in case this dickhead turns out to be smarter than he looks," thought Friedman.

Just as Friedman was about to ring the bell again, the little guy appeared from the back of the store and now had a pissed-off-looking chubby little Hispanic woman in tow. Friedman figured they were doing the nasty in the back, which was disgusting to consider because they were like a pair of trolls. He walked over to a desk and began to shuffle some paperwork around, just to let him know who was in charge, as he pointedly ignored the uniformed cop outside his business. Friedman didn't take the bait and stood relaxed on the sidewalk. He finally walked over and stood behind the PT Cruiser and pretended to run the license plate with communications on his ROVER. That got the reaction he expected. Little Guy and Chubby Girl came running quickly to the door as Friedman hit the button on the DICV recorder on his belt.

He quickly assessed them and determined that Little Guy owned the business due to his cheap flashy clothes, slicked-back hair, and his boots made of some strange animal's skin. He figured that Chubby Girl worked at the business but wasn't the wife—maybe a girlfriend on the side—because husbands and wives didn't do the nasty at midnight in a storefront business. Whatever their relationship, he was obviously pissed and she was obviously egging him on.

"What the fuck do you want?!?!!" said Little Guy, as a start to their conversation.

"Good evening, sir. Is this your vehicle here?" said Friedman, motioning toward the PT Cruiser.

"Of course it is. Are you stupid? Look at it."

"Sir. How did you manage to get it inside the perimeter of the carnival? There are signs everywhere prohibiting parking for the next three days, and all the streets are blocked with barricades and crime-scene tape. I'm going to have to ask you to move it." said Friedman.

Keeping his cool and speaking to Little Guy like he was a moron was having the desired effect. He could see the guy burning up inside. He could tell that Chubby Girl was dying to put in her two cents, too.

"The last time you had this fucking carnival we parked on the side street and someone broke all the windows in our car. I'm sick of losing business and then becoming a victim, too. I never heard from detectives about the windows, neither. I know you guys don't give a shit about solving crimes committed against legitimate business people," whined Little Guy.

"Well, I don't know about last year. It sounds to me that since they broke *all* your windows, it might have been you were specifically targeted rather than a random crime. Did you try to assist the auto detectives with a list of possible suspects? I guess the list could be rather long. Some folks might get upset when they figured out how much your services really ended up costing them," countered Friedman.

"What the fuck do you know about our business?" hissed Chubby Girl, finally unable to keep her mouth shut.

Little Guy turned to her and began speaking Spanish. That sort of thing happened to Friedman all the time. Most of the Hispanics in Southern California were Mexican, Salvadorian or Guatemalan, and since the majority were from rural areas and were often uneducated, the assumption was that if you weren't short and brown you couldn't speak Spanish. There had been countless times when suspects got their stories straight right in front of Friedman, thinking he couldn't understand them. He never let on that he spoke Spanish unless it was absolutely necessary. It was always fun to see the look on people's faces when they found out.

"Don't say shit to him," commanded the Little Guy in Spanish. "This motherfucker and his coconut partner are screwed big time. We're gonna file a complaint for harassment and racism with the big Gringo's boss. That red cop sitting in the car is the one that arrested Luis about a year back. We filed a false arrest complaint, but the Mexican Internal Affairs guy told Luis he had a right to arrest him. He said he *knew* that most of the cops on patrol were racists, but he'd never been able to catch one. He said if the same guy fucked with Luis again to call him and he'd make sure he got fired. That detective was down with *La Raza*. The Red might be able to say he's Hispanic, but this asshole can't.

"We'll tell his boss that he called us 'dirty wetbacks' and they'll both get fucked. The Gringo for saying it and The Red for not reporting he said it. This'll be the second time for The Red—it'll look like harassment for sure."

"What about the outside cameras? Aren't they recording what we're saying right now?" said Chubby.

"Nah. The cameras still work, but the recorder hasn't worked for a while. The video will show they were talking to us, and that'll be enough for the Internal Affairs cops. They'll believe us for sure. They'd love to catch some racist street cops."

"We ain't moving shit," said Little Guy, turning to Friedman and switching back to English. "This is harassment. I want to talk to your supervisor."

Friedman knew their plan, obviously, but he was worried that if the right person didn't take the complaint then things might not go like he'd hoped they would. He wanted to give the Little Guy enough rope to hang himself so he suggested, "Of course, Sir. Let me call you a supervisor to come out, but it could take a little while for him to get here. If you want to walk over to the station, you can talk to the watch commander. He's the lieutenant in charge of the whole watch. It's only a block. Tell me what you'd like me to do to help you."

Friedman also knew that Lt. Short was working tonight and would absolutely *love* to take a biased policing/racial discrimination beef from these two idiots. He would ask the perfect questions with such zeal that

Little Guy and Chubby Girl would be beside themselves with glee at having screwed a couple of street cops with their false complaints. He knew Lt. Short would ultimately end up looking like an asshole after the complaint was investigated (once Friedman's own audio from the DICV had been heard), and Little Guy and Chubby would get put on the IA's chronic/false complainer list. That would protect other cops from their bullshit in the future. It was a win-win. He didn't want Redbone to know they were going to complain, however, because he figured Redbone might give them something to complain about, and that would defeat the whole purpose.

"That's even better. I hear'd how your sergeants take care of you and don't report it when citizens try to tell how they've been abused. We're gonna go right now. And if you touch my fucking car while I'm gone I'll add another complaint," sneered Little Guy.

"Sir, your car is subject to impound at this time, but I'll wait until I hear from my lieutenant before I take any further police action," Friedman said in his best 1-Adam-12 voice.

Friedman walked back over to the black-and-white as they stormed off down the sidewalk at a pace that would have been likely to kill them both if they had had to walk more than one block.

"So what was the verdict?" asked Redbone, looking up from his Sudoku. "Where'd they go?"

"He told me that the car wouldn't start, so I told him just to leave it there tonight as long as it was gone first thing in the morning. They walked down to the taco stand at 83rd for some post-coital Mulitas. I'm gonna swing down to South Bureau and transfer a captain to Pacific Division. Why don't you finish the loop and meet me back at the front in about 20 minutes. Cool?" said Friedman.

"You got it. Why'd you let that guy lie to you, Bro? You and I both know he drove that thing in here. It runs and you know it."

"Got to pick your battles, dude," said Friedman as he turned and walked down Broadway toward the station.

The morning-watch cops at 77th Street Division all used the South Bureau Headquarters bathrooms at night. They were clean, smelled good and always had good, soft toilet paper instead of the cheap stuff the City bought for the dirty masses that used the working side of the building. Since there was never anyone in South Bureau after 5 p.m., Friedman always used the women's restroom for his business. It was even nicer.

He was walking out the bureau front door about 15 minutes later when he overheard Lt. Short at the front desk assuring Little Guy and Chubette that he had all their information and he would personally ensure that Internal Affairs would contact them shortly. While he was fawning all over them, Friedman walked by and all three shot him dirty looks. Friedman laughed and waved as he walked out the front door of the station.

He was walking northbound on Broadway on the east sidewalk about to cross 76th Street when he saw his black-and-white coming southbound on Broadway in the No. 1 lane. It was up around 73rd Street and cruising slow, as Redbone checked the barricades and equipment on his way.

He heard panting and the pitter-patter of little boots coming up from behind, and when he turned he saw Little Guy pulling Chubby Girl up the street by the hand.

"You're fucked, asshole. We filed all sorts of complaints against you and your coconut partner. I hope you got another job lined up, 'cause your career is over. And your boss said that we can leave our car in front of our business as long as we fucking feel like it," breathed Little Guy with obvious triumph.

"Well, you won, partner. Congratulations," replied Friedman. It was all he could do to keep from telling them how badly their plans were going to backfire, but before he could say anything else he heard tires screeching from up north of their position.

All three turned to look up Broadway, and what they saw stopped them dead in their tracks. The black-and-white was swerving side to side, nearly colliding with the west curb of Broadway, then narrowly missing the carnival attractions in the middle of the wide street. Friedman could see Redbone swinging his arms wildly around inside the car and could hear him screaming profanities. He wasn't going too fast at first, then all of a sudden the car's engine began to scream as it accelerated rapidly. It made two last quick swerves, then a sweeping left-hand turn eastbound across Broadway, picking up speed as it went. It careened between the "Domain of Death" puke-maker and the "Dare-you-to touch-the-walls / 290's Delight" funhouse and struck Little Guy's PT Cruiser exactly broadside.

The sound was deafening as the crunch echoed off the businesses in the quiet of the closed street. The impact was terrific. The big Crown Victoria struck the tiny PT Cruiser with such force that it broke both its axles and made the entire car about a foot and a half thinner when it pinched it up against the curb. The PT flipped up and over the curb and lay on its passenger side on the sidewalk in front of its owner's business. The black-and-white appeared to be nuzzling its underside with what was left of its front end.

Little Guy screamed and ran clip-clopping up the street with Chubby close on his heels. Friedman keyed his ROVER and broadcast a Help Call, then ran up the street after them.

Redbone didn't look good. Friedman couldn't tell how badly he was hurt, but the airbag deployment had broken his nose for sure and he was out cold. The car was a mess, both inside and out. The entire front end was wasted, and the whole interior was covered with glass and airbag dust.

Little Guy ran into his business and ran back out with an early-'90s video camera that looked as if you could have used it to film a major motion picture. He started with his dead PT Cruiser and then began to film the black-and-white. That didn't bother Friedman, but when he started trying to film Redbone inside the car, Friedman got pissed.

"This is a crime scene. We have no idea what happened here, and if you don't move away and quit interfering I am going to use the force necessary to move you," hissed Friedman into the camera as he drew his side-handle baton.

Something in the big Gringo's eyes scared Little Guy, and he instinctively backed up a few feet before the first responding units snatched him up and set him down to film outside the crime scene.

Redbone started to come around just prior to the arrival of LAFD 57's, and Friedman leaned in and hit him up.

"Hey, Bone. You OK?"

"I think so. How fucked up is my face? There's a lot of blood."

"Looks like your nose is broke. What the fuck were you thinking?" asked Friedman.

"There was a fucking bee or a wasp, maybe—bigger than a bee, I think. I tried to get it out the window, but it just kept trying to get me," replied Redbone, who laughed ever so slightly just prior to passing out again.

Friedman was relieved to see that Redbone wasn't hurt too badly. He didn't know about the bee thing, though. He'd never heard of bees or wasps flying around at night, but who could fucking tell? He reached in and turned off the DICV recorder and stood aside to let the firefighters to do their job.

It turned out that Redbone had had his own plans for the destruction of the bondsmen and had been biding his time. Friedman's confrontation with them was coincidental but provided the opportunity for the implementation of "The Redbone Plan," which resulted in the smash-up.

He'd had an idea that would allow him to use a black-and-white to wreck any car and get away scot-free. All he needed to make the ultimate finding be deemed non-preventable by the Peer Review Board would be to give them a solid excuse. Any accident would be caused by an act of God if there was a wasp or a hornet or something with a stinger to be blamed. It was actually a bit of sadistic genius on his part. The idea came to him while he was sitting on the back porch of Friedman's house, slurping up a cold Pabst. Under the second story eaves, there were several wasps' nests. Friedman had cleaned them out in the past, but they always came back, sometimes small and sometimes big, but no matter how vigilant he was, they always came back. Redbone went online to Wikihow and learned to make an extremely effective wasp trap. It was essentially a plastic water bottle with the top cut off and inverted.

He filled the bottle with a little sugar water, and the wasps went in the small opening to get to the sweet juice and couldn't find their way out again. It took him a few tries, but he managed to trap several alive without getting bitten. He had been keeping them in old-school black film containers in his war bag. They would usually last about a week before they died and dried out. He figured he could pop one out and smash it on the MDC or the dash-board, then wreck the car into anything he wanted to. It needed to be at least a bit juicy though, or the traffic guy might get suspicious. He just had to claim a wasp flew in the window, and while he was doing battle with it, he wrecked the car. Pure genius, but he'd need to deploy soon or they'd be in the wind with their winnings.

The problem, of course, was that he underestimated the impact. He knew that Friedman had turned on the DICV while talking with that asshole of a bail bondsman. He had felt the burn box vibrate on his Sam Browne and he figured Friedman was working some kind of a woo-sha on the guy. He didn't pay much attention until Friedman finished up and told him that he'd been bamboozled by that dwarf. Redbone got pissed. He closed out Sudoku on his cell and pulled out one of his film-container wasps from his war bag. Then he resumed carnival patrol. Redbone knew what he had to do and was excited at the idea of finally implementing "Operation Stung-by-the-Po-lice."

Maybe too excited. He played things up for the DICV because he knew it would be the first thing to be viewed by the traffic guys. Once he laid the foundation for the ploy, he swerved about a while, and then nailed it.

He steered the black-and-white from the bottom of the steering wheel with his left hand and made that last big sweeping left-hand turn while he floored the accelerator. He hadn't been prepared for the impact and hadn't considered putting on his seatbelt.

The pain from the airbag was excruciating. He last remembered talking to Friedman with flour floating around in the air, and then waking up in the back of the RA with the LAFD guys busting his balls about driving like Dale Earnhardt. His nose gushed blood for about 45 minutes, enough for the RA paramedics and RNs at California Hospital to remark that he bled better than most people they'd seen.

He still considered it a victory for the Blue Suiter, because there was no way he was ever going to be pinched now. Not with the combination of the wasp and the bloody nose. He was good to go, and that bail bondsman could bitch and complain all he wanted to.

"Take that, you squirrely little dwarf," thought Redbone from the comfort of his hospital bed where he was being held pending results from about $30,000 worth of scans and tests that would eventually tell him his nose was broken.

When Friedman told him about *his* hoax against the bondsman, Redbone was happy, but then realized they would try to blame him for retaliation. In the end, he figured it didn't really matter. By the time the investigation ran its course, he would be long gone.

CHAPTER 13

CAPTAIN YASUKE

"CAPT. CAPALL IS HERE TO SEE YOU, SIR," SAID CAPTAIN
Yasuke's adjutant.

Yasuke sighed. He was dealing with his own shit, and now he was
about to be forced to deal with Capall's shit, too. South Bureau Commander
Jim Boyle was up his ass about officers punching people in the face during
uses of force, officer-involved traffic collisions, low ticket-writing numbers, the cluster-fuck of the DICV, and now his own personal favorite: He
wanted Yasuke to lose weight as an example to the officers.

"You're doing a tremendous job, Reggie. Tremendous. But the troops
look to you as an example. Fact is you're out of shape. Affects morale,"
Cmdr. Boyle advised him in his clipped manner of speaking while calling
time out with his hands. He had a few weird habits and touching the tips of
his right fingers to the palm of his left hand while he talked was only just
one. Using the word "tremendous" was another. Friedman was pretty sure
he didn't realize it, but everyone else did. He would use the T-word at least

twice in any sentence pertaining to police work. It was like clockwork and always set his audience tittering.

Capt. Yasuke was Nisei—born and bred in Los Angeles but son to proud Japanese parents who believed in the American way of life. He was taught the Japanese way growing up. Sure, he was pure Americana, but the precise nature of his ancestry was instilled. To do something correctly was to demonstrate respect for the process. He was one of the few command staff that had actually worked patrol for several years before seeking promotion. He learned the job of police officer before he tried to learn the jobs of detective and sergeant. He mastered sergeant before seeking the rank of lieutenant. He was a well-respected lieutenant prior to abandoning the "enlisted ranks" and drinking the command staff Kool-Aid to become a captain. He knew he was a bit out of shape, but he also knew he wasn't obese, either. The problem was that Cmdr. Boyle was just as anal about physical fitness as he was about everything else. The man was a perfectionist and expected everyone serving under him to be a perfectionist, too. He micro-managed every decision in the entire South Bureau and couldn't bring himself to delegate watering the fucking office plants, much less the management of 77th Street. It made it almost impossible for Capt. Yasuke to run his division. Everything he did was second guessed. Everything he wrote was questioned and changed. All discipline decisions had to be made under the cloud of "What will Boyle say?" and 77th Street morale was suffering.

Now he was dealing with this complete asshole Capall. This tool of a captain had been thrust upon him by the Big Chief after he stepped on his dick by confiding to a patrol sergeant that he had created a hostile work environment. How stupid could someone be? Cmdr. Boyle was exceptionally pissed about his having been stuck with him. Yasuke's 77th Street Patrol sources informed him that officers had zero confidence in their Captain I. More specifically, he was told, "They wouldn't follow him into a water balloon fight." That was not good.

"Send him in," said Yasuke with resignation.

Just the sight of Capall with his sloped shoulders, giant head, blotchy skin and huge, face-dominating Chiclet teeth was almost more than Yasuke could stand. He wished, not for the last time, that he had the power to simply make him go away. Perhaps when he made commander he could finally decide whom he wanted working for him and whom he could dispo for being a waste of oxygen.

"What can I do for you, Pat?"

"Well, Reggie, I hate to be the bearer of bad news, but I think we've got a problem," replied Capt. Capall.

"What do you mean?" said Yasuke, completely secure in the knowledge that Capt. Patrick Fiacla Capall loved being the bearer of bad news.

"It's Friedman and Obrador from morning watch. Something is going on, and I can't figure it out. They've had some unusual complaints recently. Not to mention two suspicious TC's. I think they might have snapped."

Capt. Yasuke had known Friedman for several years and knew what he was capable of. He pitied Capall if Freidman had set his sights on him. He knew that Friedman was personally responsible for ensuring the entire 77th Street gang and narcotics units refused to sign the financial disclosure provision of the Federal Consent Decree, and that alone probably took five years off Cmdr. Boyle's life. He had influence with the younger officers, good relationships with the older officers, and the line supervision respected his tenure and opinion. Capt. Yasuke and Friedman had butted heads often, usually about Yasuke's disciplinary decisions that had been foisted on *him* from South Bureau. But Yasuke had always found him to be respectful and knew that Friedman was motivated by doing what was right on behalf of his peers. He was a good, honest, hard-headed street cop, the kind that Yasuke loved to have working for him. He knew a pogue like Capall would never understand a guy like Friedman.

He didn't know too much about Obrador except that everyone called him "Redbone," which Yasuke thought was very, very funny. He knew he'd been deuce'd recently, but that didn't mean too much. Cops like to drink, and those dirty Chippies were always fucking their brothers and causing problems. Yasuke knew if he had been partnered with Friedman for a while he must be a good cop or Friedman would have broken up with him long ago.

Capt. Yasuke had heard about the complaints that had come down the pike. He knew Obrador had single-handedly caused a riot at the front desk with his 290 experiment. He knew that stupid rookie sergeant from PAB had cut paper on Friedman for insubordination when he punked her in the field after *she* tried to punk Obrador. He had heard about the race beef and T/C involving the bail bondsmen from a few days ago.

What he suspected was that this was really stemming from the fact that Friedman had wrecked Capall's 300. He knew how much Capall loved that car. Everyone knew. It was a running joke among the other captains. Yasuke had kept his city car for the last four years since he only had to commute from Torrance. He figured it was "a point 'A' to point 'B' vehicle," and he was just glad to have finally risen high enough in the department to be ensured a take-home ride.

"What are your concerns, Pat?"

"I'm concerned that they could be loose cannons. Especially that Friedman. My lieutenant told me that he had just finished taking the face sheet for a 1.28 with some egregious racist allegations, and Friedman walked by and laughed and waved," said Capt. Capall.

"Refresh my memory, Pat. What was the nature of those egregious allegations?"

"The complainants allege that Obrador targeted them for specific enforcement and were harassing them because they filed a complaint against him prior. They said that Friedman called them 'dirty wetbacks' and he told them he was going to drive them out of business because he hated all Mexicans. The female complainant stated Friedman told her he would give them a pass if she was willing to 'perform' sexually."

"Perform?" said Capt. Yasuke.

"She used some vulgar terms for coitus and fellatio," mumbled Capt. Capall, clearly uncomfortable with describing anything sexual to another human being.

"That doesn't sound like Friedman to me. If I was a betting man, I'd suspect you'll find that those two bail bondsmen were lying. Friedman is too smart for that kind of beef. If he was laughing and waving, I'm pretty sure he's got something up his sleeve." said Yasuke.

"Reggie! We can't risk it! If he is innocent, then we should let the complaint process run its course. But if he's guilty, then we need to protect the public from rogue officers."

"And protect our take-home cars, too…" laughed Capt. Yasuke with a sideways glance at Capall.

Capall flushed red and started to open his mouth, but decided against it. He'd be sure to take care of that stupid Jap motherfucker when the department finally recognized his talents and promoted him to a position from which he could rule with impunity. Yasuke had just made his list.

"I think we should call in the SKID team to re-investigate Obrador's T/C," said Capall, changing tactics.

The SKID team was the LAPD Traffic version of Robbery Homicide Division. They were highly trained traffic officers called out to investigate any city property-involved traffic collisions that could result in extensive city liability. They were usually called out when a patrol unit went in pursuit and someone died at the termination or by influence along the way. They were the best at what they did and were serious about their shit.

"It's a little late for that. It was investigated by South Traffic and determined to be non-preventable. What makes you think it needs to be checked out again?" replied Capt. Yasuke.

"I think it was done in direct retaliation to the bail bondsman filing a complaint against them. I think he made up the wasp thing to throw us off."

"Pat. Did you see Obrador? His nose was broken for God's sake! You've seen the video from the bail bond store and the DICV…everything matches his story. How could he have made all that up? Who would damage themselves that bad to get back at someone for such a bullshit complaint? The traffic guy found a wasp on the dashboard of the black-and-white. Where would he get a fucking wasp at short notice!?" demanded Yasuke, who was beginning to get annoyed at Capall.

"I know it seems hard to believe, but I think Friedman was behind it. I think something is up. They seem too comfortable and too happy," replied Capall, flinching at his boss's profanity.

"We have already got the liability for the ruined bondsman's car, one dead black-and-white and one cop out IOD. We are not going to re-open a simple T/C to satisfy a hunch of yours.

If there was any logical reason, I would do it in a minute. Believe me, I would. It just doesn't add up to a conspiracy, and I can't figure out why it would bother you if the cops under our command were happy," said Yasuke.

"Reggie, what about Obrador causing that citizen to get horribly beaten at the front desk? The man's jaw was broken in six places! He's still in the intensive care unit down at Harbor UCLA. They had to remove his spleen! The good Lord knows when he's going to get out. My wife and I have been saying the rosary for his recovery."

It took everything he had for Yasuke to keep from rolling his eyes. He stared at the picture just over Capall's head for a full 20 seconds before he was able to speak with any sense of confidence that he wouldn't burst out laughing. He knew that Capall was pretty serious about his Catholicism, but praying for a child molester to recover from a pay-back beating was a bit of a stretch.

"IA has the case, Pat. They'll let me know if there seems to be some sort of sadistic intent. Right now it looks like a young officer made a mistake. We don't actually have a policy about registering the 290's at the desk.

Just because we've always done something a certain way doesn't mean we can hold officers accountable for policy that doesn't exist."

"The man nearly died!" Capt. Capall shouted.

"And the suspect that nearly killed him is in custody! And he was a heinous criminal of the most egregious kind! And it is not our job to pass sentence until we have the facts of the case! And if you were as concerned about the officers under your command as you were about some child-sodomizer, I wouldn't be hearing that officer morale under your 'leadership' is horrible!" countered Capt. Yasuke, who had finally had enough.

"I'm more concerned with the internal complaint," Yasuke continued. "What possessed that idiot Short to let that rookie sergeant cut a face sheet for insubordination against Friedman? That is a cluster-fuck in the making. She never gave him an order for him to refuse to obey. Her being an insecure boot sergeant doesn't equal insubordination. Now I'm stuck with having to back her play or fuck over a popular veteran officer. Morale is in the toilet now as it is. We don't need to stir the pot for nothing."

"It's too late to undo that now, Sir," said Capt. Capall formally, now butt-hurt over Yasuke's failure to see things his way.

"No, it's not. I'll leave it for you to handle. Just remember if that goes to a Board of Rights—and it will if you can't get it handled here at the divisional level—then she is going to make us look like fools who can't handle our shit. Friedman knew what he was doing out in the field, and he knows we stand to be the losers if it goes public at a Board. Set up a meeting between Friedman and Sgt. What's-Her-Name, and get it resolved in-house."

"What should I do about Friedman and Obrador's work status?" inquired Capall.

"Keep them in the field and monitor their complaints. If weird things start to happen, then we'll talk. It seems to me that there have been a couple of strange coincidences, nothing else. Don't worry. We'll get you another Chrysler, Pat."

CHAPTER 14

MILAGRO

FRIEDMAN WAS STARTING TO GET WORRIED. NO, WORRIED wasn't the right word. Concerned...that was closer.

His whole life he had moved forward with confidence. He was an impulsive man by nature, but his impulsiveness was tempered by an ability to quickly assess a situation then make the best decision that the circumstances allowed. Once he had chosen a path, he followed it with conviction.

When he married the first time, he did so in the honest belief that it was a good thing. He ignored the advice of friends and family, telling him they were both too young, and he forged ahead. When he became a police officer, he embraced the profession with zeal and quickly put it ahead of all else...to the detriment of his young marriage. When he found out she was in love with someone else, he never blamed her. He knew he had created a situation that was untenable and so moved quickly to dissolve the marriage...for the good of them both.

Several years later, when he discovered that his future second wife was pregnant with his first son, he knew what the circumstances demanded:

the right thing. They were married and briefly content. A handsome second son followed, but in spite of their perfect children they made each other miserable. They were unhappy more than they were happy, by a long stretch. Friedman stayed in a relationship that he knew was unhealthy for 10 years. He did so because he felt it was the best thing for his boys. That, and he felt that when you make a commitment you should honor it. He finally pulled the plug when a good friend told him he couldn't be any kind of a father if he was miserable all the time.

When they divorced, his ex-wife wanted to move back home to South America and wanted the boys to go with her. Friedman understood that. When shit goes sideways, everyone wants to be around family and comfortable cultural surroundings. He also knew that if he forced her to choose between her boys and her country it would make everyone miserable. The boys were still pretty young, and Friedman felt that they still needed their mom more than their dad, at least until they were older. He made the choice to let them go with her. They talked all the time on Skype and spent their summers with Friedman. His boys were happy and well adjusted, but letting them go was the one decision in Friedman's life that he constantly struggled with. He could never really convince himself that he had done the right thing. He missed them every day and always vacillated about whether or not they were better off because of his decision. The one thing he was sure about was that in the overall scheme of things, it was good for everyone but him. Dad always gets fucked, but that's his job. Hopefully, a shitload of money would soon be changing *that* situation.

No, to be worried about decisions, once they were made, was never really in Friedman's DNA. But he was starting to become concerned with the way things were going in his life now. Their winnings had changed everything, and he was starting to assess his options. He wasn't concerned about the things he and Redbone were having fun doing at work—far from it. He believed whole-heartedly in their decision to exact payback and felt they were on a fabulous path of destruction. He was concerned about the future. He had come to the realization that he loved being a police officer and wasn't quite sure that he was finished with the profession. It almost embarrassed him to say it out loud. He knew the LAPD was broken badly, but he felt it could be fixed. He believed it could be re-aligned without sacrificing the gains they had made with both the community and within the organization. The officers were better than ever. They could better articulate their actions, they were better educated, more diverse, and they exercised discretion far more frequently.

The problem was with the command staff. The generation of LAPD officers that invented the "back-alley-choke-out-contest" was now in charge. The Department was reeling from the Federal Consent Decree of 10 years and the restrictions it had imposed. The collective guilt of guys like Cmdr. Jim Boyle and Assistant Chief Sterling Anderson was causing the brass to implement foolish policies. They were undermining the historic LAPD work ethic and damaging morale with leadership by consensus. They had misinterpreted the word "transparency" to mean "appeasement." The new concept of "best practices" meant they were now taking the lead from departments like Detroit, Milwaukee, and Boston. The LAPD used to teach *them* how to enforce the law. Under Big Chiefs Parker and Gates, the LAPD was the innovator. Now the LAPD brass was looking to places like Chicago for policy. It was embarrassing. Friedman was beginning to wonder if his portion of the winnings could be parlayed into political influence to effect change that could be long lasting and ultimately more effective than crashing shops into assholes' cars for fun.

Two weeks later, with Redbone still out IOD, Friedman was working with a probationer named Montaña when they responded to a call on the eastside of the division. It was listed as an animal cruelty, but the comments of the call on the screen of their MDC were too vague to make out what the person reporting was really trying to say. While they were en route to the call, the radio telephone operator working console J6 typed them a cryptic message, stating, "You're gonna love Incident 5623."

When they arrived at the call and walked up to the porch, Friedman started to chat in Spanish with the owner of a Doberman Pincher dog named Milagro. The owner/victim, a Mr. Gomez, told them one of the strangest stories Friedman had ever heard.

Mr. Gomez stated that for the last three months he had noticed that when he was leaving for work at approximately 0600 hours, his dog Milagro had been returning home southbound on Wall Street from 82nd Street. He found this unusual, but thought nothing of it until he realized that there was a pattern to the days and times the animal returned home. After consulting with his spouse, he determined that Milagro went missing sometime near 0030 hours nearly every Thursday, Sunday and Monday nights only to return, apparently exhausted, the following morning. About the time he noticed the pattern, Mr. Gomez also noticed that when the animal returned in the morning, she would often leave a visible "trail" of viscous material on the dirt yard. Upon investigation, it was determined that the source of this viscous material was the dog's vagina.

Being at a loss to explain the situation, Mr. Gomez set up an observation post at his residence and was able to determine that on the aforementioned nights, a lone male Hispanic would walk up to the gate of his yard, feed the dog an unknown item, and slap the dog three times on the hindquarters.

The suspect would then open the gate, and Milagro would follow him out of the yard and up the west sidewalk of Wall Street toward 82nd Street.

Mr. Gomez recognized the suspect as an individual who had lived two houses north of his on the west side of Wall Street, but had moved to either 201 or 203 E. 82nd Street.

Mr. Gomez had deduced that the suspect was luring Milagro from his residence using gifts of food, engaging in vaginal sex with the animal over the course of the evening, then releasing the animal to return home. He stated that normally the dog is fairly aggressive but informed Friedman and Montaña that her demeanor had changed. He attributed this change to "shame." Mr. Gomez finished up by saying he understood that the entire situation was difficult to believe, but felt that if the suspect was willing to have sex with a dog, who could tell what type of deviant behavior he was willing to engage in with a human?

The rookie Montaña was trying not to laugh and could barely control himself. Unsure if Friedman spoke Spanish fluently enough to comprehend the situation, he asked, "Sir, did you understand the story he just told us?"

But Friedman was not amused. He was an avowed animal lover and had always felt that the two beings that garnered unconditional sympathy in the hood were the kids and the dogs. Everyone else made their choices and had to live with the consequences.

"I got it, Bro. What do you say we scope this place out and catch us a dog-fucker tonight?"

Because it was a Monday night and still relatively early, Friedman took the information for the report and asked Mr. Gomez to go ahead and leave Milagro in the front yard as usual. He told him to go to bed and forget about the situation for the night, and he and Montaña would handle things.

They sped back to the station, and Friedman had a quick chat with Sgt. Leinen. He told him they would be Code 5 doing surveillance on the Gomez residence from about 2330 until 0130 to see if they could catch a real predator. Leinen laughed and gave his blessing, with the only caveat being that if things got busy they'd need to break off. Friedman went upstairs to Detective Bureau and over to the Auto Detectives area. One of his friends kept the keys to a plain car in his desk, and Friedman would avail himself of it when he needed to snoop and poop. There was never an issue as long as he had it back in place prior to the detectives' start of watch.

They set up on the east side of Wall Street, south of the Gomez residence where they had a pretty clear view of the suspect's residence at the end of the block and the gate that Milagro would have to use to leave the yard. They had only been on the Code 5 for about half an hour when

Friedman began to wish he had a cigarette. He'd quit smoking more than five years ago and seldom missed it, but when he was doing surveillance it always reminded him of the days when he was working with his old partner Kurt Thornton.

They worked 12A66 together during the violent early 2000's, when 77th Street really jumped off. He and Kurt also worked Vice together and spent a pretty substantial amount of time doing surveillance on illegal nightclubs, prostitutes and watching their own vice officers work the corners when they were a part of the spontaneous trick taskforces.

Kurt was a staunch Republican and former Marine from Texas who was an avowed Baptist and a proud black man. He never minded if Friedman smoked in the car while working, and they used to have great arguments about religion that lasted through long hours of the night. Those were some of Friedman's best law enforcement years, and every time he sat on an observation post it took him back. Many of the things they had done while on patrol could have gotten them fired or indicted, but between being scared and exhilarated they always did their best to do the right thing by the 85 percent.

Almost to the minute of 0030 hours, Friedman saw a Hispanic man walking southbound on the west sidewalk of Wall. He slapped Montaña on the top of his head. He had fallen asleep and slumped over with his chin on his chest. Normally Friedman would have ridden his shit for giving up the ghost, but he knew the kid was not used to morning watch, much less boring Code 5 work on that watch.

"Bro, we're in business. Check out this guy. He matches the description, and the time is right. Let's see what he does," said Friedman.

The guy walked past the Gomez's gate to the northwest corner of Wall and 82nd Place and posted up. He was obviously nervous. A basehead rode by on a bike with a little jerry-rigged trailer filled with copper pipe he'd stolen from some construction site, and it scared the guy so much he nearly turned and ran. Based on Friedman's experience watching guilty people from afar, he knew they had their man. He switched to field training officer mode and started pointing things out to Montaña.

"Check out how nervous this guy is. Look at him taking his hands in and out of his pockets. Check out that yawning—he's nervous. See how his head is on a swivel? That's the thief salute. You see that, you can bet something is about to happen," instructed Friedman.

Almost on cue, the Dog Fucker (he had already become guilty in Friedman's mind) walked briskly to the Gomez's side gate on Wall Street just north of 82nd Place and pulled something out of his jacket pocket. They could see Milagro run over and eat whatever it was from the Dog Fucker's hand through the gate. He lifted the latch and started walking up the sidewalk with Milagro in tow.

"OK dude, we gotta let him get almost home then hustle up there so we can get a look-see at which house he goes in. We gotta be quiet though or we'll screw the pooch, no pun intended," Friedman said. "Sound travels far at night, so when we get out of the car don't slam the door. Make sure your cell is off and keep your ROVER turned down way low."

Montaña was wide awake now with the thrill of the chase. He was fidgeting around in the seat and could barely contain himself. He wanted to jump out so badly, he could taste it.

"Sir, he's too far away! I can't see him anymore! What if he goes in a different house? We're gonna lose him!

Jesus. Was I ever this anxious? This kid is gonna lose his mind before we even get to the fun part.

"Bro. Relax. I can see the top of his head walking by the blue truck. Watch. He's gonna pop out right behind that minivan. We got him. He should go right up into that driveway where Wall tees with 82nd Street. There he goes, he's headed that way. Let's hustle," advised Friedman.

They jumped out of their plain car and jogged up the east sidewalk of Wall, sticking close to the parked cars to stay out of sight of the target location. Friedman stopped Montana right before the corner, and they watched through the windshield and rear window of a parked pickup as the Dog Fucker walked up the common driveway of the exact house described by Mr. Gomez.

The driveway was dark, so they couldn't see which place he went in, but they could see light briefly emitting from an open door then the door shut, and it was dark again.

"Fuck! I couldn't tell which one he went in! Could you?" asked Friedman.

"Negative. I'm pretty sure it was the front one, but I'm not one hundred percent," replied Montaña.

They ran over to the property in question and crept up the dark driveway. Just as they approached the front duplex, a light came on in a rear window and they knew they were in business. They climbed over some bushes and looked in the gap between the blinds. The room was empty. Afraid the Dog Fucker had found them out, Friedman backed them off to behind one of the cars parked in the driveway, and they hunkered down.

"Now what?" whispered Montaña

"Let's just sit tight for a minute. I'm pretty sure we're in the right place. I don't think we got burned, but you saw how nervous homeboy was. Let's wait and see what happens," whispered Friedman.

Two minutes later, they heard a strange, high-pitched half-scream from the front of the residence. Friedman nearly jumped out of his skin, and Montaña flinched so badly that he was glad he didn't have his gun out. He probably would have capped off a round. The sound stopped, but was replaced with a low-pitched moaning that sounded so creepy it gave both Friedman and Montaña the piss-shivers.

"What the fuck is *that*?!" stage whispered Montaña.

Friedman couldn't hear anything else. He knew instinctively what the noise was. He was suddenly so angry that he couldn't see straight, as he broke cover and stalked over to the window just to the side of the door of the front residence.

There was just enough of a crack between the bottom of the blinds and the bottom of the window sill for Friedman to get a clear view of something he wished he'd never seen. It would be burned into his memory for the rest of his life, and every time he accidently remembered it he would feel queasy.

"Update our Code 6 and put out a back-up, partner. Remember to sound calm when you do it," said Friedman to a bewildered Montaña.

Breaching a door is an art. It comes with practice, and if done wrong can result in the breacher's leg being the only part on the wrong side of a closed door. If you kicked the middle of a door, it often just created a hole, but booting it correctly usually put the door (frame and all) in the living room of the target location. Friedman had kicked in a few doors in his day and knew that the place to put the boot was just to the side of both locks.

He was in a blind fury as he reared back and booted the door clean into the residence. He swung around to the left as he drew his baton, making the familiar metallic singing noise as the ring holder slid past the length of the business end.

The Dog Fucker had put a muzzle on Milagro and had her tethered tightly to a sturdy oak coffee table. His pants and underwear were piled on his shoes near the table, and his old blue mechanic's jacket was hanging over a chair. He was wearing only a dirty white wife-beater tank top. He was about 40 years old and built strong from a lifetime of hard work. He was on his knees behind the animal holding its legs tight in his fists as he violated her. Milagro was trying to get loose, but she was no match for the expert hold of the Dog Fucker. He looked up, but was concentrating so intently on his disgusting business that when the door burst open he didn't even stop.

This dirty motherfucker doesn't give a shit! He's trying to finish before he goes to jail! Some things must be addressed up front.

Friedman skipped forward and swung his side-handle baton with a massive power stroke, intending to strike the Dog Fucker across the chest to knock him off the dog. Unfortunately for the Dog Fucker, he finally clued in and instinctively tried to duck the blow. The last three inches of the baton cut cleanly across his mouth. He screamed as he fell backward in a powdery white cloud of what used to be almost all of his teeth.

Montaña rushed in past Friedman and tried to cuff their suspect, but he wasn't having it. Their backup request had kicked in, and the room was suddenly filled with cops who were piling onto a very drunk, half-naked, and now toothless suspect. He was much stronger than Friedman initially had given him credit for and the fight was on. It turned out the Dog Fucker realized that he was in deep trouble for his strange sexual proclivities and wasn't going to submit to the public humiliation of arrest if he could help it. With strength born of desperation, he threw off the cops who were using their combined body weight to hold him down and dove straight out the front window of his apartment. Unfortunately, he forgot about the security bars on the other side. He rebounded back into the room and as he stood to fight, Montaña hit him with the TASER. With 50,000 volts flowing through his body, he did what came naturally: He shit himself. The power of the TASER spun him around, and with no pants to contain his booze and street-meat-affected bodily functions, he sprayed the cops as if with a garden hose.

Outfitted with some sort of a kick-ass nozzle.

Turned on full blast.

Everything stopped. The electricity clicking its way down the wires into the Dog Fucker was the only sound heard for the full five-second jolt. Then the room came alive. Montaña dropped the TASER, doubled over, and vomited. One of the victim cops started screaming unintelligibly while waving his hands in the air and marching in place. Another ran from the residence and took the garden hose to himself in the front yard. Two shiny clean cops ran in from outside, and Friedman told them to put on some gloves and cuff the Dog Fucker who had both the shit *and* the fight TAZER'd out of him.

Friedman was cutting Milagro loose when Sgt. Leinen walked in the front door and surveyed the scene. He pulled out a cigar from his chest pocket, calmly lit it, then looked from the bloody, shit-covered Dog Fucker to the bloody, shit-covered cops and shook his head.

"Who's gonna unfuck this goat rope? I hope you're satisfied, Friedman. These guys are going to need to burn their uniforms, and that jackwagon is gonna need a new grill. That dog must be one hell of a piece of ass."

CHAPTER 15

THE RIDE ALONG

FRIEDMAN AND MONTAÑA WERE OVERTIME BY 10 HOURS DUE to the Dog Fucker arrest. Based on Freidman's inadvertent head strike, the whole situation became an FID call-out. This was both good and bad. The Force Investigation Division handled all categorical use of force investigations, which includes shootings by officers, uses of force resulting in significant injury or hospitalization, and all head strikes (intentional and inadvertent). It basically created a cluster-fuck. The captains needed to be notified at home, the League sent out representatives to ensure that the involved officer's rights didn't get trampled by the department, the officers were separated and assigned their own sergeant to babysit them and ensure there was no collusion. From Friedman's perspective, it was a good thing. A categorical use of force meant he didn't have to do anything at all. He sat back, got interviewed by feisty FID guys, and then they wrote all the reports and dealt with the body. And the League brought pizza.

The Dog Fucker was holed up at California Hospital getting stitched and X-rayed to death, which meant someone had to babysit him, too. The rookie FID detective team drew that short straw. The whole thing was, of course, tainted by the nature of the case. All the office pogues working FID were titillated by the fact that Friedman and Montaña had kicked the shit out of a dog-fucking deviant. The League guys were both supremely amused and very proud. Everyone was enjoying themselves except Montaña. This was his first real big spin-up, and it was making him nervous to have all the brass and lawyers around. Capt. Capall was pissed because he had been at a church event late and had just gotten to bed. Capt. Yasuke didn't even bother to make the trip. He could smell nothing-ness over the phone when he got the call.

The Dog Fucker had already demanded a complaint for excessive force against Friedman. This took a while to ascertain because in addition to being a fall-down drunk (and a fucker of dogs), he was determined to speak only marginal Spanish. It was discovered he was an indigenous Guatemalan national whose only fluent language was Q'eqchi'. It took several hours for FID to round up a Q'eqchi' speaker, and he wasn't much help since Q'eqchi' was apparently a language that utilized a lot of the tongue pressing on the front teeth to form words. But that didn't deter the boys from Professional Standards Bureau. They saddled up and sent a field team out the minute Capt. Capall called it in. Their motto was "The Truth of the Matter" and they were going to get to it. The goal was to turn the Dog Fucker into a Cop Fucker, come hell or high water. Capt. Capall didn't believe Freidman's story for a single minute. Freidman didn't give a shit.

That next Friday saw Friedman and Redbone sitting in roll call listening to Lt. Short droning on about how it should only take two officers, maybe three at most, to take down a combative suspect. He was getting verbally thrashed by Horst and Plazola, who both had witnessed several cops getting sent to the hospital by one angry female on PCP. Redbone was showing Friedman a picture on his cell of the 55-foot catamaran he was going to buy. His plan was to spend a year, maybe two, having a crew sail him around the Caribbean Sea in search of native females. He figured he could easily spend a year doing nothing, then park the cat in the Redondo

Beach Harbor and use it as a Los Angeles base of operations. Friedman was worried that Redbone would spend himself into the poor house within 10 years, but he figured the Batts Brothers would protect him.

He looked across the roll call room and saw the Brothers sitting in the back row. They were rapt with attention and fascinated by everything they saw and heard. Friedman had arranged a ride-a-long for them through the area office.

He told the secretary in charge of those things that they were thinking about coming on the job. He told Sgt. Leinen that they were friends of his who just wanted to see what LAPD officers did for a living. He also told Leinen that they were in the investment business and to make sure to get some good tips for his 401K. The Brothers Batts obviously understood the nature of things and assured Redbone and Friedman they would stick to the rules of disclosure.

"I can't believe we are actually going to get to ride around in a black-and-white with an LAPD sergeant," said Brian Batts when they first met in the lobby.

"I've been looking forward to this for weeks now," gushed Tony Batts.

What the fuck is wrong with these two? I can't believe that we're trying to escape, and these two idiots can't wait to see what we put up with every night. I swear to God. These two jokers live the Life of Reilly and they can't wait to touch the dirty underbelly of society. I've spent my whole adult life keeping the wolves at bay, and they have no idea. Is that what it's like for normal people? This is like a trip to Disneyland for them...

Friedman had given them a tour of the station and the jail. At least he tried to give them a tour of the jail. He got stopped by a civilian supervisor, who told him with an air of authority that per the new jail watch commander all tours needed the approval of the Jail OIC. Friedman just gave her a dirty look and turned around and left. He didn't feel like fighting a battle with stupid people, so he just told the Batts they could watch *American Me* on cable and get a good idea what went on below the station.

He had taken them in to meet Lt. Short, and it was fun to see him try to decide if the brothers could somehow help his career. After several probing questions, he decided they were of no use and he blew them off. Friedman laughed inwardly, because they had already told him they were having dinner with the mayor tomorrow night.

You fucked up that one, Short. These two motherfuckers have more political arrows in their quiver than anyone you've ever met...or ever likely to meet in the future. I can't wait to make sure you know you missed the opportunity of a lifetime.

Roll call ended and they lined up for their gear at the kit room. Redbone made sure they got a shop that was to his satisfaction. They loaded up their goods and were up at the pumps when Leinen hit them up.

"You dumbfucks gonna want to get some grub with these guys?"

"Sure, Sarge. What've you got in mind?" asked Redbone.

"How about Mexican? We can go hit Santa Fe and Zoe. It is Friday, but if we get there early enough, it shouldn't be too crowded," said Leinen.

They had just finished up dinner and were driving back through the Division when they heard 12A51 get a Code 3 traffic call at Normandie and Florence. The call got updated twice right away, and the RTO advised there was an overturned vehicle with people trapped inside. The last update advised that the vehicle was smoking. Friedman started rolling Code 3, knowing that A51 would at the very least need help with crowd control.

Thirty seconds later, Plazola came on the air and Friedman could tell something shitty was happening by the tone of his voice.

"51. We need FD here Code 3. Make it at least three RA's. The vehicle is burning...with at least two still inside. I have at least three others unconscious, not breathing...two ejected."

"Jesus, Friedman. That sounds like a clusterfuck," said Redbone while clearing intersections as he updated their response to Code 3 on the MDC. He had no idea how bad it was really going to be. They would both take the memories of the next 20 minutes with them to their graves. The Brothers Batts would never want to go on a ride-along again. They wouldn't even talk about it later.

Upon arrival Friedman could see things were indeed shitty. He parked their shop in the liquor store parking lot on the northeast corner of Florence and Normandie and ran over to the nearest crowd on the same corner. FD was working on a 3-year-old, who Friedman could see was already dead for sure. Redbone ran over and stopped short, staring at the little girl as she leaked her life onto the grimy sidewalk.

"Bro. Get your game face on and start shutting this thing down. Set up a containment and make it wide. Use the biggest gangsters you can find to help you clear the crowd until we get some help here," said Friedman. He could tell that Redbone needed something to do.

Friedman ran across the street to the southwest corner, where there was another crowd gathered around a small body on the ground. As he ran, he looked left and could see Plazola and Horst trying to get into the burning minivan crashed up against a pole on the southeast corner. The van was turned over on the passenger side and the flames were getting big. He could hear screaming from inside, but it stopped even as he ran by. When he got to the southwest corner, the crowd stepped aside and exposed a young boy, maybe 5 years old at most. Friedman stooped down to check if he had a pulse and couldn't find one. His head was slightly misshapen, and when he checked the boy's eyes Friedman saw his pupils were two different sizes. He knew it was useless, but he figured he should start doing CPR. LAFD ran up and pushed him away before he could begin, so he looked around to see what else needed his attention.

There was an RA leaving Code 3, so Friedman assumed that they had at least one of the ejected parties was still alive. Or maybe it was the person in the second vehicle. Who could tell? He could see the LAFD loading up the little girl onto a gurney, but that didn't mean shit—his experience told him it was too late for her. He walked over to Plazola and hit him up.

"What do you need, Al?"

"Fuck, brother, just start setting up the crime scene. These two are done for."

Friedman checked out the burned-out vehicle that FD had just finished extinguishing, then walked over and looked inside. There were two figures that looked almost like shadows. They were both reaching up toward the broken driver's side windows and were burned beyond recognition. They reminded Freidman of the ash mummies created by archeologists at Pompeii.

"Jesus," said Friedman. "How many K's are we dealing with?"

"It looks like these two and maybe some of their kids. I saw a basehead pulling a kid out of the minivan when we got here. A couple other kids were ejected. Doesn't anyone use fucking car seats or seatbelts?" replied Plazola.

"There's at least one little boy and a small girl that are KMA from what I saw," said Friedman.

"That's four for sure...we better get to work," said Horst as Sgt. Leinen walked up.

That's when Freidman saw the Batts Brothers standing in the liquor store parking lot where the command post was getting set up. He hadn't even seen them at the scene, but they must have arrived right behind them. Brian was throwing up in the bushes, and Tony looked like he had just finished.

Friedman was pissed. Not at anything particular...just the fact that he'd seen a few too many lives extinguished. Normally he didn't mind. His first exposure to violent death was when he was a rookie officer working for the Metropolitan Transportation Authority Police Department. He worked the Blue Line train for his entire three years at MTAPD, and if there was one thing for sure about that train, it was that it dealt out vicious death. It must have been his first week when he saw the results of a guy using the train to kill himself. Those trains weighed 90 tons each and didn't even hesitate when they hit a car, much less a human. The guy was spread out over about 100 yards of track just south of the Spring Street Crossing down in Long Beach. Friedman figured if he could handle that grisly mess, he could handle anything—and he'd been right. Over the course of his career, he'd seen more death than you could shake a stick at. It rarely bothered him, but seeing an entire family wiped out ate at his core.

He was contemplating his chosen profession when he heard an arrogant little sergeant fucking with a young P2 who was sitting in the passenger seat of the nearby black-and-white.

"Hey, Toblar! You want to go see the bodies in the minivan?" asked the sergeant.

"Sure, Sir, if you want me to," replied the rookie, looking up from the crime scene log he was completing.

Friedman knew that Toblar had served a couple of tours in the war. He'd been quietly finishing out his Naval career as a fireman when a friend convinced him to re-up. The friend told him that being a Corpsman was a great way to get good medical training that would help him get a job when he got out of the Navy. He needed to sign up for something like six additional years because of the extensive training, but he figured he was young so it would be worth it to have a good job when he got out. That was early-2001. Within the year, he was attached to a Marine Corps unit in Bagdad. He'd been shot in the chest with an AK47, survived an IED attack on a Humvee he was riding in, and had been blown up by a grenade.

"Oh, that's right, I forgot you been to war, you've probably seen burned bodies before," said Sgt. Superior as he walked haughtily away.

Toblar didn't know Friedman was on the other side of the shop listening to the exchange through the open driver's side window.

"I've probably burned a few too, asshole," Toblar said to himself, unaware that Friedman could hear him.

Suddenly Friedman realized that everything was perspective. The things he'd been through in life paled in comparison to some of the things others had been forced to see and do.

He was just about to get back in the game when he was approached by a female captain he'd never seen before. She had traffic patches on her uniform and short (out of policy) hair hanging down over her collar. She had an air of extreme self-importance.

"Officer. Do you have a Field Officer's notebook?" she snapped.

Friedman just stared at her dumbfounded. He couldn't imagine why she wanted a notebook and thought she was holding some kind of impromptu inspection.

"Officer. I asked you a question. Do you have a Field Officer's notebook?"

"Uh…Yes," replied Friedman finally.

"Show it to me."

Friedman pulled out his worn-out old notebook and held it up.

"Do you have a pen?"

Friedman pulled it out of his shirt pocket and held it up.

"I want you to follow me around and write down everything I say," said the traffic captain.

The captain marched away, and Friedman followed her for about three steps then turned right. He went over to see how Redbone was doing. He figured his extensive police experience exempted him from being scribe to some hopped-up She-Pogue Captain.

The crime scene wound down to the waiting game, as they always did. It seemed as if every traffic cop in South Traffic Division was there, and they were all doing something important while the 77th Street Patrol guys held the perimeter points. The Batts Brothers left with Sgt. Leinen, never to return. When Friedman later asked them if their ride-along was everything they expected, they both just shook their heads.

"I can't believe this is what you do for a living…you need to get away from this," said Brian.

"It wasn't what I'd expected. It was horrible," echoed Tony.

One of the downsides of such a major incident was that every command staff in the region came down to get their face time. The news media was out in force, and there were captains, commanders and the South Bureau deputy chief all vying to make public condemnations of the hit-and-run suspect that STD determined caused the incident.

Traffic Captain She-Pogue walked up and Friedman started to slink away, but she didn't seem to remember him.

"Officer. I need you need to go buy some coffee for the staff officers," she said as she handed him $40.

"Yes, Ma'am," replied Friedman, disgusted.

Friedman took the two twenties and walked over to the small liquor store. Their location had been completely shut down and commandeered for use as the command post, so they had lost all their evening business. They had two Thermoses of coffee left over from the morning, and Freidman asked them if he could buy them both.

The manager told him just to take them and bring them back when they were empty. They were always friendly to the 77th Street cops, and he refused to take his cash because the coffee was so old. Friedman forced him to take the whole $40 and returned to the CP. He set the Thermoses on the trunk of a shop with some small Styrofoam cups, and the traffic captain asked him for her change. When Friedman told her there was no change, she flipped out.

"Are you telling me you paid $40 for two Thermoses of coffee?" shouted the captain.

"No, Ma'am. You did," replied Friedman with a straight face. Another bridge burned.

CHAPTER 16
DOUBLE STANDARDS

THEY WERE OFF FOR A FEW DAYS AFTER THE RIDE-ALONG from hell. It was a good thing because Redbone was still talking about it three days later. Friedman told him to let it go and get drunk for a while like everyone else. Everyone knew that cops drank a lot, and the nasty things they saw on a regular basis were huge contributing factors. The Department was getting better when it came to sending officers to Behavioral Science Services after traumatic events, but referrals were always tempered by deployment needs. For example, in the case of the burning minivan and its accompanying deaths, Horst and Plazola were sent to BSS, but no one else. Everyone on-scene saw everything there was to see, but how could it be justified to take 20 guys out of the field until they got cleared by an army of shrinks? The result was that officers usually needed to suck it up and get on with their lives. Booze helped. Was it ideal? Absolutely not, but it was a fact of life. The problems came when officers succumbed to alcohol addiction and it caused issues at work. The Department was famous for talking a good game about stress management, but at the end of the day it would crucify a cop who brought disgrace on the famous badge... whether it was their fault or not. It wasn't a new phenomenon, either. Back in the '60s, the Department fired Karl Hettinger for petty theft. He was the partner of Officer Ian Campbell, who was murdered during the famous Onion Field incident. Granted, it was before PTSD was understood, but any asshole could see that a good cop doesn't suddenly become a petty thief. Officer Hettinger tarnished the badge, so out he went.

Friedman and Redbone went back to work with heavy hearts, but they knew their time was coming to an end soon. It had been a full four months since their lives had changed, and they were beginning to enjoy not giving a shit. Every day brought them closer to pulling the plug, and they coasted through each work day with the comforting knowledge that it was all just temporary.

This must be what coming up on retirement feels like for an old-timer. The difference is that we're both young and healthy...and ridiculously rich. Our lives aren't going to be tempered with concerns of stretching our retirement money to the bitter end. We get to begin a fabulous adventure while most of those old-timers just get to begin to die.

Thoughts like those were the frequent topics of conversation for Redbone and Friedman while driving around 77th Street Division at night. It was like they were living in a state of suspended animation. They were doing what they had been doing for years, but now none of it mattered. They could tell an asshole criminal what they really thought. They could do what was right for the citizens without worrying about stupid LAPD policies. They were free to be the best possible cops they could be without fear of damage to their careers from the Monday-morning-quarterbacking, second-guessing command staff. It was very liberating. Friedman often told Redbone it was what he imagined law enforcement was like in the '60s and '70s at LAPD. More doing right by using common sense, and fewer being condemned for it. The difference today was that, of course, they *would* ultimately be condemned for it. It just didn't matter. They were happy.

Then they went to a call that changed everything. It reminded them of their obligations to the victims and to their brother officers.

They got the call right out of the chute, and it was simple enough. It was a dispute between neighboring business owners that had turned into a battery when one of the parties lost his cool. They'd both been to the same call a thousand times.

They parked on the east-side access lane of Crenshaw just north of 54th and walked up to the appliance repair shop that was listed as the person reporting's location. The comments of the call indicated that the parties had been involved in a dispute over a washing machine that had not been fixed to the satisfaction of its owner. Freidman immediately recognized the adjacent business as headquarters for one of the many South Central African-American rag newspapers.

"Hey bro, just a heads up…if the problem is next door," he said to Redbone, motioning to the newspaper shop, "they're gonna be politically connected."

Redbone gave him the thumbs-up acknowledgement as they made contact with the PR.

Ms. Peña, the counter lady from the repair shop, told Friedman and Redbone that the owner of the newspaper next door had brought them his washing machine to get fixed. He wasn't happy with their work and had been in and out of the business complaining all day. He returned late in the afternoon for a showdown. He was very irate and stated that the motor didn't work so he wanted another machine in exchange. The owner of the appliance store, Rudolfo Barillas, told him he could have the one at the front of the store that he wanted, but it would cost him another hundred dollars plus the trade because it was a bigger-capacity machine.

Ms. Peña said that made him very angry, and as Mr. Barillas and the newspaperman walked through the store and out the back door arguing she heard him tell her boss, "You don't know who you're messing with! I'll send your ass back to Mexico!"

This was already following a familiar line for Friedman and Redbone. The 'Hood' was much less politically correct than the rest of the world. Insults that would never be said in polite society were regularly exchanged without a second thought. Friedman always laughed when people told him how racist the police were. Cops learned really quick to believe in Martin Luther King Jr.'s dream of judging people by the content of their character rather than by the color of their skin. It didn't really matter if the guy sitting next to you in the shop was green, blue or orange...as long as he had your back when you needed him, he was your brother. Friedman had never experienced true racism until he worked in the ghetto. Then he saw it nearly every day...from the citizens.

Ms. Peña told the officers she had watched video surveillance footage of the newspaperman discreetly breaking the knob off his own machine when he had been in their store earlier. She figured he was trying to build his case for a new machine. She and the shop mechanic, Leon Hernandez, followed them out the back of the store because they were worried about Mr. Barillas' safety. When they got outside, they could hear yelling and saw the newspaperman walking toward her boss with his fists clenched. She decided to put in her two cents. She told Friedman and Redbone that she shouted, "I saw you break the knob off your machine. On video. You had better leave Mr. Barillas alone, or I'm calling the police!" Bad plan.

The newspaperman spun around and ran right up to her with his arms outstretched and lunged toward her neck with clawed hands, she said. He was enraged and screamed, "I'm going to kill you!" Ms. Peña told Friedman and Redbone that she froze. She simply knew she was going to die and there was nothing she could do. She believed his threat completely. She started to pray that her children would forgive the newspaperman.

Very pious, thought Friedman.

Mr. Hernandez acted with astonishing quickness. He said that he had stepped between Ms. Peña and the oncoming newspaperman and that his reaction had been pure instinct. He utilized the momentum of her attacker and swept him past her, throwing him to the ground. When the newspaperman recovered, spun around, and tried to renew his attack, Mr. Hernandez gave him the old school one-two and dusted off each side of his face with a set of closed fists. The now-humiliated paperboy uttered a guttural, "I'm going to kill your friend when I'm done with you, bitch." Mr. Barillas intervened and prevented a coup de grâce by the now emboldened Mr. Hernandez and hustled everyone back inside the store. The Paperboy marched into his business holding both sides of his face.

Redbone walked out the back door of the business, searched around a bit and discovered a video camera facing the alley that belonged to the business across from the appliance store. He told Friedman he was going to head over and do some electronic work and see if he could scare up an impartial witness.

That was one of the agreements of their partnership. It didn't matter if it was a computer, a cell phone or video equipment. Redbone handled all things electronic. Friedman bore witness to the advent of video games in his youth. Redbone was born with a computer in his hand. He was 10 years younger than Friedman, and all things electronic came infinitely more naturally to him. Those 10 short years made a world of difference.

Friedman walked over to speak with The Paperboy. When he walked inside the newspaper offices, he was immediately confronted by the semi-hostile Paperboy and a lady who was apparently Mrs. Paperboy.

"It took you long enough to get here," he grunted to start off the conversation.

Realizing there could be trouble, they had called in a pre-emptive radio call strike of their own.

"Well, Sir, I wasn't aware you had called. We were next door investigating an incident that apparently occurred about half an hour ago. Can you tell me your version of events?" replied Friedman.

The Paperboy described a set of circumstances very similar to the story told by Mrs. Peña. Except he was the totally innocent victim, never attempted to attack and choke Mrs. Peña, and he never threatened to kill anyone. He finished up strong with, "I expect you'll be arresting the man who pushed me down and punched me twice."

Just before he could come up with a verbal gem about citizen expectations, Redbone raised Friedman on Simplex. He made his excuses and stepped outside for some privacy.

"You clear from newspaper guy?" asked Redbone

"Yeah. You get anything we can use?"

"Yep. The video from the place across the alley caught the whole melee out back. You want to come over and see it?" replied Redbone.

Friedman went back and told the Paperboy to stand by. He walked to the back alley and met Redbone at the rear door of the business with the video. They walked inside, and Redbone played back the tape.

The tape was clear, but with no sound. It did, however, prove that the actions of the Paperboy were consistent with the statements made by Ms. Peña. It also proved the Paperboy to be a liar.

"What do you think? I bet we got the newspaper guy for a pretty clean 422 that was foiled by the mechanic," said Redbone. "What does he say happened?"

Section 422 of the California Penal Code is defined as criminal threats. It has historically been abused by cops and citizens alike to violate people's First Amendment constitutional rights. To be legit, it requires a credible threat and the ability to carry out the threat. It also requires that the victim believe the threat. This was a pretty clear-cut case in Friedman's opinion.

"He denies everything and wants her man arrested for kicking his ass. He's gonna be pissed when he finds out he's getting done up. It's gonna be one of those, 'Let me get this straight. I called the po-lice, and now I'm goin' to jail' capers for sure," replied Friedman. "Let's get a supervisor out here for a blessing."

Redbone requested a supervisor and to Friedman's dismay a mid-watch supervisor rolled up. He knew it would exacerbate the situation because the supervisor was Hispanic. That would feed into the Paperboy's world view of the growing Mexican conspiracy. But the supervisor was already there, so they ran down what they had and showed him the video. He agreed with their 422 call, but in true LAPD leadership fashion he called out the night dicks to confirm his decision. When the veteran night detective rolled up, he was disgusted that he had been called out at all.

"What do you need me for? Friedman knows what he's doing. You do, too. You just want me in the mix so when this asshole starts screaming racism you can point the finger my way and say it was my decision," he told the mid-watch sergeant. "It's the right call. Book him 422. Put me down as advising on the booking approval."

Friedman, Redbone and Sergeant Mid-Watch walked over to the newspaper business and broke the bad news. The Paperboy was not pleased, to say the least.

"Let me get this straight. I'm the one that called. I'm the one that got beaten. And I'm the one that's going to jail. That's some bullshit."

Friedman and Redbone exchanged a look. Friedman told the Paperboy to turn around and put his hands behind his back. He reluctantly complied at first, but then started to freak out when the bracelets went on. He really began to struggle when they walked him out to the car. He launched into a tirade once they hit the sidewalk and tried to attract as much attention as possible from the gathering crowd. Friedman had to put him in check when he started to resist by trying to pull away from his grip.

"Sir, if you pull away from me or resist arrest in any further way I will have no choice but to use force to gain your compliance…and it will hurt. I promise."

This set him off. Although he apparently believed Friedman's warning and quit trying to pull free, he started shouting to his wife who had followed them out to the sidewalk.

"Call Sterling! He'll handle this shit! I'll be back here in an hour! This is bullshit!"

Friedman knew there were probably only one or two Sterlings in the world and had a feeling that he was talking about their very own Assistant Chief Sterling Anderson. It pissed him off that the Paperboy had been so emboldened by the Department's ass-kissing that he would even consider that a phone call could get him to walk free.

Bad news buddy. This is a felony beef. Even the Big Chief can't just make this thing disappear. You're gonna have to stand tall before the man before this goes away.

They drove to 77th Street and checked the Paperboy in with the watch commander. They were in report writing room "A" getting the mountain of paperwork together when Friedman saw Capt. Yasuke walk by the door.

"Redbone. Something is up. I just saw Yasuke in the station. What the fuck is he doing here on a Saturday night? I smell bullshit—we are about to lose our arrestee. He's gonna get the Brass Pass," said Friedman.

"Come on, bro. It's a legit Frank—the night dick signed off on it. Homeboy has something like 30 years on the job. There's fucking video. They can't just dispo something like that because an arrestee knows someone. This isn't 1920s Chicago. You're paranoid," replied Redbone.

"I hope you're right, but I bet you're not. You mark my words, that asshole isn't gonna spend the night."

Friedman couldn't take it any longer, so he walked into the watch commander's office with his booking approval. There was only Lt. Short in the office, so he handed him the booking approval and gave him the story. He broke down Ms. Peña's statements and the Paperboy's statements. He told him about the video and how it backed her up. He finished with the sergeant and the night detective's opinions.

"Sounds solid to me," said Lt. Short. "Does he have a rap sheet?"

"Negative," replied Friedman. "This is gonna pop his cherry."

"No, it's not," said a voice from behind Friedman. "I'm going to ask you to take an investigative report and release Mr. Hayes, Friedman."

Capt. Yasuke was standing in the doorway of the watch commander's office, and Lt. Short stopped what he was doing just prior to signing his name on the booking approval.

"Come again, Captain?" said Friedman.

"Friedman, you heard what I said, and I think you know why I said it. This isn't negotiable. He's never been arrested before, and the odds of him actually getting convicted for 422 are pretty slim."

"Cap. We arrest people all the time who haven't done anything before. That's not relevant to what he did today. And we don't get to decide whether or not he'll get convicted. We only decide if probable cause exists for arrest. In this case, a sergeant, a very senior detective and I all agree. We have more than enough with physical evidence, conflicting statements and video," replied Friedman, his blood rising. He was trying to keep his cool, but he was dangerously close to losing it right then and there. He was ready to screw the whole pooch to defy the captain.

Redbone had walked into the hallway and was shaking his head at Friedman through the glass window between the hall and the watch commander's office. He could see that shit was about to pop off and he didn't want things to spin out of control. He was silently willing Friedman to stand down.

"I'm not going to argue with you over this. He walks, and you document your investigation for detective follow-up on an investigative report. If there's something to it, they can handle it at a later time," said Yasuke.

"So what you're saying is fuck our victim because this asshole knows Anderson?" said Friedman, seething. "If he hasn't done anything wrong then, why take a PIR? I'm not stupid. It's so the investigation can be controlled from above and made to go away. All this because Billy Ray Hayes is a ghetto-press asshole and the department is afraid of what he'll write.

This is bullshit, Captain. You know it, I know it, and that motherfucker Anderson knows it."

"The captain just gave you an order, Friedman. Follow it, or you will be guilty of insubordination," chimed in Lt. Short from the cheap seats.

"I can handle this without any assistance, Lieutenant," said Captain Yasuke.

That cocksucker Short is right. If I pitch a big enough fit, they might just let me book that asshole, but I'll be done for good. It'll be a Board of Rights for me and desk duty until my date arrives. That's the end of the fun for me and Redbone. If I decide to stand up here, I might as well pull the plug tomorrow, because I'll never see the field again. And that fucking Paperboy will still walk...

"I'm not telling you this is right. I'm not telling you this is fair. I'll admit there is a double standard and I don't like it any more than you do, but I'm giving you a direct order to take an PIR and walk him out the front door of the station. This is my decision, and I'm taking full responsibility for it," said the captain.

CHAPTER 17

210 TEMPLE

"SO WHAT DID HE DO?" ASKED KAZAN.

"He stood down. What the fuck was he gonna do? The captain gave him a direct order. It was like a challenge. That little-dick Short was practically drooling. He thought for sure Friedman was gonna take a stand and fuck off Yasuke. You could see it in his body language—he was sure the time had come when he was going to get to screw Friedman," said Redbone.

They were standing in the hallway of the third floor at the Clara Shortridge Foltz Criminal Justice Center. It was the main Los Angeles courthouse and was known by its address, 210 Temple, to most LAPD officers. Like nearly every other governmental endeavor in the City of Los Angeles, it was a cluster-fuck of epic proportions.

Clara Shortridge Foltz was an early California suffragist who, among other accomplishments, was the first woman admitted to the California Bar and the first female Notary Public. In 1893, she came up with the then-radical concept of state-funded criminal assistance to defendants who couldn't afford representation. The first public defenders. It was ironic for the courthouse to be named after her because defendants at 210 Temple had been profiting by suckling at the taxpayer tit ever since.

There was very little efficiency at 210 Temple. The problems were many and varied. It was the building where the O.J. Simpson ball was dropped. The jury pool was famously shallow, and the phrase "12 rocks in a box" was heard daily. Officers packed the hallways everyday for be-there court subpoenas. They would stand around all day without testifying, as the wheels of justice ground forward at a snail's pace, only to be told to return the next morning for another session. Many of the cops worked morning watch, so they would have to work all night then stand in court all day due to some DA's inability to plan the next day's shit. The third floor, which was where all preliminary hearings were handled, was especially problematic. The assistant district attorneys who were assigned prelims were mostly rookie DA's, and it could be very trying for the veteran cops to deal with them. They would call and tell officers that they needed to be in court for prelim and then let them stand around all day with the pithy admonition, "This is part of your job. You're getting paid overtime to be here, anyway." They never stopped to consider that LAPD officers hadn't been getting cash overtime for years, and were compensated by the banking of overtime hours to use at a later time with "TO's." TO's were regularly denied due to deployment needs, so they really went to court for free.

There were badass DA's at 210 Temple for sure, but most of them worked hard-core gangs or other special details like JSID (Justice System Integrity Division - the dirty cop cookers). The main idea was for the DA's to do their time and get the fuck out as quick as possible. The best went to other court buildings like Long Beach or Airport Court, almost anywhere but 210 Temple.

Friedman and Redbone were there on a nickel-rock caper. South Central was covered in rock cocaine, and it was sold everywhere in small $5 chips. Hence the term "nickel rock." It was like shooting fish in a barrel, and even a halfway decent street cop could pull a nickel rock observation arrest every night if he or she wanted to. Lots of cops did, but Friedman hated drug arrests. First of all, he was an avowed Libertarian who felt drugs should be legal, but mostly he was turned off by the fact that all 11350 H&S (Health and Safety code for cocaine) arrests meant be-there court. That equaled standing in the hallowed halls of 210 Temple on his day off or when he should be sleeping. Not to mention that drugs had been so decriminalized through programs like Proposition 36 that no one ever went to jail anyway. It was a waste of everyone's time.

The only time they arrested anyone for drugs was if they had no choice in the matter or if the guy was an asshole and they had nothing else on him and he needed to go.

Friedman was running late, so Redbone was hanging out in the hallway with Ponich and Kazan shooting the shit.

"The guy got a straight pass. It was bullshit. He walked out the front door with a shit-eating grin on his face 'cause he knew he'd won and there was nothing we could do. It was pretty hard to take," intoned a disgusted Redbone.

"That's fucked up," agreed Ponich. "But you guys did the right thing. Friedman would have been fucked if he'd fought it. That's an automatic Board of Rights. Those weasel captains on the Board will fire your ass in a heartbeat if they think you didn't ask 'How high?" when one of their homies says jump. You gotta kiss the ring."

"That's bullshit. It was an unlawful order. He didn't have to stand down, he could've...What the fuck is that?!" said Kazan, checking himself mid-sentence and pointing down the hall. "Look at this guy and his church suit!"

There was a commotion near where the elevators opened onto the main hallway. Suddenly the multitudes of cops in the hall were cat-calling and hooting at a guy in an absurd purple suit. It was the color of royalty but with thick white pinstripes. Its owner had accessorized with a matching purple Biltmore Derby hat, complete with a long white feather, purple snake-skin boots and a matching snake-skin belt.

"Dude. That's fucking Friedman," said Ponich, erupting in laughter.

"Where?" said Redbone.

"He's the giant pin-striped grape, bro. That's him strutting down the hall!" answered Ponich.

And strutting he was. Friedman was crip-walking through the crowd, complete with a white cane—and he was owning it. He was high-fiving old friends and acknowledging accolades from hysterical Blue Suiters as he made his way down the hall toward Division 38. The royal wave was in effect.

He swaggered up to where Redbone was hanging out with Kazan and Ponich and struck his best pimp pose.

"What the fuck is this?" said Redbone, laughing. "You're crazy if you go in a courtroom dressed like that. Haven't you seen *My Cousin Vinny*? The judge is gonna shit a pickle on you, dude. You look like Dolomite."

"Come on, bro. What's the matter? You don't like the new threads? I've always wanted a suit like this."

Friedman stood with his arms outstretched and spun around in a circle. The suit's jacket was a big double-breasted affair that hung down almost to his knees. Between the purple with pinstripes, white silk tie and handkerchief, cane, hat and shoes, Friedman was dressed to the South Central church-going nines. At least four cops were busy snapping pictures with their cell phones for posterity. Friedman indulged them with several old school Bitch-Better-Have-My-Money poses.

While Friedman was playing ghetto model and the others were laughing, a young female DA walked out of Division 38 and shouted out, "Officer Friedman?! Officer Obrador?!"

Redbone flagged her down, but he didn't really need to. Her eyes were glued to Friedman, and she seemed to be unconsciously steering toward them.

"I'm Obrador, and that gentleman is Officer Friedman."

"What's wrong with him? Is he working undercover?

"No, Ma'am. He's here to testify on the Daniel case. It's an 11350," replied Redbone, who was thoroughly enjoying the look of disbelief on her face.

"Judge Bisdigian is not going to like this at all. I've never seen him laugh in the four months I've been here. He's not a funny man," said the DA.

"Why are you wearing those clothes, Officer Friedman?" she asked.

"What do you mean, Ma'am? This is my best suit. I recognized the importance of this case and its implications on society as a whole," replied Friedman.

"I can't continue this case. We are at 10 of 10 days. I don't even have a legitimate reason to dismiss it. The judge will want to know why. I can't Prop 15 Officer Obrador, because you are here and you discovered the cocaine during the pre-booking search. You're going to have to testify. In that. We are going to be in for a world of hurt with Judge Bisdigian," said the DA, practically close to tears.

"I have read my report and am completely ready to testify to its contents. Let's get this done," declared Freidman.

The DA scuttled back into the courtroom, and it was only a minute or two before her law clerk came out into the hallway and called Friedman to the door to testify. For some reason, he seemed to know exactly who Friedman was.

Almost instantly, there was a mad rush by the idle officers in the hallway to get into Division 38. Nobody wanted to miss the show that was surely only about five minutes away. Friedman had to wait for the doorway to clear before he could make his way in.

When he opened the door to the courtroom, the silence was deafening. The room was packed as if there were a celebrity trial going on. The only thing missing was a media presence. It was so quiet that the defendant, seated on the left next to his attorney, sensed something and turned around to follow everyone's gaze to Friedman. His eyes nearly popped out of his head, and he waved gaily before his attorney could stop him.

Hudson Daniel actually really liked Friedman and Obrador because they were always so decent to him when they crossed paths. They'd arrested him for his warrants after he'd gotten into a fight with a security guard at a liquor store over on Manchester and San Pedro. The guard was a real shit-bird, and Friedman knew it. Instead of booking him for battery, they arrested him for his drinking-in-public warrants. Things took a turn for the worse when Friedman emptied his pockets in front of that asshole watch commander and a couple of rocks fell out on the floor. Before he could discreetly step on them, the lieutenant snatched them up.

You'd have thought he'd won the fucking Lotto. He made Friedman book him for felony cocaine possession. Friedman and Redbone apologized through the whole booking process. It was really his fault. He'd forgotten he'd been holding them for his homegirl. He didn't even smoke. He just drank—a lot.

Friedman strolled down the aisle with his hat in one hand and his cane in the other, as he nodded to friends smirking from the bench seats.

Judge Bisdigian was going through some papers on his bench when the small swinging gate that divided the spectators from the main show broke the silence in the room. The noise it made when Friedman walked through it must have been accentuated by the silence, because the judge jumped a little and looked up. He looked right at Friedman and then back to his paperwork. It must have taken him a second to register what he'd seen, because he quickly looked up again and his mouth fell open.

Freidman placed his derby on the DA's table and leaned his cane against the side. He sauntered over to the witness box and raised his right hand. The court clerk was a 67-year-old black woman who didn't even miss a beat.

"Please raise your right hand (he already had, but it was part of the speech she'd been giving for 40 years and she wasn't about to change it). Do you solemnly swear that the testimony you are about to give before this court is the truth, the whole truth and nothing but the truth?"

"I do," affirmed Friedman.

"Please take your seat and state and spell your name for the record," said the clerk.

Friedman started to walk around the backside entrance to the witness box.

"Stop!" commanded Judge Bisdigian. "Officer, what is the meaning of your attire?"

"I'm sorry, Your Honor?" replied Friedman in the most innocent voice he could muster.

"Do not attempt to be humorous with me, Officer. Your attire is not professional. You are dangerously close to being held in contempt at this very moment. Explain your behavior at once."

"I'm not sure what you mean, Your Honor. I wear this very suit to church every Sunday at the Crenshaw Christian Center down on 79th and Vermont to hear the Reverend Price preach the Good Word. I would assume since my attire is sufficient to please the Lord, it would also please the Court," replied Friedman with a straight face.

The crowd started snickering but stopped short with a dirty look from Judge Bisdigian.

"Take the stand," said the judge, apparently not willing to publicly debate religion with Friedman. "But be advised I will be speaking with Assistant Chief Anderson regarding your courtroom behavior. I have a standing dinner engagement with him every third Thursday, and you will most definitely be a topic of discussion."

The crowd murmured disapproval at the very mention of Anderson's name in public. Someone actually hissed. Friedman stepped up into the witness box and stated and spelled his name slowly for the court reporter.

Defendant Daniel was all smiles as the prosecuting DA laid out the case against him. Friedman ran through receiving the call, detaining Daniel based on the description provided by the comments of the call, their in-field investigation and the discovery of the nickel-rocks during the pre-booking search.

The public defender couldn't have been more than 24 years old and had the look of a self-assured liberal activist. His disdain for the police was obvious, and the fact that his client continued to wave surreptitiously at Friedman wasn't helping matters.

He started with a sarcastic, "Good morning, Officer Friedman."

"Good morning, Sir."

"Did you prepare the report in this case?" the PD asked.

"I did."

"Have you had time to review your report?"

"Yes."

"Is it a complete and accurate depiction of events as they relate to the arrest of Mr. Daniel?"

"Yes."

"You testified earlier that you first observed my client standing in the Valero gas station on the southwest corner of San Pedro Street and Manchester Ave."

"I did."

"How did you know he was the individual involved in the incident at the liquor store?"

"He was named in the comments of the call, and I recognized his name from multiple prior contacts."

"That's true!" chimed in Defendant Daniel. "Officer Friedman has jacked me up a bunch!"

That drew guffaws from the crowd, a dirty look from his attorney and a stern admonishment from Judge Bisdigian about how letting his lawyer do the talking was in his best interest.

"How far away were you when you first saw my client?" continued the public defender.

"We were traveling eastbound on Manchester Ave. approaching San Pedro when I first saw him."

"Manchester Ave. is three lanes wide in both directions with an island in the middle. Do you expect the court to believe that you could see my client's face and recognize him from such a distance?!" demanded the rookie public defender, springing his trap with a big shit-eating grin and an air of triumph. "Exactly how far can you see, Officer Friedman?"

"Well, Sir. I am a runner and I like to get my daily exercise out of the way early in the day before it gets too hot."

The public defender was about to object with a bewildered look on his face, but Friedman continued.

"When I wake up in the morning and sit on my front porch, enjoying a cup of coffee and a banana, I frequently watch the sunrise. It's my understanding that the sun is millions of miles away..."

CHAPTER 18
PAT AND STERLING

"SO HOW IS 77TH DIVISION TREATING YOU, PAT?" ASSISTANT Chief Anderson asked amiably as Capt. Capall settled down into one of the comfy chairs in the chief's office.

The Assistant Chief was second in command of the LAPD. He'd had a meteoric rise in the last 10 years. He'd always had a weakness for women, which had caused some hiccups early on in his career, but he'd mastered the political nature of the LAPD and knew how to use outside influences to achieve his personal goals. He'd been cultivating loyalties, both inside and outside of the Department, for several years and had a formidable army of sycophants that he could rely on to help keep him in power. He definitely knew where the bodies were buried. The Big Chief hated him but was forced to keep him at his post because of his political connections, mainly to Council District Eight down in South Central. He had a deep power base in the black community and was a useful ally when things went sideways, which they sometimes did.

When Capt. Capall stepped on his dick with the hostile work environment beef, the Big Chief was going to demote him to lieutenant and give him an admin transfer. He figured it would be a valuable lesson to other supervisors who thought they could do whatever they wanted. But where others saw problems, Anderson saw opportunity. He convinced the Big Chief to give Capall a lateral transfer and let things lie. He knew from reports by some of his informants within the Department that Capall hated field cops and was ambitious. He would most likely prove to be a valuable hatchet man for Anderson's dirty work. He could be molded into an Anderson-esque protégé whose loyalty could be counted on to trump integrity every time.

"It's fine, Sir. Just fine. I really do have to thank you again for sticking your neck out for me. If it hadn't been for you, I'd probably be looking for a sergeant job at some po-dunk little town down in the Bible-Belt," replied Capt. Capall.

"Well," said Anderson silkily, "Call me Sterl. All my friends do. We need to take care of each other. Just remember me if I ever need your help. Would you like some coffee? Let me get some coffee in here."

"April," said the chief into the intercom on his desk. "Will you bring Capt. Capall and me some coffee? Black OK, Pat?"

"Uh, yes, Sir," said Capall. He hated coffee, and when he drank it he drowned it with sugar and cream, but if the chief liked it black then so did he.

Moments later, the assistant chief's adjutant appeared through the office door carrying two cups of coffee on a tray. She was a beautiful light-skinned black girl in her early thirties who had risen through the LAPD ranks by coat-tailing Anderson. She was a Sergeant II and had her eyes on being a lieutenant within the year. Working for the assistant chief was demeaning and she hated how she was treated, but if one wanted to advance to captain and above there was only one way to get it done quickly.

It had taken Anderson three weeks to give her a choice between her marital vows and her career.

"Thank you, April," said the assistant chief as his elevator eyes made both Capt. Capall and the sergeant uncomfortable.

"Love me some of that light brown sugar. How about you, Pat? You like to split the dark oak?" Anderson asked. The sergeant was still in the room and looked with embarrassment at Capt. Capall, who wasn't entirely sure if the question was rhetorical or required an answer.

He'd never been with anyone but his wife since they'd been married at 19 and 18, respectively. He decided that a positive nod and a slight chuckle was the most politically expedient thing to do, even though his stomach churned at the assistant chief's behavior. He'd heard about his proclivities.

"Well, we'll have to see if April has any friends. Maybe we can get together for a little rendezvous sometime," smiled Anderson at the captain's obvious discomfort.

When the sergeant closed the door, Anderson leaned forward and said, "What do you know about some P2 in your division named Friedman?"

Capt. Capall was taken aback by the question. He found it hard to believe that a lowly P2 would ever come to the attention of a mighty assistant chief without some sort of a media catapult. He suddenly realized that his boss had his ear to the ground, and most likely very little escaped his attention. It made the captain nervous.

"Well," he stammered, "*I* think he's a loose cannon. I tried to tell Reggie Yasuke that he needed watching, but he told me that he wasn't dangerous. I got the distinct impression that he liked him. Friedman is insolent and thinks he's too smart for his own good. He prides himself on being a professional patrol officer, if you can believe that. What brought him to your attention, if I may ask?"

Anderson was pleased. He could smell the contempt oozing from Capall. He didn't give a flying fuck about some uppity P2 working morning watch down in the ghetto, but the captain was still low on the totem pole and had to touch the dirty masses on a daily basis.

"I had lunch the other day with Judge Bisdigian, and he told me that Friedman wore some sort of a monkey suit to court. Said he was a smart-ass that needed to be put in check. I would take it as a personal favor if you'd keep me apprised of his behavior. I like to keep the judge happy. He's been a good ally to me, and you never know when you might need a Superior Court judge on your team, right? Why don't you go ahead and cut a face sheet on him for unprofessional court behavior. A couple days' suspension should probably get his mind right, don't you think?

Capt. Capall was more than eager to put some paper on Friedman, but he doubted that a couple days of suspension would be an effective check on Friedman's arrogance. He knew that Friedman was a problem, but he also knew that he didn't really worry about a little stain on his TEAMS report. He'd heard him talking in the locker room and knew that he didn't want to promote. Capall couldn't understand how anyone could be so lacking in ambition. He would need to deploy some out-of-the-box thinking if he was going to put any kind of hurt on him.

"He's had some strange complaints with his partner lately. An Officer Obrador ... the one they call Redbone. I tried to get Capt. Yasuke to bench them, but he insisted the incidents were coincidental and opted to leave them in the field," said Capall.

"His partner is black?" Anderson asked.

"Uh, no. Why do you ask?" replied a confused Capall.

"Because they call him ... never mind," said the assistant chief, realizing how square Capt. Capall was. "Tell me about these 'strange complaints' they've gotten."

Capt. Capall spent the next hour telling the sordid tale of Redbone and Friedman. Anderson probed and questioned, and Capall filled him in to the best of his ability. He covered the whole gambit, from the TC's to the race beef, and from the front desk riot to the insubordination. After it all came out, Anderson leaned back and sipped his coffee. Capall copied him, choking down the black poison as if he loved it.

"I had to call down and have a chat with Reggie the other day. One of my childhood friends, Billy Hayes, had a misunderstanding with one of his neighbors and ended up being mistakenly detained for criminal threats. I asked Reggie to make sure the right thing was done. He wasn't very receptive at first. He tried to tell me that it had been investigated thoroughly at the scene and there was probable cause to arrest. Told me that some sergeant and a detective reviewed the facts and agreed. I was practically forced to order him to let the man go," said Anderson.

"What is the world coming to? When an assistant chief of the Los Angeles Police Department can't even expect his suggestions to be followed without question by some divisional captain? There is definitely a problem there," Anderson continued. "He never mentioned it was Friedman and ... what was his partner's name?"

"Obrador, Sir."

"...Obrador. I have a feeling you could be right. I think Capt. Yasuke might be covering for them. He's been known to have questionable loyalties. I think he spent a little too much time working patrol. He's gonna need to pick a team," said the assistant chief thoughtfully.

"I've actually been wondering if he was the right man for the job," Anderson said. "I know that Jim Boyle thinks his shit doesn't stink, but if he's siding with patrol cops over chiefs then we may need to re-evaluate the decision to make him the divisional captain of 77th Street. That fucking division has always been dirty. The only cops who want to work there are nothing but thugs themselves. We need someone with their mind right in charge."

"I agree completely, Sir. But what can we do? The whole division can't be admin transferred, and Captain Yasuke can't just be moved without some kind of cause," replied Capall, hoping against hope that the "someone with their mind right" meant him.

"Well, I agree with you about transferring the whole division. But we can give Yasuke just enough rope to hang himself. I think I'd like to keep this Friedman and his partner in the field. It sounds to me like they are a couple of fuck-ups who will really step on their dicks if we just give them enough time. When they've choked on it enough, or if they get in to a real clusterfuck, we can drop the bomb on both of them at the same time. Either way, it's a win/win for us. If Capt. Yasuke isn't interested in regulating these two assholes, then we'll just wait for the inevitable and blame him for failing to take appropriate action to prevent a culture of deviant/defiant behavior. What do you think?" Anderson asked Capall, almost forgetting to include him.

He knew if he didn't keep Capall involved and believing he was in on things, then he wouldn't be able to throw him under the bus somewhere down the line if things went shitty with the plan. Always keep a buffer between yourself and the shit, he reminded himself.

"I think that's a capital idea, Sir!" squealed Capt. Capall. "I can't think of a better way to kill two, or hopefully three, birds with one stone. If we give them time, they're sure to make a mistake that will put nails in their coffins. Even if there isn't a big single event, a collection of little issues could be used to justify a Board of Rights for both of them based on a pattern of conduct."

Who the fuck says things like 'That's a capital idea'? thought the assistant chief. *This ugly cracker motherfucker is creepy. But he sure gets excited about fucking people over. He needs to be well handled, or he could get too big for his britches and come back to haunt me.*

"Then I'll just make sure that whoever sits on their Board is really interested in making commander. They'll be gone quicker than shit through a goose. Once they get done up, I can put that Yasuke out to pasture and we can get someone in that spot who really knows how to regulate a division," said Anderson as he popped on his best "You're in my inner circle" smile for the captain.

Captain I Patrick Fiacla Capall was sitting on the edge of his chair in total rapture over the assistant chief's words. His moment had finally arrived. He was going to begin the next stage of his career, and he had a powerful sponsor. Sure, that sponsor was a deviant sex-monger who had no ethics or values, but that could be justified. He was moving in the right direction, and once he'd taken over Reggie Yasuke's position, he could focus on the next step. The assistant chief's sordid personal life would probably take its toll before too long and create another opening for upward advancement. And he'd get some payback on Friedman for wrecking his Chrysler.

CHAPTER 19
SHAR PEI AND GANGSTER JACK

"HEY, BRO," SAID REDBONE, "YOU SEE THAT GUY RUN THAT light? That was a big 'fuck the police.' Let's have a chat with him."

They were rolling westbound on Florence Avenue, approaching 8th Avenue. It was about two in the morning, and they were on their way to grab a cup of coffee up at the 7/11 at Slauson and Overhill. The vehicle in question was an Audi A6, and it had pulled up to the red tri-light facing northbound on 8th Ave. The driver had decided not to wait and blew the mid-phased light to go northbound through the intersection. Unfortunately, Friedman and Redbone were far enough away to appear as just another set of headlights to the A6, but they were close enough for it to seem like a "contempt of cop" maneuver on behalf of the Audi. The last thing either of them wanted to do was get involved in a bullshit traffic stop, but sometimes you just gotta be the po-lice, so the debate began.

"He's probably deuce, man," replied Friedman. "Why you want to deal with that shit? We're gonna spend the rest of the night dealing with his drunk ass if we jack him up."

"I agree with that, bro. Let's just give him a quick attitude check."

"Fair enough, but what if he fails," replied Friedman, "Then what? What if we end up having to fight him or something? It could potentially fuck up our coffee break."

"Sounds reasonable to me. Fuck it," decided Redbone.

They were past 8th Ave. when another vehicle heading eastbound on Florence started flashing its headlights at them. When they got closer, Friedman and Redbone could see it was a black-and-white. They slowed, and when it pulled up next to them they saw it was occupied by Lt. Short.

"Are you just going to let that car run the red light right in front of you?" Short demanded. "I could see it from all the way back near Crenshaw, so I know you saw it, too."

"Well, Sir, you see … we were just on our way to get some coffee …," replied Friedman slowly, hoping that if he delayed long enough the A6 would be gone.

"What!?" shouted the lieutenant. "You go pull that car over and do your job! I can't believe you two are so lazy that you aren't willing to take a free citation when it falls in your lap! Get to work. That's an order!"

The lieutenant sped away eastbound on Florence as Freidman flipped a U-turn and headed toward the now-ordered traffic stop.

"Jesus Christ, Redbone, that stupid motherfucker can't see the forest for the trees. If this stop goes sideways, I'm gonna lose my shit. I was really looking forward to that cup. What the fuck is he doing out at this time of night, driving around by himself? He's gonna get hurt. He better hope he doesn't need a backup. A lot of our homeboys would take the slow road to get there."

They accelerated eastbound on Florence to northbound on 8th Avenue. Redbone and Friedman were in sight of the A6, but still quite a ways away.

"Let's hit 'em with the red light, and maybe they'll run. In for a penny, in for a pound. At least we might have some fun if they bolt," suggested Redbone.

Friedman activated their overhead, forward-facing red light and bopped the siren to get their attention. But instead of running, the driver of the A6 pulled over immediately.

"No such luck, gangsta," said Friedman.

The Audi pulled to the curb just south of 67th Street, about two long blocks north of Florence. Friedman and Redbone pulled up to the rear, slightly off set, with the black-and-white's take-down lights activated, as well as the hand-held side spots—like always.

Citizens often complained about the amount of light used during nighttime traffic stops, but the reality of patrol was that a criminal always had the advantage. By lighting the vehicle up like a Christmas tree when the cops approached, it mitigated the threat. If the occupants were interested in a shootout, at least they'd be blinded and have to take some time to acquire a target. Since a patrol cop can never tell the intentions of the occupants during a traffic stop, they treat them all the same until they've got more information.

People will do some of the stupidest shit during traffic stops, and Friedman was always surprised that more citizens didn't get hurt by nervous rookie cops. They'll jump out of the car, reaching in their pockets for their ID. They come out of the car screaming they're being wronged as they rush to confront the cops to plead their case. They'll refuse to roll down their tinted windows, or turn off their car. The list went on and on.

When Friedman had transitioned from his "Take-away 2000" city-issued holster for his old Beretta 9mm to a new triple-threat retention holster, he had just such an experience on a traffic stop.

He had been driving, when his partner Kurt had pointed out a stop he wanted to make. They conducted the stop, and just as the driver had pulled over he opened his driver's door a crack. This type of action is a big red flag from the point of view of a cop, because the driver gains the advantage if the intention is to come out shooting. Normal citizens don't really do it unless their windows are broken. Either way, a cop on a traffic stop won't take a chance.

Freidman shouted out a warning to Kurt just as the driver's side door flew open and the occupant came running back toward them with his right hand outstretched. Friedman tried to draw his Beretta, but since the triple-threat holster required several manipulations he couldn't get it out. He hadn't practiced enough, and his muscle memory hadn't yet been trained. Thinking he was about to die, Friedman pulled his Sam Browne clean out of the leather keepers that held it to his inner belt and jerked it up around his chest before he realized the driver was trying to give him his driver's license. His lack of practice probably saved the driver's life. He took his Sam Browne home, and drew and holstered his weapon on his days off until it was second nature. Lesson learned. Kurt never let him forget about it and busted his balls relentlessly over the gaff.

Friedman ordered the driver of the Audi to turn off the engine and roll down the windows. Like every other car in the hood, they were tinted with limousine tint so people outside couldn't see shit.

Redbone started to walk up on the passenger side to check things out.

All cops do traffic stops a little differently, and it usually just depends on what is agreed upon between partners. Redbone and Friedman liked for the driver officer to hold fast back in the 'V' of the open driver's door while the passenger officer approached the passenger side of the stopped vehicle. They figured if shots were fired, the driver officer could empty his shit into the car from cover while the passenger officer redeployed.

The passenger officer would walk up and check things out and get the occupants' attention focused on him while he gave the driver the 'Code 4' fingers, signaling the OK to leave cover and approach. That way, while the driver officer was dick in the wind he'd stand less of a chance of getting smoked. It's always easy for a criminal to shoot an approaching cop by reaching over their left shoulder and emptying the chamber out the window. It's a little harder to acquire the approaching passenger officer through windows, over seats and through the blind spots of most cars.

The driver of the Audi started to roll down the front windows, and then stopped. Because the Audi was such a new car with so little engine noise, Friedman didn't think the A6 was turned off. The combo hinked him up, and his instincts started flaring.

"Hang tight, Redbone. Something's wrong."

Redbone backed up to his position of cover, now on full alert.

"Driver! Turn off the vehicle, and roll down all your windows! Front and back!" shouted Freidman to be sure the driver of the A6 got the message.

The brake lights of the Audi lit up, and it was on. It pulled away from the curb with the tires screaming as they swerved into the northbound lane of 8th Avenue.

"Motherfucker!" shouted Friedman.

"Sweet!" shouted Redbone.

The driver of the A6 had decided to run and had been trying to lure them up to the vehicle, probably so they'd have an advantage when he split. The two cops would have had to spend time running back to their car, and that would have given the Audi a good head start. Since they both had retained their positions of cover, it was easy for them to drop into their respective seats and slam the doors shut. The Audi was pulling away quickly, though, as Friedman dropped the black-and-white into gear and took off after them.

"What do you want to broadcast?" asked Redbone.

"Let's go with possible DUI driver. Who runs red lights at 2 a.m. except drunks?" replied Friedman.

The LAPD had changed pursuit policy several years back in response to media criticism over traffic deaths by influence during pursuits. Officers could no longer initiate pursuits for infractions. Only misdemeanors or felonies would cut the mustard. Of course the media wasn't willing to blame the asshole that was running from the cops. It was somehow determined that it was the LAPD's fault for chasing someone into a traffic accident that killed or maimed an innocent motorist. The reality was that the innocent dead guy's family would always sue the City and the LAPD because theirs were the deep pockets. The asshole criminal being chased was just an asshole criminal. Shifty ambulance-chasing lawyers knew they couldn't get blood from a turnip, so they attacked LAPD and its pursuit policy.

It almost always garnered a big cash reward for the family who suffered the loss because the 12 rocks in the box were bamboozled by the sharks. The argument was always based on the reason the pursuit was initiated.

"Mr. and Mrs. John Q. Public's son or daughter was killed because the vicious LAPD couldn't resist chasing down a guy that ran a stop sign. These cowboys killed their baby for their own personal enjoyment," would be the line used to hoodwink the people too stupid to get out of jury duty.

It would be conveniently left out that, yes, the asshole ran a stop sign and that was why the officers initiated the pursuit, but the reason he ran was because he was a parolee at large wanted in connection with a string of robberies. This would come out later, but it wouldn't matter. The damage was done, and the cash was dispersed to the grieving victims of the asshole's selfish behavior. Someone had to pay. The facts were that the majority of people who ran from the police had felonious reasons. There were exceptions, but they were few and far between. One of the biggest mass murderers in United States history, Timothy McVeigh, was captured after a pursuit over a traffic stop for a broken tail light. Under LAPD policy, some office pogue watch commander would have called off that pursuit in a New York minute to protect his career, and who knows where that asshole McVeigh would have ended up.

Patrol officers all knew these facts, and because they couldn't initiate pursuits for infractions, they did what the Department's policy was designed to make them do. They lied. A driver that ran was always either drunk or reckless. The Brass knew the statistics as well, but they had to do something to show they cared. So they created a policy that relied on a patrol officer's innate sense of doing right, even at the expense of his or her livelihood. The command staff knew that officers would chase a guy who ran because it was the right thing to do. It was a win-win for the Department. If things turned out well, they could say that the officers followed policy. If things turned out badly, they could crucify the patrol cop in the media and then fire him. It would give them the plausible deniability they needed to protect the City in civil suits stemming from an officer's egregious behavior.

Redbone initiated the broadcast as they screamed up 8th Avenue after the Audi, which was pulling away from them like they were standing still.

"12Z4…show us in pursuit of possible DUI driver northbound 8th Avenue from 67th Street, requesting a backup, airship and a supervisor," intoned Redbone into the microphone. "The vehicle appears to be occupied two times." He provided the license plate and vehicle description to the RTO.

The Audi was making the turn from 8th Ave. to Southwest Drive. They were hauling ass, and the black-and-white seemed to be bogging down.

"What the fuck is wrong with this car?!?!" shouted Friedman as he tried to figure out why they were topping out at around 70 miles per hour.

"Dude, you got it in first gear!" laughed Redbone.

In his rush to get on the Audi's ass, Friedman had dropped the gearshift all the way past drive into first gear. They were going just about as fast as they possible could in that gear, and when he slipped it up into drive the black-and-white lurched forward, released from its transmission-induced stupor.

They made the corner onto Southwest Drive and saw that the Audi had gained considerable ground. Friedman cranked the black-and-white up to about 110 miles per hour to try to close the gap, but since he knew the streets like the back of his hand he knew he couldn't maintain that pace.

"Bro, if this dick-fuck doesn't slow down, he's never gonna make the curve at Van Ness. If I don't see his brake lights come on in just a second, I'm gonna ease off. We're gonna be picking up the pieces for sure."

Redbone was broadcasting their location, the direction of the pursuit and clearing streets as they blew past them, as was his job as passenger officer. Friedman realized that the driver of the Audi had no clue what was coming up since he hadn't slowed at all.

Southwest Drive, aptly named because it runs in a southwest direction along the path of the railroad tracks that bisect 77th Street Division, turns into 62nd Street at Van Ness Avenue. Sixty-Second Street runs east/ west in the traditional square blocks of most of 77th as designed by the original real estate developers and city planners. This transition created a sweeping right-hand curve that the driver of the A6 approached at approximately 100 miles per hour. He was doomed but didn't know it. Friedman and Redbone did.

Friedman began braking hard in anticipation of the turn, and they could see the taillights of the Audi light up as the driver realized too late that he had miscalculated in grand fashion. The car slid sideways for a brief second, Tokyo drifting as he tried desperately to make a turn he stood no chance of making. Friedman and Redbone had closed the distance sufficiently to witness the show, and it was spectacular.

When the A6 struck the curb sideways, it jumped up about two feet in the air and slammed into the building on the northeast corner, then caromed off. It began an end-over-end tumble that sent it in a southeast direction, through the 6-foot wrought-iron fence into the rear side of the two-story house stretching the length of the southeast corner. Their speed was such that the party wasn't over. It bounced off the house, tearing a fantastic hole, and rolled sideways out into the middle of 62nd Street, pitching car parts, glass and construction materials as it went. It came to rest on the driver-side door, in a north-south direction, with the bottom of the car facing Freidman and Redbone as they went Code Six.

"12Z4. The vehicle has TC'd at the corner of Van Ness and Southwest Dr. Get an RA rolling to our location, and have responding units start setting a perimeter in case we have runners. I'll need units at Gage and Van Ness, Gage and Hass, Gage and Cimarron, Gage and Wilton, also at Hyde Park and Van Ness and Hyde Park above the railroad tracks. I'll need the first unit to respond to 62nd Street and Wilton," said Redbone in his best monotone, even though his heart was in his throat and adrenalin was coursing through his veins. It was important to sound as if he were reporting the weather because other officers from all the surrounding divisions would have switched their ROVERs to the frequency of their pursuit. He knew he would be judged by his broadcast and didn't want to make 77th Street look bad by sounding like a little girl screaming into the microphone.

The quiet when they exited their vehicle was eerie. Friedman and Redbone began to approach the A6 in a manner that was as tactically sound as possible. There was nothing in the LAPD manual that dealt with clearing a car that was resting upright on its driver's side door, but they did the best they could. There was no sound, but the distant sirens of the units en route to help made the whole thing seem like a movie.

Friedman rounded the rear end of the Audi, "slicing the pie" with his Glock to minimize his exposure to gunfire. The first thing he saw through the shattered rear window was a Hispanic man in the back seat of the car. Rather, his body was in the back seat of the car. He had been partially ejected through the driver's side rear window, and his head was pinned to the asphalt by the roof. The weight of the car had popped his head like a pimple, and his shaved scalp (the part that could be seen) looked like the skin of a Shar Pei.

There was a rapidly growing puddle of blood and brain matter approaching Friedman's Danners so he stepped back and refocused on the rest of the vehicle.

"I got one K'd, Redbone," said Friedman, "I can't see the other one. Look around and see if he got ejected. If not, he's gonna be a runner."

Suddenly, another Hispanic man popped up out of the front passenger side window, exposing his head and upper body. He then quickly disappeared back inside the Audi, and the roof prevented Friedman from seeing what he was doing inside.

"Show me your fucking hands!" warned Friedman.

Redbone hopped up onto the left rear tire of the Audi and stepped up on the driveshaft, which gave him sufficient height to be able to see down into the inside of the car. It also added his body weight to the load already being borne by Shar Pei's head. Under later scrutiny of the front DICV camera of their shop, the SKID Team investigators could see a little sliver of Shar Pei's head and it appeared that Redbone was bouncing up and down on the car, further squishing the unfortunate gangster. He was actually trying to get a better stance so he didn't slip off. His friends thought it was very, very funny. Capt. Capall wasn't amused. Redbone didn't care. IA took the complaint.

The other gangster kept popping his head up and out of the passenger window then back inside, like some sort of onion-headed Jack-in-the-Box.

"If you don't show me your fucking hands, I'm gonna shoot you in your fucking face!" shouted Friedman, who'd had just about enough of Gangster Jack's bullshit.

That little comment was the topic of some conversation during the Big Chief's de-briefing of the incident. Cmdr. Boyle came to Friedman's defense, pointing out the Department policy on "tactical language" and how Gangster Jack was failing to comply with officer commands during a dynamic situation. This caused Assistant Chief Anderson to raise an eyebrow at the commander, but he said nothing. Friedman never heard anything about it later on, so it must have just been a footnote in the SKID team investigation.

Additional units were arriving on scene, and a couple of old timers from Southwest Division were the first to arrive. They had ignored Redbone's request for the responding units to take up perimeter positions, but Friedman figured it was because they were ancient. The first one out of the car walked up with his giant 6-inch revolver out and started using it to give Gangster Jack directions.

"Get out the car, ya dumb mothafucka!" shouted the old timer with the salt-and-pepper natural as he waved the hand cannon in the direction he wanted G-Jack to go. He was about 6-foot-5 and couldn't have weighed less than 300 pounds. Certainly not fat, but not slender, either. His partner was slightly taller, if anything, but about the same age. Both were P2's.

Jesus Christ, thought a momentarily distracted Friedman, *this Gee Chee motherfucker is straight country. I bet he didn't even wear shoes until he was 12 years old. God bless South Carolina. I wonder how much time he's got on—can't be less than 30—he and his partner are definitely a product of the old hiring standards.*

While Freidman was contemplating the old timers, the dynamics of the situation changed. Gangster Jack, who'd had his bell rung in grand fashion, finally realized what the cops wanted him to do. He started to try to climb out through the smashed windshield, but his "I'm cooperating fully" train of thought was debunked quickly by the old black cop whose hair matched the police car.

The old timer holstered up his roscoe and snatched Gangster Jack from the vehicle with a speed that astonished Friedman, Redbone and the criminal. He grabbed the unsuspecting onion head (who must have weighed all of 130 pounds) by both ears and lifted him up and out through the smashed front windshield. While holding his head, he spun around with such force that Gangster Jack's legs were extended horizontally. Then he let him go like a hammer thrower in a track and field event at the

Olympics. He went flying away from the A6 and bounced along the 62nd Street asphalt like a perfectly round, thin stone on a still pond after having been thrown by Major League Baseball starting pitcher. Friedman and Redbone burst out laughing as other responding units walked over and hooked him up.

Gangster Jack's vehicle extraction, while discussed at length the next morning over beers at the Desert Room, was completely blocked from view of the DICV camera by the upturned Audi. The position of Friedman's car prevented the camera from capturing anything of value at the termination. Consequently, the extraction was ultimately attributed to Friedman when the newly reformed criminal complained that his treatment by the arresting officers was unkind. He told the IA investigators that the officer was huge, black and old, but that didn't jibe with the MDC check they had run to determine who was at scene. The two old timers from Southwest, the only two officers in South Bureau who matched the description, were actually Code 6 on an abandoned stolen car on the north end of their division at the time of the incident, according to their computer. There was no way they could have been the officers in question. IA was coached by Capt. Capall to look in the direction of Friedman and Redbone anyway. It was never considered that Freidman didn't have the physical strength to skip a human being along the street like that. The two old guys had hopped into Friedman's shop and played back the DICV recording of the termination and realized they couldn't be seen because of the angle of the camera. Since they hadn't gone Code 6 at the termination of the pursuit, they just got back in their car and drove away. Old-school LAPD style for sure—the same way the command staff used to play ball.

CHAPTER 20
PUFFYFACE

THE AFTERMATH OF THE PURSUIT THAT ENDED IN A DEATH by police influence was staggering. Even Friedman was surprised by the magnitude of the investigation. He figured he'd have to provide a statement and write some sort of synopsis for the traffic unit that would be investigating, but he was wrong. Way wrong.

The Department had finally realized they needed to begin building their defense against civil lawsuits right from the start, and thus the SKID team was deployed on all incidents likely to expose the City to significant liability. The female P3 that was in charge of the scene knew her shit and wasn't shy about telling the brass to pound sand and quit fucking up her program. When Cmdr. Boyle arrived and tried to put up barriers around the body of Shar Pei, to preserve the sensibilities of the lookie-loos watching from just outside the crime scene tape, she lost her shit.

"Who gave you permission to put those things up?" P3 SKID asked the two P2's who were trying to figure out how to assemble the PVC pipes and black canvas pieces.

The P2's just pointed at the commander and shook their heads.

Cmdr. Boyle used to be a hard-ass, high-speed, low-drag, field cop. He'd worked just about every special detail the Department had to offer before, during and after he promoted. To hear him tell the story of how he began his meteoric rise to the top, he'd been in Metropolitan Division "B" Platoon and was a practiced bitch & moan specialist like everyone else. One day he was approached by a legendary LAPD warrior captain who told him that if he was going to make a difference he needed to promote. If not, he needed to shut the fuck up. He decided to promote. The problem was that once out of the field, people changed. They had to drink the Kool-Aid to join the exclusive command staff ranks, and things usually went downhill from there.

There is a saying at LAPD among the working officers: There is no such thing as a good captain—just some that aren't as bad as others. Cmdr. Jim Boyle had been a decent, conscientious captain at 77th Street, and Friedman had high hopes that he would be the impetus for change that would bring the LAPD back to its former glory. He had Patton-esque bearing. He was the kind of guy that walked into a room and people unconsciously sat up straight in their chairs. He oozed command presence and natural leadership. Friedman knew from his sources in then-Capt. Boyle's office that his first concern was the protection of the street cop. He was always trying to massage uses of force or complaints in a way that would make them acceptable to the South Bureau command. He had the potential to get that fourth star and run the show from the Big Chief's office.

But things began to change when he made commander. Rank was funny. It changed nearly everyone. Some people changed when they made sergeant, but not most. Lieutenant changed many of the people who sought that rank. To join the captaincy at LAPD changed all but the most stalwart of individuals. Commander and above was the kiss of death. Friedman hadn't seen anyone survive intact. There were just too many political decisions that came from above, and too many times it was decided to sacrifice working cops. Anyone who refused to do the dirty work, or who even seemed reluctant, would never be allowed into the club. Cmdr. Jim Boyle was rapidly becoming one of the most hated individuals in South Bureau, and Friedman wasn't sure if he even knew it. He had always liked and respected the commander personally, but he was Friedman's biggest disappointment professionally. He could have made a real difference and left a lasting legacy, but he'd lost his way and it was doubtful that he'd ever find it.

"Well, break that shit down and put it away. It's fucking up my scene, and I don't answer to some commander," snapped P3 SKID.

The P2's did as they were told, smiling at what they knew was going to be a showdown between a P3 and a god-like commander. While they were putting the barrier back in its package, they started taking bets on who would win. They gave up because they both decided if some P3 was that brave, she must have some serious juice.

Cmdr. Boyle saw them stop assembling the barrier and with incredulity witnessed them actually packing it up.

He marched over to find out just exactly who those P2's thought they fucking were. P3 SKID intercepted him and blocked his path.

"Sir. Those barriers are not part of the original crime scene and could compromise my investigation. They will not be assembled," she told the stunned commander flatly, with her hands on her hips.

The P2's started tittering because the P3 couldn't be more than 5'2" to the commander's 6'2" frame. The visual of them squaring off created a very funny picture.

"You guys leave that shit and go set up more flares on 62 and Wilton. They're almost burned out," ordered P3 SKID, completely stealing the commander's authority.

The P2's sheepishly did as they were told, unsure if they were being given an order, a suggestion, or asked a favor, but were pissed that they were going to miss the show.

"Officer. I'm sure you didn't know it, but I gave them the order to screen off the deceased from public view," started Cmdr. Boyle. "It's tremendously important we consider the public's sentiments and do our utmost to demonstrate sensitivity."

"Well, Sir, I can understand your point of view, but my job is to conduct this investigation with an eye toward limiting City liability. Anything that could create any sort of doubt in the eyes of a jury can have a devastating fiscal impact later on in civil court," replied P3 SKID.

"I don't think you understand. I want those barriers put up. I gave those officers an order, and they were doing as I instructed. I am the ranking officer on scene, and I'll be making the decisions."

"I do understand, Sir. I'm sure you didn't know it, but I answer directly to the chief of police and the city attorney's office. I am *highly* trained in my field of expertise, and *I* am in charge of this investigation. Unless you intend to officially relieve me and conduct it yourself, with the accompanying responsibility, of course, then *I* decide how the investigation proceeds. Are you relieving me, Sir?" asked P3 SKID with a raised eyebrow.

Now, Jim Boyle was accomplished at many things. He'd worked metro, he'd worked air support, he'd worked gangs. He'd worked most everything. He'd just never worked a traffic division. That was mostly because he thought traffic divisions were for pussies. He knew he was being baited, and his ego was only just barely checked by the logical side of his brain. He sensed that if he relieved the smartass bitch it might feel good for a second, but it would end up biting him in the ass later.

He knew she would make sure the investigation got fucked up, and then he'd get the blame from the Big Chief. That could prevent him from achieving what every commander at LAPD wanted: a deputy chief spot.

He needed to keep his eye on the prize. "Make no decisions that could be construed as controversial" was the LAPD climber's mantra.

He seemed to remember having heard something come down the pike about SKID investigations, but since he never read shit like that he wasn't sure what it was. The commander wished his sneaky office-pogue adjutant were there. He'd have known the policy for sure. He'd have to make a note to ensure that when he went in the field, that little weasel would have to follow along. Even from home if need be. This whole fucked-up situation with the smartass P3 split-tail was most likely his adjutant's fault. He was sure he'd figure out why by the following day.

Trapped like a rat by the salty bitch, he did what he had to. He caved.

"Of course I understand your responsibilities when it comes to this investigation, Officer. You're doing a tremendous job. I wouldn't want the City to suffer undue liability because of my interest in the community. What can I do to help?" he said through clenched teeth.

"Stand clear and be available at the command post, Sir," replied P3 SKID, as she turned and marched off in search of something else to conquer.

Friedman and Redbone had to sit down and write their statements with the help of a League attorney, and then they got to go home. They were both ecstatic because normally such a clusterfuck would have caused them hours of paperwork.

"Bro. Some asshole should put himself to sleep on every pursuit. Think how much money he just saved the taxpayers. No court, no jail time, no overtime for you and me, no more crime committed by him. The only cost was for that chick from SKID to come out and handle the whole show. I bet we get some kind of medal for this shit," declared Redbone as they were walking into the parking structure at 77th Street.

"Don't hold your breath, homeboy," replied Friedman.

They were off work for a couple of days due to their regular days off, but before they could return to work they needed to see the department shrinks. They had both been ordered to BSS, which was standard procedure for officers involved in any kind of traumatic event. Friedman thought it was pretty funny for them to be ordered for a TC in which the suspect had killed himself because he couldn't drive.

Redbone spent most of his time with the shrink talking about the traffic accident back at Florence and Normandie. It had affected him more than he'd realized. He couldn't get the images of the dead little girl to go away completely. That confession earned him a standing weekly appointment with the BSS guy, who was elated that he'd finally found a cop that needed fixing. He'd gone to school forever to become a head shrinker and was none too pleased that the only place he could find a job was BSS. But $110,000 worth of student loans for his Ph.D. in psychology demanded a paycheck. So, he was stuck listening to a bunch of cops who told him fascinating stories but weren't really interested in becoming "normal." This Officer Obrador represented the first cop who seemed genuinely interested in therapy. Most of the cops he saw had gotten into some kind of trouble on or off duty and were trying to save their jobs via counseling.

Redbone just wanted to be sure that his brain was OK. The BSS doctor was going to do his best to hold on to him for as long as possible. He released him for full duty because he didn't feel his PTSD caused him to be a danger to the public, but he couldn't wait to deploy some psych tactics on his ass.

Friedman had drawn a female doctor that he found fascinating. By his best estimation, she had had her lips enhanced, her breasts enhanced and her chin adjusted. She was a Botox monster. He also figured there was some sort of liposuction involved, because he couldn't imagine her working hard enough to achieve her level of physical fitness. He was astounded that someone with such an obsession with physical appearances would take the career path of psychology.

This chick is bat-shit crazy, thought Friedman when he walked in her office. *I've never seen someone so carved up. She looks like that chick from the Jerry Springer show that has some sort of an addiction to plastic surgery. How the fuck did she decide this profession was a good idea? Fuck it ... those who can't do, teach.*

"So tell me, Officer Friedman, how do you feel?" started Dr. Puffyface.

"I'm feeling pretty good, Doc. Maybe a little sleepy. I'm not too used to being up this early. How're you feeling?" replied Friedman, actively working to not stare at her absurdly frozen facial features.

"I'm fine, just fine. I was referring to how you feel about having been involved in the death of another human being," countered the doctor.

"Uh, I wasn't really involved, Doc. I was doing my job, and he was doing his. I'm just better at mine."

"That seems awfully callous. I've read the report pertaining to the death of Mr. Lopez and your involvement in it. You were in a high-speed pursuit, and he was killed when the car he was driving crashed," droned Puffy.

Friedman caught himself staring at her face after she had finished speaking. He hadn't even heard what she'd just said because he was trying to figure out how she managed to say the word "pertaining" without closing her mouth.

"Well, I've seen a lot of death, Doc," recovered Friedman after a moment of uncomfortable silence. "I really can't believe they ordered me here for this. I've seen and done things on this job that were a thousand times worse than chasing some non-driver into a TC. My point of view is that bad things happen when you run from the police."

"I agree with your assessment of bad things happening when someone runs from the police," said the Doctor (again without closing her mouth on the word "police"), "but it happened to you. How does that make you feel?"

This fucking bitch is starting to get on my nerves. I'm about two seconds away from asking her if she's been in a car accident lately that caused her face to swell. I gotta just tell her what she wants to hear, or I'm gonna end up on the rubber gun squad. I hope Redbone remembers what we'd talked about before we got here. If they don't think we're good to go, they'll keep us out of the field for six months. We'll end up going out with a whimper.

"I think I understand what you mean now, Ma'am," said Friedman giving her his best "You're Fucking Stupid, But You Think You're Fucking Smart" voice. "I feel that the death of any human being is a tragedy. I can't help but wonder what that young man might have become if he'd had different opportunities in life. For him to have been struck down so young and for me to have had a part in it is difficult. Through my support system of family and friends, I imagine I will come to realize that, while doing my job is sometimes difficult, my actions that night probably saved lives. I fully intend to pray about this matter with my parish priest, Father Peter Casey, and to reflect on the fragility of life."

Puffyface scribbled furiously on her notepad with what Friedman interpreted to be a look of contentment on her face—but since it didn't move, he couldn't be sure.

CHAPTER 21
DEAD OR IN JAIL

"YOU SEEN HIM YET?" ASKED SHOWANNA

"Relax. I told you, I heard Vice put a pimping case on him, and he's in the County," replied Jackie.

They were back on the track and it had been a long time, but not long enough for Showanna. Her left eye was still a bit numb, and every time she blinked it tingled. She was surprised that Jackie could be so cool after the ass-kicking she'd taken. She was sure their former daddy was just around every corner, ready for payback because they'd run with his money. They both knew the risk they were taking, but they had to eat and the Figueroa Track could generate a thousand bucks on a Friday night.

"Quit being silly and go get that trick over there. He looks like a white boy. Charge him double," said Jackie.

It was often asserted that Caucasian officers couldn't work Vice in any of the ghetto divisions. The prevailing wisdom was that since there were hardly any white people in South Central, they would stick out like a sore thumb. The hookers would know the minute they came into contact with them that they were cops and wouldn't even give them the time of day. The truth was that the whores loved white tricks. They were safe. Most were squares from the Internet out looking for a good time with their first black girl. They were unlikely to rob them, beat them or kill them. And the girls always charged more because *their* prevailing wisdom was that white people were rich. True, it was always possible a white trick could be Vice, but all the girls knew LAPD was diverse. Anyone could be a cop. Street-walking Figueroa prostitutes liked whites, Asians, Hispanics and blacks, in that order. Cash was king, and anyone who had it needed to be considered viable.

Showanna walked over to the older Jeep Grand Cherokee and leaned in the passenger-side window.

"Show me your dick," were the first words out of her mouth.

Showanna Johnson was only 20 years old, but she was no rookie whore. She'd been arrested more times than you could count, and she'd been schooled by plenty of defense attorneys, other hookers and stupid flirting cops. She knew that an LAPD undercover cop couldn't show his penis. Long Beach cops could (she learned that lesson the hard way), but it was LAPD policy for Vice operators to not expose themselves. They were not allowed to touch a girl, either, even if she asked him to. That made it simple for the streetwise working girl.

Showanna's Jeep John whipped out his dick quick as quick could be, so she hopped in and they were off. She directed him to the Furst Motel above Slauson because he wanted "half and half," common street vernacular for oral copulation and straight sex. Apparently, the white boy was no rookie, either. He was going to take his time, and Showanna was going to have to earn her double fare. She shot a quick text to Jackie, letting her know she'd be out of the loop for a while, but Jackie didn't hit her back. Showanna figured she was busy with a customer, but she was wrong—very wrong. By the time Showanna and the Jeep John pulled into the parking lot of the motel eight blocks away, Jackie was already in a world of hurt.

Jackie thought she must be slipping. She had figured that by working up in the 40s area of Figueroa instead of down at their regular post on 68th Street they wouldn't have to worry. She hadn't even seen him pull up. Of course he didn't have the same black Chrysler 300; now he was in a maroon Dodge Magnum station wagon, but he looked exactly the same.

She'd been concentrating on waving at cars with lone male occupants driving southbound on Figueroa and hadn't seen him until he popped out from behind a nearby parked minivan. She never stood a chance.

"Sup, Jackie? Where yo homegirl at?" said her former daddy, right before he punched her square in the face with a closed right fist.

Jackie's lights went out. She woke up in the back seat of the Magnum, and near as she could tell they were driving south on Figueroa somewhere below Florence. She was starting to panic, as she realized how much trouble she was in. The man driving the Magnum was as hard as she'd ever seen. There were lots of gorilla pimps in the 'hood, but he was vicious. Cold and vicious. He didn't want sex, only money. That was unusual, and both Jackie and Showanna had figured it was because he'd acquired a taste for man ass in prison. Either way, it created a dynamic Jackie wasn't used to. For as long as she could remember, men had wanted sex from her and when they didn't it made her nervous.

She knew they had committed an unpardonable sin in the world of Figueroa prostitution—they had skipped with their pimp's money. Under normal circumstances, she knew that the penalty for keeping money from a pimp was an ass kicking. She was OK with that and understood it to be part of the rules. She'd seen other girls get stomped for holding out and always thought it was justified. But she knew this situation was unlikely to end up in a simple beat down and was starting to think she might not see tomorrow. Her face was a wreck. He'd hit her hard. Like a man. He was about 6 feet tall and weighed close to 240 pounds. When compared with her 5-foot-4, 120 pound frame, there was no contest. It was like being hit with a sledge hammer right in the nose. From the force of the blow and the damage it surely caused her face, she also knew he wasn't interested in preserving her working beauty. Most pimps wouldn't damage a girl's face too badly because it could affect her money-making potential. This motherfucker wasn't interested in putting her back on the streets to make money. Something else was wrong.

"You awake? I just got out the County, bitch," said the pimp. "Someone snitched me out for havin' bitches on the track. One of my homeboys from Eight Trey Hood's got some bitches his-self. He in for some bullshit warrants and tells me one of *his* bitches say it were you and yo hoe partner. Funny how you went missin' and I gets picked up next day. Guess you wasn't countin' on a DA reject, huh, bitch? I get out a little too soon for ya'll?"

Now Jackie was scared. She understood the whole situation and started to do the math. She figured there was only about a one in 10 chance she'd live. He thought they'd snitched. That was bad. Just about as bad as it could be. Lots of girls got pissed at their daddies and threatened to go to the police, but they rarely did. Even if they screwed up the courage to make first contact with vice, they never went to court to testify. It was simply too dangerous. If the pimp didn't get convicted, the girl was dead. Even with the heavy sentencing guidelines for pimping and pandering, a pimp would be out of prison in less than five years due to overcrowding. That wasn't enough time to make a new life, even if a girl wanted to. If he went away for a long time, one of his homies would get the girl for him. A pimp's bottom bitch had been known to get working girls that snitched. It was just too dangerous a prospect.

Jackie knew that it wasn't her or Showanna that had ratted him off. It was probably one of the other girls in his stable. It could have been anyone, because he was such a violent asshole. But none of that mattered now. He thought it was them, so it was. There was no use in trying to plead a case or appeal to his logical side. He was just an animal with an animal's instincts for survival. They hurt him, so they must be prevented from hurting him again. Neither mercy nor sympathy was to be expected or given.

Rudy Gomez, aka Big Sniper from the Tiny Jokers set of Florencia 13, had been out of prison for exactly two weeks. In his adult life, he'd never been out of prison for more than three months in a row. He was OK with that because all his friends were in prison, too. The outside world moved too fast for him anyway. Every time they paroled him off, he just fucked around with the little homies until he got caught up in some bullshit and sent home. He liked showing the youngsters how to put in work. To them he was a legend. In prison he was a legend. He was, without a doubt, a legendary hardened criminal killer. In the real world, he was just a middle-aged loser.

Florencia had been making inroads into traditional black gang territory for years. It was easy now. The Mexican drug cartels controlled the dope. The Mexican Mafia controlled the distribution. The Mexican street gangs pared it down and sold it in quantity to the black gang's shot callers. The black gangs cut it up and sold it on street corners to their own people. Once upon a time, the blacks would have never let Mexican gangsters into their 'hoods without a fight. Now, with the Mafia controlling the jails and prisons, the black gangs only existed because the Mexicans let them. They were nothing more than a useful tool to make money. God help the LAPD if the Mexicans ever tired of the current system. If a true and outright war was ever declared, there would be a bloodbath in L.A. The black gangs have many hard members per set that would kill if need be, but most were play hard and their gangs were unorganized. It was every man for himself, and money was king. The Mexican Mafia was organized. They could have relatives in prison killed (or out in the real world, for that matter) if a gangster failed to obey. That meant that *every* Hispanic gang member was a guaranteed shooter. The black gangs talked a tough game, but they were hopelessly outnumbered.

Big Sniper was supervising some of the little homies as they hit up Florencia 13 on the back of a big building near the northbound 110 Freeway on ramp from Manchester Avenue. The building was a public storage self-store center that was accessed from Grand Ave. and butted up against the on ramp for the 110. The 6-foot-tall "F13" (in Old English lettering) with the accompanying mandatory "Roll Call" of all the homies from their set would be seen by everyone leaving the hood all day long.

'Hey Sniper, someone is pulling up over next to the freeway. They're getting off the car right now. It's a big llanta. He's dragging some bitch out the back seat," advised Tiny Smiley, who had been assigned perimeter security by Big Sniper.

The most racist individual in the known world is the Mexican gang member. They have innumerable derogatory terms for blacks. "Llanta" is Spanish for "tire," so called because tires are black. They use words like araña, mayate, and tinto also, and the list is ever-growing and ever-changing.

Grand Ave. parallels the 110 Freeway on the east side for much of its journey through South Central. It stops and starts depending on the cross streets and it's usually a haven for illegal dumping and illicit activity. The section of Grand that Tiny Smiley had been assigned to watch was a short cul-de-sac off Manchester Ave. that dead-ended into the northbound 110 on ramp. Its only purpose was to provide access to the public storage facility and to act as a condom depository for in-car prostitution.

The on ramp was fenced off and covered with a fair amount of typical freeway-adjacent foliage that afforded Tiny Smiley a position of concealment from which to conduct his observations.

Big Sniper walked over to Tiny Smiley to see what was up. He was proud of Tiny Smiley. He was his little sister's youngest baby, and at just 11 years old he was already down for his 'hood. Sniper looked up over the bushes and saw Jackie getting dragged by her hair out of the back seat of one of those Dodge Magnums. She was screaming for help, but with the freeway noise there was no way anyone was going to hear her.

"Fuck it, Holmes. It's just some nigger and his puta. They ain't gonna be worried about what we're doing. They might get the cops over here, though, so keep an eye on them and let me know if anything crazy happens," decided Big Sniper.

Tiny Smiley was pleased with himself. He was putting in work like a big homie, and with a sponsor like Sniper he was right in the life he always wanted. Gangster shit was fun. No more homework, no more teachers, no more rules. His abuela kept telling him he was gonna end up dead or in jail, but he wasn't scared. He knew his homies would always be there for him. Fuck it, Holmes. Who needed to know how to read anyway?

Tiny Smiley was contentedly watching the black guy repeatedly punch and kick the girl on the ground. She was screaming and doing her best to get away, but she really didn't stand much of a chance. Tiny got a good look at her face once, and even though her nose was gushing blood and she had a cut above her eye, he thought she was a pretty good-looking light-skinned black girl.

The pimp landed a particularly vicious blow to Jackie's stomach, knocking the wind out of her. While she was trying to recover, he walked back to the Dodge and began to rummage around under the front seat. Tiny Smiley saw him come out of the car with good-sized folding knife, and when he walked up to the girl she had apparently recovered her wind.

"No me matas! Por Favor! Suéltame!" screamed Jackie.

Jackie rarely spoke Spanish anymore. Her English had devolved into the horrible ghetto slang favored by pimps and hookers, but she'd grown up speaking Spanish in the house. The only time she spoke it now was job-related—when a trick couldn't speak enough English to get the deal done. Her family disowned her in junior high, when they found out she'd had sex with a black classmate, so Spanish always reminded her of that hurt. She could still remember her proud Mexican father telling her in Spanish how she was no longer his daughter and that he never wanted to see her again.

She was 12. Now, it seemed he'd been right. When faced with her death a mere eight years later, she reverted to the language of her carefree youth.

Tiny Smiley was stunned. This obviously changed things. It was one thing for a black guy to be kicking the shit out of a black girl, but a whole other thing if she was Hispanic. He was pretty sure that broke some kind of 'hood rule. Plus, it looked like the guy was going to kill her. Sniper had just finished his second 40-ounce Miller Genuine Draft and was about to throw the bottle up on the freeway when Tiny Smiley came running over.

"Hey Sniper, the bitch that mayate is fucking up is a Ruca. I hear'd her scream in Spanish. I think he's gonna shank her. Shouldn't we do something?"

Now, Big Sniper was no hero. He was, however, an avowed racist. He thought it over for a second, and using Miller beer logic, came to the conclusion that the circumstances called for action. They had a moral obligation to defend the sacred honor of the Hispanic female. That guy could kill all the black bitches he wanted to, but he wasn't going to get a single Mexican on Sniper's watch. He told Tiny Smiley to gather the homies as he stalked over to the cul-de-sac to confront the situation.

Jackie's pimp had decided he'd fucked around enough. He was going to put her lights out permanently and go find Showanna up on the track. When he was done with her, the word would be out on Figueroa. He'd never have to worry about getting snitched on again.

Jackie screamed when he stabbed her in the left side of her upper torso. He'd been going for a liver kill—prison style—but she was squirming too much and he'd missed his target. The pimp was concentrating so hard on his killing business that he didn't even notice the five onion heads until the biggest one kicked him in the face.

"You fucked up, Holmes. This is Florencia 'hood. Niggers don't kill Mexicans here. It's the other way around, fool."

Big Sniper had landed a running soccer-style kick to the pimp's face. He'd been in lots of prison fights and had long ago learned that the most vicious cheater was usually the one to survive. He could tell that Jackie's pimp had done prison time, and it would be dangerous to give him even a slight chance. One of the older homies grabbed the knife from the street after it flew out of the pimp's hand. Two of the other gangsters grabbed Jackie and carried her over to the other side of the cul-de-sac and leaned her up against the exterior wall of the public storage building. They tried to find out how she had ended up with the pimp, but Jackie was bleeding bad and too hurt to talk.

"Don't worry, Heina. You just sit here and watch the show. We're gonna teach that mayate a lesson for you," advised one of the gangsters.

Big Sniper was in his element. He was going to use Jackie's pimp as a learning tool for the little homies. The pimp had recovered sufficiently from the boot to the head to get up on all fours. Big Sniper toe-kicked him as hard as he could in the throat.

"If he can't breathe, he can't fight," lectured Big Sniper. "Drag that motherfucker into the street and put his feet up on the curb."

The pimp was clutching his throat with both hands, trying desperately to get air through his rapidly swelling wind pipe. Things were definitely not going as planned, and he briefly wondered if someone was going to call the police to come and save him. The Florencia gangsters dragged him off the curb and laid him out on his back with his feet up on the curb. The pimp was trying to squirm loose from their grasp, but without air he was weak as a newborn calf. He quit struggling, and in his head he was trying to figure out why they were going to such pains to make him comfortable by putting his feet up.

Big Sniper jumped as high in the air as he could and landed squarely on the pimp's right knee. With his feet up on the 12-inch curb and his back on the street, the pimp's knee had a long way to travel in the wrong direction. The noise was sickening, and Tiny Smiley had to look away. Sniper tumbled into the street, and the pimp momentarily forgot about his throat because of the excruciating pain in his leg.

Big Sniper stood up and dusted himself off. He walked over so he was standing directly over the pimp's head, and he leaned down to look him square in the face.

"See what happens to niggers in Florencia 'hood, Holmes? Put his other leg up on the curb, Esse."

The second knee job wasn't going to be such a laissez-faire event. The pimp's survival instincts kicked in heavy and it took three of the gangsters to hold him down. Big Sniper called Tiny Smiley over.

"It don't take much weight to break a knee like that, Holmes. It's your turn. Do him up."

Tiny Smiley had nearly thrown up when he heard the pimp's knee break. He was 100 percent sure that gangster shit wasn't fun anymore. He was wondering how his Abuela had gotten so smart, and he was planning on waking up early for school Monday morning. It was new leaf time for Tiny Smiley, aka Dionicio Agapito Gonzalez Gomez. He looked up at Big Sniper and started to cry.

Weakness. Big Sniper hated it. He must have been wrong about his little sister's baby.

"Fuck it, Holmes. I'll put this fucking mayate out of his misery for you. I thought you were down for the 'hood. If you're what's coming up, Florencia is fucked."

Big Sniper knew it was life lesson time. He reached in his right front pants pocket and pulled out the small .25 caliber semi-automatic he carried for protection while the homies were hitting up. He walked over, leaned down, pressed the barrel against the pimp's left eye and squeezed the trigger.

CHAPTER 22
OPEN EYES

REDBONE WAS PENSIVE. HE'D SPENT A LOT OF TIME LATELY thinking about what he was going to do with his life now. He knew he never had to work again if he didn't want to. He knew he would never have to worry about money. He knew that his mom and dad and older sister would never have to worry about anything again. He also knew that people with too much money and too few worries tended to self-implode. He was a smart man and knew that if he didn't have some direction in life, he'd end up a rich drunk like in that Dudley Moore movie "Arthur." He didn't want to waste the gift they'd been given.

"What's on your mind, Redbone?" asked Friedman. "You seem out of it. You worried about something?"

The truth was that Friedman was worried about his partner. He'd told him that he was meeting the BSS head shrinker because of that T/C on Florence and Normandie, but really he just thought it was a good idea. Friedman was mostly afraid that their winnings would destroy Redbone. He knew Redbone was a natural drinker and party animal. Unchecked by financial worries, Redbone's habits could spiral out of control and destroy him, Friedman figured. They were thinking almost the exact same thing at the exact same time…like partners often do.

They were rolling around the division, just kind of cruising. The radio was dead and the whole place was quiet, so they were doing laps until end of watch.

"Did I ever tell you that my sister had cancer?" asked Redbone out of the blue.

"Negative. Never mentioned it. It must have been a long time ago… what kind?"

"She had breast cancer. It was about 10 years ago, and since she was so young the doctors didn't think it was cancer…they thought it was a cyst. They finally figured it out, but by then she had to have a double mastectomy. We all thought she was going to die for sure. I guess luck runs in our family."

"No shit," replied Friedman.

"She does some breast cancer 5K charity run every year to remind herself that she should be dead. I've been thinking that someday I'd like to donate big to a good cancer charity. Do you think the Batts Brothers would be able to help me out with that? I know some charities only use like 20 percent of donations for the actual cause and the rest is used up in administrative bullshit. I don't want to give money to a charity so their CEO can make 400 grand a year."

"I'm pretty sure that's the kind of shit they'd be real good at," said Friedman. "Give them a call on Monday and see what they have to say. I bet they'll know exactly what needs to be done to get some cash into the right hands so it would really help people."

Friedman was actually shocked by Redbone's charitable thoughts, because he'd never really seemed like a "get involved" kind of guy. He'd mostly been talking about traveling and buying toys since their lives had changed. Friedman knew something else was bothering him but figured Redbone would bring it up when he was ready.

"I've been thinking about a lot of things lately," started Redbone. "Mostly about what to do with my life now that I don't have to worry about money. It's funny how you never really think about how much your identity is tied up in your profession."

"Yeah? How's that?" replied Friedman.

"Well, this job is one of the only jobs in the world that people introduce you to someone at a party and they say, 'This is so-and-so. He's a cop.' Know what I mean?"

"Yeah, I hate that. You're right though. That's what has your brain chugging along?" said Friedman.

"Kind of. Indirectly I guess. I've spent the last two or three months dreaming of buying shit and having fun, and I guess I'm kind of over that. I just realized the other day I can go wherever I want and do whatever I want and buy whatever I want. But after all is said and done, I'm going to end up in the ground just like everyone else. This job is honorable. We make a difference in people's lives. I want to keep doing something that makes a difference."

"Are you worried about your legacy, dude?" laughed Friedman. "That's some very introspective shit."

"Negative, asshole. Well, maybe. Who fucking knows? I just don't want to waste this opportunity on bitches and toys. I want to make a difference somehow. You know what I'm saying? I don't want to be Martin Luther King Jr. or anything, but I think I have an obligation to effect some kind of change in the world."

"Listen to this motherfucker! He's been rich for 10 minutes, and now he's a fucking philanthropist. I'm in the car with a Carnegie!" shouted Friedman out the window of the black-and-white to a group of baseheads huddled on a bus bench.

"Look here, ya stupid motherfucker, I know you agree with me. I know you think just like me. That's why we're doing all this shit we're doing here — to have some fun, for sure, but also to get some revenge for the guys who can't. To put some shit right. That's called making a difference, dick," replied Redbone.

"I hear you, Bone. I'm just fucking with you. I've been thinking the same things lately. I'm not too sure that what we're doing is making a difference. It's fun, no doubt. But I've been looking at ways to make a long-term difference around here. Smashing cars isn't gonna get it done. You know what I'm saying?"

"Dude! Are you thinking about staying? You're fucking crazy!" said Redbone, twisting sideways in his seat to look directly at Friedman.

"I don't know, Bro. A part of me thinks I should. I could be like a kind of sleeper cell. From the inside I could see the things that need to be made right, and then use cash to bring influence to bear and fix them. If I could bring the LAPD back to its former glory without sacrificing all the positive changes of the last 20 years, maybe that could be *my* legacy."

"That is the stupidest thing I've ever heard! This place is broken beyond repair, Dude. Look at what they call leadership! Look at who they call leaders! You'll never change the culture that rewards the people who were never cops in the first place. You're gonna get fired for all the shit we've done since we hit the numbers, anyway. You're career is over, Dude. It's a bit late to change your mind," pointed out Redbone.

"I don't know about that, man. It's pretty fucking hard to get fired unless you do some criminal shit. I'll be a P2 forever, that's for sure, but we'll see what happens. I think I'll just ride this whole thing out all the way. If they fire me, then they do. But if they don't, I'll make some decisions."

The MDC message light lit up, and they received a call to respond to 555 E. Hardy Street in Inglewood to meet the victim of a stabbing.

"Fuck. Centinela. I hate that place," said Friedman.

"And you want to stay here doing this kind of shit. You're a fucking idiot," replied Redbone.

They pulled into the rear of the hospital and parked. They headed to the ER, because that was where they usually needed to go when summoned by the Hospital Gods, but the surly LVN working the center counter couldn't figure out who had called or why. Redbone walked out to the car and got the call-back information, and when the LVN checked it out he told them it was the main lobby that had called.

They had to walk through the maze of hallways to get to the main lobby desk. When they got there, the security guard told them they'd been asked by the charge nurse in ICU to call the police because one of their patients had woken up and could talk. He thought the patient had been dropped off by a ghetto ambulance the other night and was a stabbing victim, but he wasn't sure. He gave them the room number, and they headed for the bank of elevators.

The RNs in the Intensive Care Unit were a little better to deal with when compared to the ER staff, but not much. They suffered from the same delusion that every person in the hospital was a patient and never stopped to consider how they ended up there. Friedman had to put a couple of them in hard check one time when he was guarding an asshole rapist that had shot a cop while trying to evade capture. The nurse in charge of the criminal tried to order Friedman to remove his handcuffs to make him more comfortable. She also demanded that Friedman allow him to watch whatever he wanted on television. (Friedman had turned it off). When Friedman told her to pound sand, she ran and got the charge nurse who gave it her best shot, too. He told them that their "patient" had shot and almost killed a friend of his and there was no way possible that the cuffs were coming off. The nurses lobbied on behalf of their charge until Friedman told them the reason he'd been wanted in the first place. Apparently the rape was a bigger deal for them than their patient trying to murder a uniformed police officer. The next thing Friedman and the asshole knew, it was catheter time. The television was off the menu, too.

They walked into the ICU and were greeted by a desk full of Filipino nurses. One of them walked over and hit them up.

"You guys here for the stabbing victim?" he asked.

"Not sure. We just got a call to come to the hospital. The security guard downstairs sent us up here. He thought it might be about a stabbing. What do you know about the situation?" asked Friedman.

"Well, she got dropped off at the back door of the ER last week. I'm actually really surprised she lived. The ER docs said that she had lost over 40 percent of her blood volume and her organs were shutting down when they got her on the table. They called the police from the ER, but the two officers from Inglewood PD told them to call back later if she lived. She's finally awake and seems to be aware of what's going on."

"Did she tell you anything good?" asked Redbone.

"The whole time she was unconscious she kept talking nonsense in Spanish, begging her dad to forgive her and complaining about spiders. Her dad must own a mechanic shop because she went on and on about bad tires. When she came around, she told the day nurse that she'd been kidnapped up on Figueroa, so that's why we called you guys," said the nurse.

When they walked in the room, they were shocked at the appearance of the victim. Her face was swollen horribly and was mostly covered in gauze. It was sort of an über Newton turban. She was buzzing and beeping, hooked up to everything, and appeared to be just about as bad off as they'd ever seen. But her eyes were open, and when they walked up to the bed she spoke out strongly, if somewhat distorted from the swelling.

"Friedman? Redbone? What are you guys doing here?" asked Jackie.

"You know us, Ma'am?" replied Friedman.

"It's me, Jackie."

"Jackie!? Jesus Christ! What the fuck happened!? You look like you got run over by a train!" blurted out Friedman before he had a chance to think. He was stunned by her appearance and couldn't fathom how she got like that and managed not to die.

She started to cry as she realized how badly her face must be damaged if they couldn't recognize her. She was a wily, streetwise, Figueroa prostitute, but she was still a girl. Her self-esteem was just as appearance-based as any 20-year-old, and she was worried people wouldn't want to be with her if she was disfigured. Like all the girls on Fig, she too harbored dreams of finding that Mr. Right who would take her away from all the bad. "Pretty Woman" was just a bullshit '80s movie, but it was based in reality for sure. Every whore on the Figueroa Track was looking for their own personal Richard Gere.

"Easy, baby..." said Redbone, as he shot Friedman a dirty look. He walked over to the other side of the bed and gently picked up her hand and held it. She looked at him through her tears and sobs and just shook her head. She couldn't calm down and she couldn't stop crying. He gave Freidman the "Get-the-Fuck-Out-of-Here" nod and sat down on the edge of Jackie's bed.

Friedman backed out of the room, ashamed of his inability to read the situation and proud that his partner could. He went to the nurse's station and gathered up all the information he could for their report. Then he looked in on Redbone and mouthed he was going down to the ER to see what he could find out from them. Redbone was still sitting on the side of Jackie's bed, holding her hand and talking gently to her. Friedman had never felt like more of an asshole. The filter between his brain and mouth sometimes got fucked up, and he periodically lost his way.

Redbone has progressed like a champion. Too bad he's not gonna be a cop anymore. He's about the best I've ever seen when it comes to understanding people. He's got a gift. The LAPD is losing a good one — educated, street-smart and a firm grounding in patrol. A guy like him would make a fine command officer. He could have gone a long way here. He's gonna make someone a hell of a husband and father someday, though…and that's an even better use of his talents.

Friedman hit up hospital security, and much to his surprise they were not only able to play back their surveillance video of the back doors of the ER, they were also able to burn him a disc. The video was crystal clear, but it didn't show too much. Whoever it was that dropped Jackie off was no idiot. He was a rather nondescript male Hispanic. He looked to be about 40 years old with a shaved head and a big hey-brother moustache that could be seen clearly even from the video. He was obviously strong from the way he picked Jackie up from the back seat with seemingly no effort. Considering she was dead weight, that was no mean task. The car he used was an equally nondescript mid-nineties Honda Accord with no plates. There'd be no tracing that lead. Friedman could tell by the way he moved that he was a convict. When he walked coolly away from the back doors after handing Jackie off to a security guard, he moved slowly, as if he wasn't worried or concerned. Friedman had never seen him before, but that didn't mean a thing. There were thousands just like him.

Back upstairs, Redbone was making much more progress than Friedman. He got Jackie to calm down and start talking. He already guessed who was responsible for her condition, but she surprised the shit out of him with how it all went down.

Jackie wasn't sure if she had been more terrified by her former pimp or the old-school Mexican gangster that had saved her. She had watched everything transpire in the cul-de-sac on Grand Ave. From her position, she'd had a clear view of the whole program, including the grand finale. For a girl who had seen some brutal things, she was caught off guard by the brutality of it all. She was street-smart, too, and realized she was an untrustworthy witness to a homicide. When the old cholo shot the pimp in the face, he immediately looked in her direction. She had instinctively closed her eyes at the gun shot, and with her being so banged up he must have thought she was unconscious. She played that card to the hilt. Big Sniper had picked her up off the sidewalk and loaded her into a car. He told the other gangsters to take the strap and get back to the barrio and he'd be along in a bit. She remembered them arguing briefly about what she'd seen.

"I think the heina saw you blast that mayate, holmes," warned one of the gangsters. "What if she talks?"

"We saved her from him, holmes. She won't say shit. She ain't gonna make it, anyway. I seen homies in the pen stabbed like that before. They *never* make it when they get stuck up high like that."

Jackie had lost so much blood by that time, she didn't need to pretend to be unconscious. She didn't know anything that had happened until she woke up in the bed she was lying on at that very moment.

"Redbone, I can't be involved in that shit. Those Mexicans were hard. The one that killed that asshole was cold. He didn't give a fuck. If he thought I was involved in helping the police, he'd kill me in a second. You know how often I go to jail. I'd be dead in a week. I don't want any part of it. Please don't tell the detectives I was there," pleaded Jackie.

"Jackie. You must have bled all over the place. That pimp is gonna have your blood on his knuckles and shoes. Your blood is gonna be on the sidewalk where you were sitting. You know you get swabbed every time you get arrested. We're talking about homicide. They're gonna rush DNA, and they'll get a hit on you for sure. They're gonna have your name and picture running up and down Figueroa if we don't bring it to them first," replied Redbone.

Friedman went back up the elevators and into the ICU. He walked over to Jackie's room and peered in. Redbone gave him the "OK-to-Enter" nod, and he walked over to Jackie's bedside. He listened intently as Redbone broke down the whole story, and with Jackie occasionally chiming in he got the full and complete picture. He knew what needed to be done. The situation called for The Right Thing. He figured the pimp got what he deserved and Jackie was saved by the hand of God. Even if the tool he used to save her was another asshole. He had several friends working South Bureau Homicide. He'd ask around and see who was handling it and find out what they had.

CHAPTER 23
TEX-MEX

FRIEDMAN HAD WORKED WITH AND AROUND THE TWO homicide detectives in charge of the pimp murder for nearly 15 years. They were they type of guys who worked as partners in patrol and continued on in their careers together. They'd worked Vice at 77th Street and had taught Friedman the ropes when he first joined the team. He'd worked patrol with them before that. They both took the detective's test at the same time and landed in band four or five. They were promoted almost simultaneously, and after they each did some time working tables, they became partners in Criminal Gang Homicide Group together. The name of the homicide units and their areas of responsibility changed with nearly every regime. They were on divisional homicide teams. They were bureau homicide teams. They were under the CGHG umbrella with various teams assigned to various divisions. Friedman could never keep it straight and didn't really care.

He'd thought about trying a loan up to Homicide a couple of times, but he loved his 3 day/12 hour per week schedule too much to give it up. Those guys were always subject to call out and worked a shitload of overtime.

He also thought the DIII in charge of CGHG was one of the few people you could actually touch who was personally responsible for the Federal Consent Decree that stemmed from the whole "Rampart Scandal" bullshit. In the late '90s, the DIII (then a lowly worker bee) was part of the investigation that was dealing with the fallout from Rafael Perez and his small crew of criminals. He was one of the group of idiots who believed everything that Perez told them hook, line, and sinker. That group destroyed many lives and careers, and created the myth of a corrupt LAPD based on the stories fed to them by an admitted perjurer and attempted murderer. The media fallout resulted in federal oversight of nearly all daily working aspects of the department via the Federal Consent Decree and devastated the reputation of the LAPD. Even after the facts showed the "scandal" to only involve Perez and a couple of his friends (who never should have been hired in the first place), the damage had been done. Friedman believed the consent decree and the people responsible for failing to stand up against it had created the leadership vacuum in the LAPD. He had worked in the same building where the Rampart investigation was headquartered and remembered seeing the DIII and his friends high-fiving when the media announced indictments of several (ultimately determined to be innocent) Rampart officers. He knew he wouldn't be able to keep his mouth shut around someone like that, so Freidman declined offers to loan up to CGHG at least twice.

"Friedman! What the fuck, bro?!?! The word on the yard is that you and your red-rookie partner have gone plum loco!" shouted Matt Stations, as Friedman walked in the back door of the bar.

Det. Stations was a transplanted Texan, and it showed in his every word and deed. He was boisterous and outgoing but quick to take offense. He and his partner had been responsible for the two years of Friedman's career during which he'd had the most fun—in 77th Vice.

"I heard he has at least two Boards pending and that he doesn't stand a chance," chimed in his partner, Herman Schäfer. "You must be some kind of stupid gringo to start fucking up this late in the game."

Det. Schäfer was born and raised south of the border. When he showed up at his hiring oral exams, one of the Hispanic sergeants on the board tried to challenge the fact that he had claimed Hispanic on his application because of his last name. He'd been born in Mexico to fourth-generation Mexicans, and having lived there through high school, he quickly punked the sergeant. Turned out the La Raza asshole sergeant couldn't even speak Spanish. Schäfer got hired quickly.

Friedman had called them up and asked them to meet him at the Desert Room in Gardena. They used to spend a lot of time drinking there back in the day after morning watch ended, and he felt it was a safe location for their chat.

It was a dive bar in the truest sense of the word. In a state where smoking in bars had been prohibited for years, you could still find ashtrays behind the counter. They had an old-school token system in case you wanted to buy a friend a drink, and the décor was strictly '60s. They opened at 0600 hours every day, and there was always a crew of regular old-timers there right when the bell rang. Friedman loved it. Suzie, the owner, was a true friend of 77th Street, and they always held their off-probation parties and unofficial (no one over the rank of lieutenant) Christmas parties there.

"Yeah, yeah, yeah, so it's been raining a little bit lately. You pussy detectives just forgot how it feels to be judged by the Monday morning quarterbacks," countered Friedman, as he pulled up a red Naugahyde bar stool to the table Matt and Herman had already commandeered.

"Fuck me, brother. From what I hear, it sounds like you just don't give a shit. Everything cool?" asked Schäfer.

"Yeah, man. I'm good. You know how it is. Trouble comes in waves. It's no thing."

They shot the shit for a bit about old times and old crimes. They hadn't really sat down and hung out since the boys had split Vice for bigger and better things. Like always though, with good friends, it seemed as if no time had passed and they were as tight as ever. Vice was a funny assignment. They had been through some dangerous things together on patrol, but working Vice had created a bond in a strange way. Vice is always right on the line of illegal and legal. The officers who share a successful Vice tour tend to get really close.

"All right, bud," said Stations. "We didn't get called all the way down here to walk down memory lane. We live the other way in Sagus, remember? What the fuck is going on?"

"I hear you guys drew a homicide over on Grand Ave. In that cul-de-sac just above Manchester. A head shot?" started Friedman.

"Yeah. Seems like a pimp caper. It might be a trick, or maybe one of the bitches in his stable got out of control. Not sure yet," said Schäfer, leaning forward. It was pretty unusual for a patrol cop to seek out a detective on a homicide case. It happened, but not all the time. Herman Schäfer knew Friedman really well and was pretty sure that if he was here to chat about a dead guy, he had a good idea of who they should be looking at.

"You know how much I trust you guys, so I'll just say it. I have an eye witness, but you can't use her," said Freidman.

"What the fuck does that mean? If you got an eyewitness, then you need to sound the fuck off," said Stations. His blood was rising quickly, and Friedman could see it. So could Schäfer, so he intervened before his partner fucked things up. He knew that Friedman didn't do anything he didn't want to, so if he came to them it was most likely to help.

"Why like this, bro?" Schäfer asked. "First tell us what you have, and I'll tell you what we know."

"Well, for starters I know you're going to find her because her blood is everywhere at the crime scene. She's been swabbed a shitload, so it'll only be a matter of time, if you don't already know. This one is special. She's kind of a friend of mine. She's a good girl and she almost died, and she's terrified because of what she saw," said Freidman.

"Her name is Jacqueline Arreola," said Schäfer.

"Man, what the fuck?" said Stations. "Now you gonna just open the fuckin' murder book, too?"

Homicide detectives learn right off the bat to keep their cards close to their chests. For Det. Schäfer to give up information like that, even to a long-time, trusted friend, was a major breach of homicide protocol.

"Do me a favor and please tell me you aren't fucking her," Schäfer said to Friedman.

"Fair question. I'm not fucking her. She's just one of the girls on the track that I know and trust. She gave my partner a shitload of info, but I promised her we would help to keep her out of the loop. I'm talking to you now to see what we can do about not making me a liar," Friedman said.

"Well, since Herman here apparently doesn't give a fuck about the rules, I'll break it down for you. This has to stay between us, bud. You know how things work. We get caught compromising an investigation, and we'll be handling radio calls right alongside you," said Stations.

Det. Stations told Friedman that the storage facility had good video of the murder. It obviously had good video of Jackie's stabbing, too. They knew she existed right from the start and didn't know for sure, but assumed she'd seen the finish. The gangsters had picked her up and moved her out of video range, so the detectives couldn't see what she had been in a position to witness. The expedited DNA search popped up her name right away. Her rap sheet was what made them lean toward the pimp/whore theory. They just didn't know where she was. They had checked the ERs at all the hospitals, but for some reason no match emerged. The other gangsters at the scene were still John Does. She was the one they wanted and starting tomorrow they were going to canvass Figueroa and the other tracks with her name and picture.

Friedman pulled out the DVD from Centinela Hospital security and gave it to Stations.

"This is your shooter. He's a parolee named Big Sniper from Florencia. Not sure what set. Jackie doesn't know anything more about him, but she watched him dust off the pimp. Him and the other cholos saved her after the pimp had kicked her ass and stabbed her for snitching."

"What did she snitch about?" asked Schäfer.

"She didn't, but he thought she and her homegirl had snitched him out for pimping. He'd gorilla pimped them a while back, and me and my partner sort of intervened," said Friedman.

"No good deed goes unpunished, right?" said Stations. "Why them, bro? You've seen plenty of victims on Figueroa. What's in it for you?"

"Nothing. Well, maybe I'm getting old, and it would be nice to actually save just one or two before I leave, know what I mean?" replied Friedman.

"Before you leave? You got another 15 or 20 years left, home slice. You're our age—that's not old yet," laughed Stations.

"What do you want from us?" asked Schäfer

"You know who your suspect is now. Do him up without her. Tell your boss you canvassed the tracks and couldn't find her. Tell him she's probably dead in a dumpster because the shooter either killed her or left her to die from her stab wounds because she was an eye-witness to the homicide. If she shows her face in court, she'll be dead the week after. That gangster was old school and hard for real. Break down one of the other onion heads that were there for the show. Someone always talks. There has to be other evidence at the crime scene that links this to Big Sniper some-how. Find it … as a favor to me," Friedman implored.

"Bro. You're asking a whole hell of a lot. Fucking with a homicide investigation is serious business. We get caught withholding a witness, and an eye-fucking-witness at that, that asshole could walk. That would end me and Matt forever. Our careers would be over. You OK asking us for that?"

"We go way back, and I wouldn't ask something of you that didn't need asking," said Friedman. "I know this is a hell of a favor, but if you can solve it and close it without using Jackie, I'd like to ask you to try."

"I tell you what. We'll pursue the case as if we can't find her. It stays between us. We'll present it without her if we can. You've got to promise me, though, that if things start to fall apart, you will produce her and make her comply. We can always say we had been looking the whole time and just found her. We'll give you our word, but you gotta give us yours. Things get fucked up, then she comes in, stands tall in court and drops the fucking bomb. For now, she stays out of the book. Fair enough?" said Det. Stations with an agreeing nod from Det. Schäfer.

"And this conversation never fucking happened," said Schäfer.

With Big Sniper's moniker and gang in their possession, it wasn't too hard for them to work backward. In some ways, though, it was harder. They obviously had to keep their information secret until they could officially tie Sniper to the crime scene. People would ask questions. They couldn't use the video at the hospital tying him to Jackie and, therefore, the crime scene without giving up Jackie. They couldn't just run him on Cal Gangs, because an audit of the murder book would show they looked him up prior to establishing him as a possible suspect. That would never fly. The biggest problem was how to put him there by name.

The public storage video showed a partial view of the shooter wiping his mouth after he'd jumped the fence at the corner of the storage facility, as if he'd just finished eating or drinking something. Crime scene photos showed a 40-ounce bottle of Miller beer perched on top of a flat rock near some tall bushes that had a clear view of the cul-de-sac. Det. Schäfer had it tested, and Big Sniper's DNA was all over it. From there it was easy. The Cal Gang database gave them everything they needed to know about him. His tattoos, his homeboys, his clique and his entire gang history were there for the taking. Their supervisor was sorely unimpressed by their inability to find Jackie, but he did a quick about-face when they miraculously got a good lead from the DNA off the 8-ball bottle. In reality, it was still really good police work. They got in touch with his parole officer and had a warrant issued for his arrest. The 77th Street Gang Enforcement Detail snatched him up within a couple of days. Like any good gangster, Rudy Gomez, aka Big Sniper, refused to provide a statement.

They, of course, knew Sniper was the shooter, but despite the good video and the DNA putting him at the crime scene, the DA wanted more before she filed. It was night, and one old-school gangster pretty much looked like another in the dark, she argued. He could have been hanging out back in the bushes drinking a beer the night *before* someone who looked just like him shot a pimp in the face, she said. "Bring me the gun," she demanded. "Produce the girl in the video. I need a confession or an eye-witness."

Det. Stations asked her if it would be OK for him to invent a time machine, take her back in time, position her up on the roof of the self-storage building, give her some popcorn and a comfy chair, and then nab Big Sniper Gomez as he committed the crime right in front of her. Would that be sufficient for her to consider jeopardizing her 98 percent conviction rate?

Friedman was going to have to hold up his end of the bargain and produce Jackie. Det. Schäfer was reaching for the phone to call and give him the bad news, when Stations got off the phone at the next desk.

"You ain't gonna believe this, bud," said Matt, as he reached over and hung up Herman's phone. "That was the front desk downstairs. There's an 11-year-old onion head with his grandmother and a priest who want to talk to someone about a black guy getting shot. Said it happened a week or two ago by the freeway. Said his Uncle Rudy shot the guy in the face right in front of him. Sounds like the abuela took him to confession Saturday, and he spilled the beans to God's own representative on Earth. Seems Jesus wants him to do the right thing and roll. We're in business.

CHAPTER 24
THE SECOND WIN

THE MAN IN THE BLACK CHRYSLER 300 HAD BEEN IN MEET-
ings all day. He'd started the day at Valley Bureau headquarters, where
he'd attended a luncheon for a retiring commander. He'd always hated that
motherfucker and was pleased as punch to see him go. While the speakers
droned on and on about what a wonderful leader commander Zimba had
been, he'd been silently running through a list in his head. Who would
be an effective replacement? He'd never really had a good foothold in the
Valley, and this wasn't an opportunity to be wasted.

Then he had to be at an event in Watts. That was the price he had to
pay for being the "Official Community Liaison." He'd always hated Watts. It
was dirty and cramped. The people were low class, and the activists down
there were exceptionally shifty. That's saying something in a city like Los
Angeles, where activists of all types had their hands out. He'd been forced
to go to some sort of a fundraiser at the Watts Towers. He especially hated
that place. He could never understand how a sculpture made by some bat-
shit crazy Italian could mean so much. It was cheap and ugly and was so

poorly designed and built that the City had to spend a shit-ton of money just to keep it from collapsing in on itself. It was the pride of a neighborhood that had no pride. He always figured that if he gave it half an effort, with three empty cat food tins and some baling wire, he could create an idol they'd all worship.

It ground on his nerves how everyone vied for his attention and demanded photographs with him. It was like he was celebrity. The activists all wanted to shake his hand, and more than half of them stunk on ice. He always made sure to have a full bottle of Ghetto-Be-Gone in the glove compartment. He was positive that sooner or later one of those dirty motherfuckers was going to give him scabies.

By the time he'd managed to pry himself loose from the old ladies and cake, he was already late for his last meeting at the Mark Ridley-Thomas Constituent Service Center up on 84th and Vermont. It was an annual local businessmen's meeting, where he got dragged over the coals for every little thing that went wrong in the area. He was the guest speaker every year as was ordered by the Big Chief. Last year, there was some old asshole who owned a dry cleaning business just up the street and kept asking him about the deployment of department resources. He must have had family on the job or something, because he kept asking questions that hit too close to home. It was as if he'd been given inside information and prepped by someone who knew how shifty the Department really was. His questions were way too patrol focused for him to have come up with on his own. He hoped that the old coot was dead by now.

He cruised the 300 over to Imperial Highway, then up Figueroa to get from Watts to South Central. He knew every prostitution track in the city and was well aware that Figueroa, from Imperial Highway to Vernon Ave., was hooker headquarters. He could afford high-priced tail now, but there was always something extra exciting about buying it off the corner. He stopped just north of Colden Ave. and chatted with a hot young black girl who flagged him down. She was caramel-skinned and about 18 ... just how he liked them. He told her he needed to go to a meeting, but he'd be back in an hour or two. She said she'd be out all night and to be sure to hurry back. When he asked her how much she charged for half and half, she told him 100 even. That was a little expensive, but he figured if she was there later he could negotiate.

When he got to the Constituent Center, he parked in the pay lot (but refused to pay) adjacent to the north side of the building. He used to have a bad habit of leaving his car unlocked, but after it disappeared while he was in a liquor store one time, he changed his tune.

It had taken some explaining to the Big Chief how his City ride was gone with his gun and badge. I took just a bit *more* explaining to justify exactly what the fuck his car was doing in front of a liquor store in Lynwood right off the Long Beach Avenue track at 0145 hours. With the engine running. Of course there was no one in the car, he'd told the Big Chief. Such is life. Lessons learned: Lock the fucking doors. Take the fucking keys.

The meeting was another arduous exercise in community-based policing. He really missed the old days, when he could just tell people to fuck off. He had to sit and listen to each and every small business tycoon bitch and moan about base heads in the bushes and missing inventory and take-over robberies. The old man who owned the dry cleaner up on 84th Place and Vermont wasn't dead as he'd hoped. That son-of-a-bitch actually asked him if he had recently intervened in a felony arrest on behalf of the owner of a newspaper over on Crenshaw. The old man said it sounded unlawful and against department policy if it had actually happened. Said he was worried about the rights of the victim, and he'd heard that the whole thing went away because the newspaperman was a friend.

If I EVER find out that motherfucker Yasuke put him up to this, I'm going to have his balls in a jar on my desk for all to see, thought the man from the 300. *That's a fucking well-informed question. Too well informed. Finding out this son-of-a-bitch's source is gonna be that creepy cracker Capall's first assignment.*

He spent the next 30 minutes assuring the crowd that no, he hadn't intervened on behalf of anyone. This was the modern LAPD and not 1920's Chicago. Things like that just didn't happen, and if he found out how such an egregious rumor got started, he'd be sure to take action. One of the department's core values was "Integrity in All We Say and Do." It was his personal motto, and he lived it daily. Blah, blah, blah.

When he finally managed to extricate himself from the meeting, he was exhausted. It was nearly 10 o'clock at night, and he'd been going all day. He couldn't wait to get home for a cocktail and some sleep. He rolled eastbound on Manchester Avenue from Vermont, and as he passed Hoover Street he remembered that little light brown sugar he'd seen earlier down on 95th.

Maybe just one pass …

The black Chrysler cruised slowly down Fig. It was just his luck that the bitch was gone. There were a couple of other whores working the track, but not a single one of them weighed less than 300 pounds. He'd done some chubby chasing in his day, but the fat hookers were always nasty and rarely practiced what he considered to be acceptable feminine hygiene. You could usually smell them when they got in the car. It was disgusting. He'd not been that desperate in a long time.

Maybe just one trip up Fig to Vernon, then over to the 110 …

He rolled the 300 northbound up the Figueroa track slowly … like a panther on the prowl. There was no one out in the 60s. That was unusual because there were always whores out on 68th Street, right in front of the Prince Liquor. The 77th Street Vice unit had cautioned the workers at Prince to stop letting the girls use the back room to hide from the cops and to quit letting them trick in the small room that was accessed by the back stairs. It would work for a while, but then the vice unit would have to drop the hammer on them to make sure they understood. Letter of the Law ABC enforcement could be crippling to a business that made its living off two-for-one 22-ounce beers and single cigarettes. The Alcoholic Beverage Control laws were very ticky-tack.

In the long run, though, no amount of enforcement could stem the prostitution tide. It was as if Vice were sticking its finger in a dam. Eventually the dam burst and hookers spilled out everywhere.

He was nearly up in the 40s and about to give it up when he finally caught a break. On the southeast corner of Figueroa and 52nd, he saw a girl he thought would do nicely. He turned right at the light on 51st and then another right on Flower Street, just adjacent to the freeway. He swung around onto 52nd and hit the north curb just east of Figueroa. After a brief discussion through the window, which included a little word game and the showing of breasts and penis, respectively, the girl jumped in and they were off.

"Hey, Bone. You see that black 300 grab up that girl?" asked Friedman.

"Yeah, so what?"

They had been laying off quietly, watching Figueroa for the last couple of nights and looking for any sign of Showanna so they could give her the good news about Jackie. They knew she would be worried, and since Jackie was too fucked up to let Showanna know she was OK, they thought they'd handle that for her.

"Let's jack them up and see if the girl knows where Showanna's at. Whaddya think?" said Friedman.

"Done and done, bro. Go get 'em ..."

Friedman swooped the black-and-white down onto Fig from the north-south alley just west of Figueroa. They'd been parked just north of 52nd Street behind a low wall, watching the track. They caught up with the black Chrysler on eastbound 51st, just as it passed over the 110 Freeway. Friedman lit them up as they turned north on Grand Avenue from 51st.

"12Z4. Show us on a traffic stop on a black Chrysler 300, no plates. We'll be northbound Grand Avenue from Five One. It's occupied at least twice," Redbone advised communications.

Friedman offset the car, and Redbone approached the passenger side. The driver had already rolled down all the windows and turned on the interior lights, which clearly indicated to Friedman that he was either a professional criminal or a cop. He was hoping for a criminal. During his Vice days, he'd encountered several cops on Figueroa. He'd never book a cop unless he had to, but he didn't feel like dealing with the shame and pleading looks right now. It was always so pathetic. He didn't blame the guys. He didn't even care that they were picking up whores. He just didn't like having to deal with their begging.

Redbone gave him the four fingers, so he walked up to the driver-side window. The instant he hit the driver's face with his über-light, he knew his identity. He'd seen him too many times doing too much fucked-up shit to not know. It only took him a short second to realize he'd just won the lottery a second time. Friedman had been dreaming about this moment for more than 10 years, and it was simple dumb luck that it came to fruition. His mind was spinning, but he recovered quickly and his plan of action seemed to materialize right in front of his eyes. Thank God they didn't know the girl. That would make things easier when the shit hit the fan.

"I'm going to need to see your ID, Sir," said Friedman with a straight face.

"You don't know who I am?" asked the driver with a smile as he handed Friedman his California driver's license.

"I've never seen you before … should I know who you are, Mr. … Anderson?" replied Friedman as he glanced at the Cal ID.

"Well, I guess that would be Assistant Chief Anderson to you … officer," replied Anderson with a self-assured smirk on his face.

"Stay seated in the car and don't move, Sir."

Redbone couldn't see what was happening on the driver's side of the vehicle, but he'd already gotten the girl out of the passenger seat and was talking to her on the sidewalk. Friedman gave him the signal to cuff her up and a head nod in the direction of their black-and-white. He didn't know what was wrong, but something on Friedman's face told him there was some kind of a problem. He cuffed up the prostitute and put her in the caged back seat on the passenger side as Friedman walked back holding an ID in his hand.

Friedman unclicked his belt mic and motioned to Redbone to put his burn box belt recorder with his on the trunk of their shop. He grabbed his elbow and moved him to the front of the car.

"Redbone. Do exactly what I tell you 'cause we don't have time to fuck around. That's Assistant Chief Anderson driving that 300. When I get him out of the car, pretend you don't know him. Turn down the radio in the shop, and go put your burn box behind the driver-side headrest in the back seat. I'll distract the whore. It's time to make history, brother. We're having chief for dinner."

While Friedman talked to the girl as he prepped her seatbelt, Redbone opened the driver's side rear door and slipped the DICV mic behind the headrest before taking the seatbelt from Friedman and clicking it in. They shut the doors, and Redbone approached the 300 again from the passenger side. Friedman grabbed his mic and walked up almost simultaneously to the driver's side window, leaned down and looked inside.

"I believe I'll be leaving now, Officer. Give me back my license," said Chief Anderson.

"Step out of the vehicle, Sir."

"I don't think so. I'm giving you a direct order to give me back my license and let me go on my way," replied the chief.

Anderson either didn't know or didn't remember—he was so disconnected from the realities of patrol—that all the cops in South Bureau were wired for audio and video via the DICV. Maybe he thought they were

Newton cops and therefore from Central Bureau, so they didn't have DICV. They had stopped him in Newton Division, after all. Either way, Friedman knew, and he was going to use it to crucify him.

"Sir, you are being lawfully detained for investigation of soliciting a prostitute. Your order is unlawful and, therefore, per the LAPD Department Manual, I am not required to comply with it. *I* am ordering *you* out of this vehicle, and if you fail to comply with my lawful order I will use force to make you comply."

"Well," chuckled the assistant chief as he unbuckled his seatbelt and opened the car door. "I don't think there will be any need for force."

"Why don't you go ahead and request a supervisor over here, Officer … Friedman?" Anderson said as his eyes bulged slightly when he recognized the name from the tag on Friedman's chest. "So you're Friedman. I've heard about you and your partner from Capt. Capall. I see why they call him Redbone."

"I've already called for a supervisor," lied Friedman. "One will be here shortly. Turn around and put your hands behind your back, Sir."

The assistant chief hesitated for a brief second but changed his mind when Friedman grabbed his elbows and spun him around. He watched as Redbone slid around his Chrysler and smoothly grabbed his right arm, then slipped his boot to the back of the chief's right heel while Friedman pulled out his hooks.

This rookie oorang motherfucker is actually getting ready to leg sweep me, thought the chief.

"You gonna let your partner ruin your career, boy?" said Anderson to Redbone as Friedman cuffed him up. "There is no way this is gonna end good for you. All this is gonna do is fuck up your life. His career is over, anyway. I'm gonna see to that. You need to open your eyes and think for yourself."

"My partner is in the process of making a lawful detention for a misdemeanor crime. I am in complete agreement with his actions. I would ask you, Sir, to continue to cooperate with our investigation," replied Redbone.

"Suit yourself, you ignorant bastard. When is that goddamned sergeant going to be here?" demanded the chief as Friedman walked him back to the driver's side of their black-and-white.

"There is a supervisor en route right now, Sir. I'm going to ask you to be seated in the back of my vehicle for your safety while we wait," said Friedman.

"You're gonna put *me* in the back of a *black-and-white*?!" asked Assistant Chief Anderson incredulously. "You have lost your mind. This is the end of everything you've ever known. I'm going to end your careers! You'll never see your pensions!"

"Sir. If you do not cooperate and sit down inside my car, I will be forced to make you sit down inside my car. It will not be pleasant. Please cooperate with me. The supervisor is on the way. If you feel you are receiving disparate treatment, you can discuss it upon his arrival," said Friedman.

"Don't you threaten me, you son-of-a-bitch! I'll have your badges! I'll have your way of life! You've messed with the wrong motherfucker!" exclaimed the chief as he slid into the back seat of the black-and-white.

Friedman closed the rear door and set the safety lock. He pulled his DICV mic off his Sam Browne, tossed it on the front seat and closed the driver's door. Then he walked with Redbone to the sidewalk, where they stood near the passenger door of the 300, apparently waiting for a supervisor.

"What's the plan, dude?" asked Redbone.

"What did the girl tell you?"

"She didn't know Showanna. She said the Chrysler pulled up and the driver threw out a hundred for half and half. She told me she didn't agree to anything. He wanted to see her titties. She said he pulled out his dick and showed it to her without being asked," replied Redbone.

"Then we've already got enough to arrest him right now. Maybe not a conviction, but probable cause for sure. We're just gonna let them sit in the back seat together for a bit, then check the DICV later and see what they said. I guarantee that arrogant motherfucker is going to hang himself.

After that, I'm gonna get us an audience so Assistant Chief Anderson doesn't get to cover this up and make it go away. He's gonna have to do some explaining to fix this shit. We'll give them two or three minutes. That should be enough."

"You gonna call that supervisor now?" asked Redbone after a short time.

"Better. Watch this shit," replied Friedman as he hit the orange button on his ROVER.

Beep, beep, beep went every radio within hearing distance of South Bureau.

"All units," intoned the RTO, "officer needs help. 12Z4's ROVER has been activated. 12Z4 verify your location."

The first units to arrive were from Newton, but within one minute the street was packed with LAPD officers. Nothing brings the troops like a help call. There were units from Southwest Division, 77th Street and Newton Street. There were vice units, narco units, night detectives and even a couple of Chippies who had been nearby and monitoring the LAPD frequency. The 77th Street bicycle unit came skidding up. Friedman was silently hoping that everyone got there without getting hurt because he knew how crazy cops drove to a help call. He let the crowd get big before he broadcast a code 4.

"All units cancel the help call. Code 4, accidental activation only," was the broadcast from the RTO.

The Ticket

"What the fuck is going on, Friedman? You forget how to work your radio?" asked Sgt. Leinen as he walked up.

Before Friedman could respond, the on-scene chatter became overwhelming as their back-seat prize was recognized. Suddenly, officers were fighting for a peek at the treasure Friedman and Redbone were holding. Phones began snapping pictures as Assistant Chief Sterling Anderson squirming in his seatbelt, trying to avoid being photographed in the back seat of a black-and-white while sitting next to a hooker. His seat-mate was smiling and duck-lipping in every single photo.

CHAPTER 25
LEMONS

"OK, FRIEDMAN. YOU AND YOUR PARTNER HAD BETTER HAVE your shit together because this is a serious clusterfuck in the making," said Sgt. Leinen. "I will back your play if it's legit, but you and I both know it's going to get snatched from above in short order. If things don't work out in your favor, it's gonna end all of our careers. This motherfucker better be airtight."

When Sgt. Leinen had realized who was in the back seat of Friedman and Redbone's black-and-white, he ordered everyone to clear out. He had Kazan and Ponich transport the prostitute back to 77th Street after Friedman told him they had her for a solid 653.22 PC – loitering with the intent to prostitute. The assistant chief was yelling something at him from the back seat cage, but he wanted to talk to Friedman first.

Friedman told them what they had, how they observed it and what they wanted to do. He felt he had solid probable cause to arrest the assistant chief for 647 (B) PC, based on the statements of the prostitute and their observations. He told the sergeant that he would need about five minutes to review the DICV to see if they had any more.

"You're gonna gamble everything on the hope that he said something incriminating to the hooker?!" said Leinen. "You're a fucking idiot! You want me to back you on a weak-ass 647 (B) against the assistant chief of the LAPD?! Your observation and a hooker's statements won't hold water with the Brass or the city attorney. It'll be a CA reject and disappear. It would be a waste of time. I'll give you two minutes. I'm gonna go get yelled at by that asshole for *two fucking minutes* on your behalf, Friedman. If you don't give me the high sign, he walks right here and right now. Don't even think of fucking with me on this. If he doesn't hang himself with the in-car video, then I'm gonna trust you to back *my* decision. Fair enough?

"You got it, Sarge," replied Friedman.

Sgt. Leinen walked back to their shop and let the chief out. He walked him over to his black-and-white and took off the handcuffs. He asked Anderson to sit in the front seat so they could have a private discussion about how to resolve the situation.

"I don't know what kind of watch you're running here, Sergeant. I stopped to give a young girl a ride home as a courtesy, and now I'm being accused of soliciting a prostitute?! This is the exact sort of thing that gives our organization the reputation it has in this community. This is harassment, pure and simple. Thank God it was someone with credibility and not some innocent citizen who was having their rights violated. What do you intend to do about this?" demanded Chief Anderson as they sat in Sgt. Leinen's shop.

"Well, sir ... based on what the officers observed, and statements provided by the prostitute, it appears they had a legal right to detain you," replied Leinen.

"Let me make this clear, Sergeant. I will not allow this to happen. The Department will not allow this to happen. *You* had better not allow this to happen, or I will end your career. Do we understand each other?"

"With all due respect, Chief, I have exactly nine months left on DROP and then I'm retired. I'm not afraid of what you can or can't do to me. If Friedman and Obrador want you booked and they have probable cause to do it, you're gonna need to find someone else to break the law for you. I won't intervene on your behalf," said Leinen through clenched teeth.

Friedman and Redbone exited their black-and-white with huge smiles on their faces. Leinen knew right away they got what they were hoping for. When Friedman walked up to the passenger side of his shop and opened the door, he knew what was about to happen. He could see the green light of their DICV belt mics glowing.

"Sterling Anderson, you are under arrest for violation of section 647 (B) of the California Penal Code: soliciting a prostitute. You have the right to remain silent ..."

Freidman insisted that the chief be handcuffed and transported in his black-and-white like any other trick. Leinen acquiesced, over the objections and threats from the chief, and agreed that Redbone should drive the chief's 300 back to the station rather than impound it. It was a City car after all, he opined.

When they got to the station, it was eerily quiet. They parked in the booking stalls and were immediately met by Lt. Short. Sgt. Leinen had called him on the way back to the station to apprise him of the situation. He was not happy. The lieutenant had ordered everyone out of the station, including the front desk personnel. He had the station front doors locked and the lobby lights turned off. It was like a ghost town.

"Friedman! What do you think you're doing? That is Assistant Chief Anderson! Are you insane?" screamed Short as Friedman exited their shop.

"I know exactly who he is, Sir. He's an arrestee today. I have probable cause to book him for 647 (B), and I intend to. I would advise you to tread lightly right now, Sir. I would hate to see you get caught up in providing special treatment to an arrestee because of his position," Friedman said evenly.

"Uncuff him immediately!" ordered Short as Redbone walked over and assisted the chief out of the back seat. "I'm truly sorry, Chief. I'll make sure this gets handled correctly."

Sgt. Leinen motioned the lieutenant off to the side with Friedman as Redbone walked Assistant Chief Anderson toward the rear station entrance, still cuffed.

"Tell him what you have, Friedman," said Sgt. Leinen.

"Sir. We were conducting an observation post on Figueroa for prostitution-related activity. We were specifically monitoring an individual we believed to be a working prostitute on the northeast corner of 52nd Street. We observed what ultimately proved to be Assistant Chief Sterling Anderson's black Chrysler 300 pulling up to that same corner. The girl leaned in the passenger window and engaged the driver in conversation. She then stood back and exposed her breasts before getting in the passenger seat of the vehicle. We conducted a traffic stop and interviewed the prostitute. She told us the chief demanded to see her breasts, offered her money for sex and exposed his penis as an act of furtherance."

"That doesn't mean a thing! How dare you detain the assistant chief on the word of a prostitute! I would never sign a booking approval based on what you have! I am going to personally see to it that you never see the street again, Friedman," shouted Lt. Short before turning on Sgt. Leinen. "And you! You've always been too close to the officers to be an effective supervisor. You might as well pull the plug tomorrow and save yourself the humiliation of the complaint that's coming."

"Lieutenant, I've never really liked you. I think you're a suck-ass office pogue who would have been fired on probation if I'd had my way. Your unwillingness to back your officers in order to further your career is embarrassing but understandable, because you've never been a real cop. That being said, I think you need to rethink your position on this matter. Our beloved assistant chief broke the law. He is not special in any way. He is subject to the same standards of arrest as anyone else. Probable cause exists in this case, and that is all that matters. I've known Friedman for over a decade and based on his extensive Vice experience if he likes Anderson for this then he has my support," replied Leinen.

The lieutenant turned and stormed off after Redbone and the chief. Leinen and Friedman were close on his heels, but he was hard to keep up with.

"Thanks a lot, boss. That took balls," said Freidman as they trotted after Short.

"Don't start jerking me off just yet. This is far from over, partner," replied Leinen. "I shit you not, Friedman, that DICV had better be the smoking gun or we're fucked."

"It's better than you could possibly imagine. You're gonna be a fucking hero."

Friedman, Redbone, Lt. Short, Sgt. Leinen and Chief Anderson were all back near the holding cells arguing over whether or not the chief should be subjected to the humiliation of being housed in one, however temporarily. Capt. Capall followed their shouting like a bird dog and discovered his worst supervisory nightmare come alive. His sponsor was in handcuffs. His ass-kissing lieutenant had lost control of the situation. His most senior sergeant was taking the side of his nemesis—and that rookie Obrador was laughing.

He'd received the call from Short exactly 35 minutes ago, and in that time he'd managed to get out of bed, get dressed, drive to the station at Mach 1 (in his piece of shit plain-wrap Crown Victoria), and run the length of the station only to witness his career in a full-blown meltdown. He realized this situation required tact and a calming influence. It was time to make some lemonade.

"Officer Obrador, would you be so good as to go to report writing room A and make sure there is a fresh pot of coffee on? I have a feeling it is going to be long night," said the captain.

"No problem, sir."

"Lt. Short? I believe your duties at the watch commander's desk are being neglected. Please see to it," admonished Capall.

"But, sir…"

"Now, Lieutenant."

"Yes, sir," replied Short meekly as he slinked off in the direction of the WC's office.

"Sgt. Leinen, I think we were one supervisor in and one out tonight, and I just heard a request as I was walking in. Could you go handle that and then come back in and see me, please."

"Right away, sir," replied Leinen as he turned on his ROVER and advised communications to cancel the outside supervisor and show him en route to the request.

"Officer Friedman, would you please uncuff Chief Anderson? His alleged crime is a misdemeanor and no matter the outcome, the worst case scenario is he will be released on his own recognizance. He has no record and poses no flight risk," said Capt. Capall smoothly.

"I'm not so sure about the flight risk part, Captain," said Freidman as he unhooked the chief. "He was ordering me to let him go in the street earlier. I'm worried he'll be given a pass without having to answer for his crime because of his status as an LAPD staff officer."

"Obviously, this situation will need to be handled delicately," advised Capt. Capall.

"You are goddamned right it needs to be handled delicately!" screamed Anderson while rubbing his virgin cuff-wounded wrists. "I can't fucking believe you run this division like this! Your P2's think they make the rules! I make the fucking rules!"

"No, Chief. You *don't* make the rules," said Capt. Yasuke as he walked around the corner.

He, too, had been notified by Lt. Short, and he, too, had made it to the station in record time. The difference between a captain I and a captain III was that while Capall was driving like a maniac to stem the ebbing tide of his career, Yasuke was on the phone with the Big Chief. Real time Analysis and Critical Response Division had called the Big Chief at home and told him that they had been contacted by a sergeant from media relations. The sergeant had received a call from a source at a local Los Angeles AM talk radio station who revealed that he had video (and audio) of Assistant Chief Sterling Anderson in the back seat of a 77th Street black-and-white with a prostitute. The video was damning, said the senior detective who was the officer in charge at RACR. He hadn't seen it, but the source had played the audio over the phone for the sergeant. Media relations was of the opinion that there was no way to explain away the assistant chief's behavior. It was going public, and if they failed to act it would be an indictment of the entire Department.

It was the opinion of the Big Chief that those bastards at the League were behind it and had specifically chosen a Media Relations sergeant as a not-too-subtle hint of what could be expected if the Department failed to act accordingly. He ordered Yasuke to view the video, and if it was as bad as it sounded then ensure that Assistant Chief Anderson was booked for the appropriate charge and released on his own recognizance. The Big Chief would deal with him in the morning.

"Please try to ensure things are done discreetly," were the Big Chief's last words to Yasuke on the subject.

CHAPTER 26
AFTERMATH

THERE WAS QUITE A BIT OF NEWS ACTIVITY FOR A COUPLE OF weeks as the media sharks battled it out with the activist sharks. In the end, like always, things went by the wayside. The Big Chief quietly announced the retirement of Assistant Chief Sterling Anderson. Even the powerful machine that had kept the assistant chief untouchable for so long was silenced by the DICV. The only activists that rallied to the assistant chief's side were the "recovering" types. When interviewed by local news, they did more damage than good.

"Who doesn't like a little slice of strange every now and then?" demanded one.

"You tell me which one of you hasn't paid for some lovin' in one way or another?" proffered a second Anderson champion.

"Are we going to forget all the good done by this man because he couldn't keep it in his pants?" was Friedman's personal favorite.

The video and audio were damaging beyond belief. Even aside from the initial illegal orders and threats of retaliation all captured on Friedman's burn box, it was hard to stomach. The command staff knew what the assistant chief was like, but they couldn't believe he would be so stupid to as to hang himself out to dry with little backseat DICV gems like:

"We'll be out of here as soon as their sergeant gets here. You meet me over on Broadway and 51st in 20 minutes. I'll give you twice what we agreed for your trouble. When was the last time you made 200 for half and half, huh baby?

Or

"Don't worry, brown sugar. When I'm done with these two stupid motherfuckers, they'll be begging me to stop. *I* make the law. *I* decide who goes to jail. *I'm* the motherfucking judge around here."

Or

"What the fuck?! Those motherfuckers put out a help call! Friedman!!! I'm gonna kill you, you son-of-a-bitch! Don't look at the cameras! Get the fuck away from me, bitch!"

Or

"What's that box!? Why is there a camera in the backseat!? Is that thing working!? Oh, shit. We're in South Bureau."

Redbone had filmed the in-car playback screen with his cell and forwarded it to his childhood friend Leonard Ericson, who was an investigative reporter for one of the biggest AM talk-radio stations in Los Angeles. The Brass leaned heavy on the corporate executives at the radio station to try to force Ericson to give up his source, but he stood his ground. He knew he had the backing of the United States Constitution and its historical protections of the press, so he held firm. Everyone knew where it came from anyway. The reality was that the Big Chief was so relieved to be rid of Anderson that he told IA to just quietly let it go—for now. It could wait until things slowed down some. He even gave a sideways compliment to Friedman and Redbone during an interview when he acknowledged a question by a reporter asking about the status of the arresting officers.

"Their actions that night were in the best traditions of the Los Angeles Police Department. They put aside personal loyalty and made the difficult choice to arrest one of their own. They knew what the Law Enforcement Code of Ethics demanded. "Integrity in all we say and do," a core value of the LAPD, was clearly demonstrated that night. They are back working patrol on behalf of the grateful citizens of this fine city."

Friedman and Redbone almost peed their pants laughing at that one. They were at the bar in the Desert Room when the interview came on TV. They hadn't bought a drink since their coup d'état. Coppers from several generations had been stopping by the Desert Room to put cash down for drink tokens on their behalf. They had been receiving gift certificates, flowers, and thank you cards at the League office ever since the news broke. The 77th front desk looked as if someone had died, there were so many bouquets. Whenever they walked in a room, spontaneous applause erupted. Roll call was a circus. They'd told and retold the story so many times, they were already getting sick of it. Sgt. Leinen was being treated like a god by the officers at 77th Street. He could do no wrong.

In the after-action meeting with Capts. Capall and Yasuke, Cmdr. Boyle and the South Bureau deputy chief, Friedman and Redbone were roundly praised for their actions that night and their willingness to stand firm and take the hard road when confronted with a moral dilemma. In the after-after-action meeting with Capt. Capall, there was a slightly different take on things.

"If you two think you are going to get away with what you did to the assistant chief, then you are sadly mistaken. You might be heroes today, but I know who and what you really are. You can't fool me. You've damaged the LAPD organization with your unwillingness to be reasonable. You caused an embarrassment on my watch. You both have so many complaints pending that you'll never survive. I'm going to make sure of it."

Lt. Short was slightly less vitriolic but no less understated.

"I will put up with you for as long as I have to, but if you think this changes things, you are sadly mistaken. I would suggest you both stay out of my way from now on. There are several complaints pending against you, and I will not be tolerating any more. I have to keep you in the field for now, but as soon as I can, I'll be pulling you. While I'm in charge here on watch 3, you'll be heavily scrutinized."

Captain III Reggie Yasuke walked over to the commander's office and knocked on the partially open door. He was well aware that this meeting was coming, and he was dreading it. He knew for sure that Friedman and Obrador would never be allowed to survive snubbing their noses at the Big Blue Machine. They unseated the second-highest-ranking member of the Department, and that made a lot of command staff nervous. If a pair of P2's could take down Anderson, then anything was possible. They would have to pay. It wouldn't be right away, of course, but they could not be allowed to survive intact. Their peers must learn their place. Friedman and Obrador would be held up as a not-so-subtle example of what happens to those who think they can step beyond the natural order. Sgt. Leinen would need to go, too. His example was a dangerous one in the eyes of the Brass. There was a concerted effort under way by The Command to pick and choose new sergeants whose department loyalties trumped personal loyalties. Old-school leaders like Leinen undermined that practice. Yasuke was disgusted with the whole process but knew there was nothing he could do. To stand up would put him out of the loop and end his career. He'd sacrificed too much to give up now. Friedman, Obrador and Leinen would still get dispo'd—with or without Yasuke—and he knew it. He hated it, but he was a realist. He had to be to survive all these years. He knew how things worked.

"Come on in, Reggie," said South Bureau Commander Jim Boyle, cupping the receiver. "Have a seat. I'll be done here in just a second."

Yasuke closed the door behind him and plopped into one of the two comfy leather chairs on the opposite side of the business end of the commander's enormous desk. He scanned the walls of Boyle's office and marveled at the art work. It wasn't really art work, per se. It was more of an homage to the greatness that was Jim Boyle. He had LAPD photos of every ilk. Boyle with a helicopter. Boyle in tactical gear. Boyle with big "rescue" vehicle (read: tank). Boyle with Metro K9. It went on and on. They covered nearly every space on every wall. It was kind of strange. It read like a who's who and what's what in the world of the LAPD specialized unit.

No pictures of the commander pushing an "A" car, thought Yasuke. *No photos of him standing a corner on a perimeter or in the hallway of 210 Temple at 08:30 after working all night. No action shots of him taking a battery PIR or handling a traffic collision. I guess that kind of everyday police work is just a little too mundane to warrant a photo op. Funny how a guy like Friedman has spent his whole career doing the shit work of policing, with nary a thank you, and now they're going to throw him out like it never happened. I've known Leinen for 20 years—one of the best supervisors I've ever seen. All for nothing. These people could never understand the amount of trouble guys like Leinen and Friedman have prevented in their careers. How many times they didn't pull the trigger. The circumstances when they used remarkable restraint. The number of times they smoothed ruffled feathers before things went public. All the times they shouldered the burden without complaint only to be shit on later by Monday morning quarterbacks when everything didn't go perfectly. Just so we could attend the next COMSTAT meeting and brag about* our *accomplishments. I wonder how many people were promoted based on the work of guys like Leinen and Friedman? Most everyone, I would guess. What the fuck am I doing here? What am I hoping to accomplish—change? In this organization? The days of positive change have passed ...*

Yasuke was quietly mulling over his chosen path while Commander Boyle was busy yes-sir'ing on the phone. The entire command was in a frenzy over Anderson's departure. It created an unprecedented opportunity for advancement. The No. 2 spot required someone to die or retire before it was open. Anderson managed both—public career death followed by quiet retirement. It was not an opportunity to be missed, and every scheming pogue in the organization was on their "A" game. The obvious conclusion was that the rising tide lifts all ships. Lower pogues saw a lieutenant opening, lieutenants saw a captaincy, captains saw commander, commanders saw a deputy chief spot, and the lucky few vied for the assistant chief. All had their eye on the ultimate prize: the Big Chief. Many a climber surreptitiously sent Friedman and Redbone a heartfelt thank-you to the League—anonymously, of course.

"Well, Reggie," said the commander as he hung up the phone. "That was the South Bureau deputy chief. The word has come down from the police administration building, and it's just about what you would expect. Friedman and Obrador are going to be pulled from the field Monday morning at the end of their Sunday night watch and assigned home pending a Board of Rights. They will be with pay for the first month, then without for the duration. I'll be speaking to Bob Leinen personally on Monday. The chief wants me to ask him to retire quietly to prevent a media resurgence."

"What are the charges going to be against Friedman and Obrador? I assume the Department has come up with something better than 'Screwed Anderson with his own cock,'" asked Yasuke, momentarily forgetting himself.

"IA has confirmed the video acquired by Leonard Ericson came from their in-car DICV play-back screen. It will be easy to prove they released sensitive Department materials without authorization. That, coupled with their pending complaints, will be sufficient to support termination," responded Boyle with a sideways glance. He knew Reggie Yasuke had a soft spot for patrol, but he was going to need to make sure it wasn't affecting his judgment. There might be a call to have some sting operations applied to be sure his loyalty was in the right place. The South Bureau deputy chief was the front-runner for Anderson's job. Boyle would be damned if that vacant South Bureau deputy chief spot didn't come his way. No one was going to fuck up Jim Boyle's rise to the top. No one.

"You know, Jim, the holidays are coming up. The Department is going to put two cops out on the street with no pay right before Christmas just because they didn't follow an unlawful order. If they had released Anderson in the field, none of this would be happening. Does that strike you as fair?"

Loyalty stings were now a foregone conclusion. He wasn't sure he liked the cut of Yasuke's jib.

"Reggie. Fair doesn't enter into it. The integrity of the organization must be protected. You know that. Where would we be if a pair of P2's were allowed to cut the head off the serpent without consequence? This Department exists on the back of discipline. You know how important discipline is. If we don't make an example of them, where does that leave us? We must maintain control," replied the commander.

"I don't like it any more than you do," he continued. "When I was only a divisional captain like you, and I had fewer worries, I could afford to care more about the individual officers. You'll see when you move up, Reggie—the needs of the individual become subordinate to the needs of the Department. The higher you go, the clearer that becomes."

Shut your mouth. There is nothing you can say that will change his mind. All you are going to do is make a fruitless stand against overwhelming odds. You will lose, thought Yasuke.

"I understand," replied Capt. Yasuke. "It just seems that this whole thing could be used to benefit discipline. I think it supports the DICV and its relevance. You and I both know that Southeast Division is practically in open revolt right now. Morale at 77th is in the toilet. A big part of that has been our failure to follow the "Meet and Confer" agreements we arranged with the League pertaining to the use of the DICV. We've been coming down hard on every little violation by the officers. Internal Affairs has been using the DICV to add-charge chicken shit beefs to every complaint, despite what we've told them. The officers haven't embraced the technology because they view it as a "Gotcha." They fear it. We could use this instance to demonstrate our sense of fair play. They would see that it's a tool to enforce and reward good, honest behavior while punishing the unacceptable. Equitably. We could actually demonstrate we *really were* looking at the big picture."

"Come on, Reggie. Don't be naive. You know the rules as well as I do: Command never makes mistakes. Command is never wrong. Command never admits guilt. Command never apologizes. That's the natural way of the LAPD. Every time one of *us* breaks the rules, we end up looking weak to *them*. The troops must be led. Who's going to do it—some worn-out P2 like Friedman? Some washed-up, ambition-lacking, old-time sergeant like Leinen? If we don't take a strong stance here, we'll end up looking like we think what happened was OK. It will look like we approve. We can sell that shit to the media, but in our own house we'll lose respect. The officers under our command must respect our authority. There is no alternative."

"It sounds like 'fear' and 'respect' are interchangeable in our world," replied Yasuke. "It seems to me it would be better and more beneficial to the organization for the officers under our command to *want* to do what we ask of them. It feels like they do what we ask because they are afraid of the consequences."

"You can call it whatever you like, Reggie. The fact remains that you are going to relieve Friedman and Obrador Monday morning. The decision has been made, and you *will* follow orders. I'll be honest with you. There are a lot of questions being asked from above about your loyalties," said Commander Boyle.

Captain III Reginald Yasuke stared at him open-mouthed.

"My loyalties!? I have sacrificed my family and friends for this organization, all in the hope of being able to make a lasting difference. I have done every shit job asked of me for years. I have disciplined good, hard-working street cops against my better judgment because YOU told me to. I've done some of the most underhanded shit you could imagine on behalf of 'the greater good,' and you want to question *my* loyalties!? Where is your fucking loyalty?" demanded Yasuke.

The dam had broken. He suddenly decided he'd had enough. He knew things were over, but the realization was liberating. He was done, so he might as well let it all hang out.

"You worked Metro with Jim Leinen! How can you just toss him aside? Friedman and Obrador have been making good, solid arrests for years, and we've been getting the credit!" he spat, standing up as he pointed an accusatory finger at the commander. "You have been going to roll calls for ages, telling the officers that if they did the right thing you'd have their backs. You know this is wrong. Compared to some of the shit we did when we were young cops, these guys are saints. I know things about you that would make a hooker blush. You have balls of steel to take the side of the Department over honest men like Friedman and Obrador. Those guys did the right thing, and we're going to fuck them because of "orders?!" I'm embarrassed to be a part of this. I know it will never make a difference, but I'm done dancing to the Department's music. If you want those guys relieved, you can do it your goddamned self."

Reggie Yasuke turned and walked out of his commander's door and through the halls to his office on the working side of the building. He sat down at his desk and pulled out the bottle of Gentleman Jack he kept in the bottom drawer. It was late on Friday afternoon, but his adjutant always stayed late on Friday to avoid traffic. She knocked on his door, entered and set a cup of ice on his desk. She'd seen the look on his face when he'd walked by her desk and heard the bottom drawer open after he'd closed the door.

"Is there anything I can do for you, sir?" she asked.

"No. I'm actually real OK. Thanks for asking. I think my time is done here at LAPD, so you might want to start looking for another assignment. I'll do my best to help you, but I'm pretty sure that my recommendation isn't going to go too far."

"Oh, sir. It can't be that bad. Things will look better Monday morning, you'll see. Good night." replied his adjutant as she closed the door behind her. But something on the captain's face made her stop and think for a second: *Is he serious? What if I have to go back to patrol?* The panic started creeping in.

Across the building as he picked up the phone, Commander Boyle was laughing to himself about the foolishness of Yasuke's Last Stand. He was right about everything, of course, but that wouldn't stop the locomotive once it started down the tracks. The LAPD was a paramilitary organization, and orders were orders. Too bad, though. He'd had high hopes for Reggie Yasuke.

"Pat? Jim Boyle. Good news. I have a tremendous opportunity. As of right now, you are the acting command officer in charge of 77th Street. Well, you don't need to worry about that. He's made some career choices, and those choices have created an opportunity for us to continue doing tremendous work. Remember the mission. Here's the first thing you'll need to do Monday morning ..."

CHAPTER 27

DIRECTION

"WELL BONE, OUR TIME IS ALMOST UP. IT'S BEEN NEARLY SIX months…we're about due to implement the next phase of the plan. I emailed Henry this afternoon, and he said we can execute at any time. They've been monitoring the news and the Lotto websites, and there hasn't been anything about our win for a long time. Our pending lawsuit is handled and we're in the clear. It's up to us, but he thinks the time is just about right," said Friedman. "Whaddaya think? Have you had your fun? Is it time to ride off into the sunset?"

It was Sunday evening and they'd been clear of roll call for a while. It was getting dark early now, and there was a chill in the air. Long-sleeve weather for sure. Friedman hated the winter months. Los Angeles never got really cold, but Friedman had been born and raised near the ocean in San Pedro, and if the weather wasn't 72 degrees at all times he was uncomfortable. The early darkness, combined with the cold, slowed 77th Street Division to a crawl. It was nowhere near as busy as it once was. It had become a weekend division, only busy on Friday's and Saturday's, like most of the rest of the city had always been. Friedman hated that the crime rate was so low. It was just boring now. There was a time when 77th hummed all year long, every day of the week. Now if things got crazy and the Watch Commander declared Broken Arrow, the kids in the locker room talked about it at end of watch as if something significant had happened.

They were just cruising around the Division, standing by to pick up any calls that the mid-watches couldn't handle. Freidman and Redbone always figured that since they didn't have to handle calls for service (being a "Z" car) they'd let the morning watch "A" cars go eat right out of the chute. They usually brought their lunches anyway, so they could eat at any time. There was nothing worse for a morning watch "A" car than to get assigned a cluster-fuck child abuse or attack investigation right out of roll call. That meant no dinner, or a shitty fast-food dinner, because everything would be closed by the time they finished the investigation.

"I'm ready, bro. I don't really think things could get any better than the Anderson victory. I've spent the last couple of weeks or so thinking about it, and I really can't think of anything else I want to get done. I mean, there were a couple of things," said Redbone. "I'd really have liked to have wrecked the Chief's car, but that's no big goal. I think that rat-fuck Short got off scot-free, but there's a ton of guys just like him all over the Department. We probably should have made a more concerted effort to crucify Capall too, but again, there are 20 more Capalls in line behind him. We can't get them all. I think we've had some fun and made some points. Nothing memorable, but a couple of small victories."

"Small victories!?" laughed Friedman. "Nothing memorable!?! We totaled Capall's 300! We fucked over that Bail Bond asshole and protected the Blue Suiters from him in the future. I'm pretty sure that kid-fucker you got tuned-up at the front desk is still in the hospital. We saved a pair of hookers from their gorilla pimp…well, a cholo actually did that…but we played a part! We ended the reign of Sterling Anderson! That will never be forgotten!"

"Friedman. You and I both know once everyone who remembers that shit is retired, it will be forgotten. Can you tell me the name of a deputy chief from 1958? How about the captain of Harbor Division from 1976? Of course not. The Organization goes on, but we just fade away. The North Hollywood shootout was the biggest thing since the SLA shootout. Can you tell me who was involved in either one? Negative. All the shit we pulled was for us. It was for our friends. It was a small gift to the people who do the thankless job of patrol," replied Redbone.

"But there was nothing historical about it," he continued. "Our historical actions are still in our future. Think about it. People are remembered for great acts. Great acts of philanthropy. Great acts of will. Great acts of courage. With the cash influence we are going to have, we can do things that will actually make a difference in ways that will *never* be forgotten. I'm excited about the future — the past has been badass, for sure — but the future is pretty fucking bright."

"Jesus, Redbone. You're a real fucking downer. I'm looking at the positive side, and you're basically saying we wasted our time. I think I'm gonna get a mulita at 83rd and Broadway. You down? I'm gonna miss those for sure. I'm never coming back to the ghetto, so it might be my last chance."

They stood and ate their mulitas on the metal counter outside the small taco shop on Broadway just north of 83rd Street. The shop was popular with everyone from gangsters to cops, and the whole neighborhood was aware of it. It was sort of neutral territory, but since they were exposed to everything, they ate like ghetto cops do: with their non-gun hand and with their heads on a swivel. It was just how things were done, and it was second nature to both. They finished up, and Friedman threw a quick compliment to the owners in Spanish. They loved it when he spoke Spanish to them, and customers always looked surprised.

They hopped in their shop and drove southbound on Broadway to cruise the Division. There was a sense of saying goodbye as they rolled slowly through the streets. They could feel their impending departure everywhere, and it made them both feel melancholy. For Friedman, especially, there was a sense of loss. He'd spent the last dozen years of his life defending the 90 percent in 77th Street. It was his home away from home, and nearly every corner held memories. Some good, some bad. Many tragic, but many inspiring. He soaked in everything as they rolled. He thought of his friends and the adventures they'd had over the years. Policing was the noblest job he'd ever done, and he couldn't help but wonder what life after it would be like. He still held out hope that he wouldn't be fired and could stay and make a difference, but he knew that fucking over Anderson was probably the kiss of death. The Department would never allow him to survive after taking down a kingpin like the assistant chief. It just wouldn't make sense for them to let it go. He'd be held up as a working-class hero until he left, and that would be damaging to the cohesiveness of command. Even he could see that. He would be a permanent thorn in the side of whomever he worked for.

They rolled the eastside first, then rolled up and down the north/souths, starting over on Central Avenue and working west. Central, Avalon, San Pedro and Main. Friedman had been to thousands of calls on the east side in his time. He remembered being at a cluster-fuck of a homicide scene on San Pedro Street the night his second son was born. The crime scene was huge. It had been a drive-by on two separate groups of Swans, and the shooters had dished out death over a five-block strip. Friedman had been assigned by an asshole sergeant to do the crime-scene sketch. Normally, Freidman liked doing the crime-scene sketches because when the case went to trial he would get on-call court for weeks, but he knew he wasn't going to make it through the shift because the baby was overdue. The sergeant didn't believe him and told him to quit trying to duck work and just do what he was told. Friedman hadn't even started the outline when he got the call that it was time to go to the hospital. The sergeant actually told him to finish the sketch first then go back to the station to change over. Friedman looked at him and laughed. He handed his clipboard to a probationer, got in his car and drove back to the station. He never heard anything about it later, so he figured someone with common sense had spoken to the sergeant.

Friedman had seen his first shooting death on the eastside. Another Swan Blood — they were a gang of professional victims. It was a simple walk-up shooting that left a young black kid dead on the northeast corner parkway of McKinley Ave. and 82nd Street. He'd been strolling along, and someone walked right up to him from behind and popped him in the melon. Very poor ghetto survival skills on behalf of the victim. He crumpled where he stood, and his life drained into the grass. It was over a decade ago, but Friedman still remembered the sound the victim's mother made when she showed up at the crime scene. One of the old coppers called it the whale song, and Friedman thought that was pretty on the mark. She sounded like the amplified recordings of humpback whale songs he'd heard on the Discovery Channel. Her grief was palpable, and it was all Friedman could manage to not stop doing his job and walk over to console her. Those feelings of empathy soon numbed, as the number of dead bodies he saw multiplied. Within a year or three, he'd been to so many homicide scenes he'd lost count of the dead and the grieving.

Homicides rarely happened anymore, and there was an entire generation of cops at LAPD that had no idea how to handle a crime scene. In the view of the Brass, that was just fine. There would always be officers like Friedman who could help the new guys.

But not any more…not me, thought Friedman.

They rolled down Florence Ave. over to the west side of the Division, up and down Brynhurst and Victoria. Friedman told Redbone there was a time when if you made three or four laps on Brynhurst or Victoria, you'd pull a G-ride without even trying. They slipped over to the other side of Crenshaw Boulevard into the avenues. They rolled up 10th Avenue, and as they passed 6329 S. 10th Ave., Friedman remembered showing up on TV after using his baton on a combative suspect in the courtyard of the apartment there.

10th Ave. was Rollin' 60s Crip headquarters. A couple of Southeast gang cops were on loan to the Division for some reason or another, and they went in foot pursuit of a 60s gangster into the courtyard of 6329. One of the cops caught a bottle on the head from one of the criminal loiterers, and a help call went out. Friedman and his partner Thornton were the first on scene, and it was chaotic. The three-story building was built with a court-yard in the middle and walkways all around on each floor. When they came running in to help the Southeast cops, who were flashlighting their suspect in the middle of the courtyard, it reminded Friedman of Thunderdome. There were people lining the balconies all the way around, three stories up. They were yelling and screaming and throwing things at the cops. There was a group of 60s trying to lynch the guy the cops were fighting with, so Thornton and Friedman drew their sticks and waded into the fray. Most of the gangsters scattered under the threat of a batoning, but one big OG was emboldened by the crowd and stood his ground. Kurt stepped forward and started chopping him up like cordwood with his PR24. Friedman put in work from the other side, and they soon had the 60 on the ground and in cuffs.

In the meantime, the courtyard had filled with cops and the Airship had shown up. Friedman and Thornton walked their body outside and told the first sergeant they saw that they'd had a "use of force" with their suspect. The idiot was either too lazy or too stupid to know what to do, but after hearing their story he told them to not worry about it.

"It wasn't a 'use of force,'" he said.

Friedman and Thornton just stared at him dumbfounded. Even their suspect, who now respected Friedman and Thornton, tried to tell Sergeant Stupid that they'd had a "use of force." He just walked away from them, so they went and found a sergeant they could trust and told him.

What they couldn't have known was that someone inside the Thunderdome had had a video camera, and that two months later it would show up on the news. It came to light right after the famous Flashlight

Shampoo video, and it made Friedman and Thornton nervous. They both knew that as they watched the news, the Big Chief was reading their arrest report in his office. If they had listened to Sergeant Stupid, they'd both have been fired for sure for failing to report a "use of force." He would have denied telling them it wasn't a "use of force" and the Blue Machine would have eaten the P2s as an example to their peers.

They almost got you with that one, thought Friedman as they rolled up to 63rd Street and headed east.

Redbone hardly heard a word Friedman was saying. He wasn't really melancholy. He was thinking about his future. His *real* future.

He knew that Friedman had policing in his blood. That happened to a lot of guys right from the start, but he knew it had taken a long time to happen to Friedman. Friedman fell into being a cop, but it suited him. It just took a while to take hold. The Chief, Daryl F. Gates, was like that too, according to his autobiography. Redbone understood that Friedman was scared and worried about the future. Policing had become a big part of his identity, and without it he'd need to start over. He wasn't worried about him, though. Friedman had taught him most everything he knew about being a cop, and even if he had doubts about his ability to change, Redbone didn't. Friedman was a chameleon. He could change the inflection of his voice depending on who he was talking to, making the listener feel comfortable. He had spent the last 20 years of his life making people feel good about getting fucked over, and from what Redbone had seen, he was a master. The stories he'd heard about Friedman working Vice were almost hard to believe. Vice was a tough assignment and to be good at it, an officer, especially a white officer in South Central Los Angeles, had to be able to think on his feet and change at a moment's notice. No, Redbone wasn't worried about his friend; he was worried about himself.

Redbone didn't have policing in his blood. He liked being a cop, but it was an exercise in frustration. It seemed to him that the LAPD management was hell bent on making it difficult for cops to do their job, while simultaneously asking them to do their job. It was all so foolish, but it was a good job that paid the bills. Nothing more. He had mostly just drifted around life. He'd never really been passionate about anything except partying. He'd always had fun living life to the fullest, and he rarely worried about consequences. Just last year he'd been kicked out of a bar for trying to piss on a girl's leg because she wouldn't go home with him. He didn't give a fuck about anything except the here and now.

But in the last six months, things had changed.

After they won, he'd sit around for hours dreaming about how he was going to party. In his mind, he'd already bought boats, houses and cars — all with an eye on getting chicks and partying with his friends. He poured over maps of the world and books about places to see, planning the rest of his life-long party. He looked through real estate magazines and started shopping for houses for his parents and sister. He'd even made phone calls inquiring about buying an island in the Caribbean. He was spending money in his mind so fast that it never occurred to him that there might be consequences for living so lavishly.

But slowly, the reality of the gift they'd been given had been setting in. He thought Friedman understood instinctively, but for Redbone it was a growth process.

He wasn't a follower, but he often deferred to Friedman's life and work experience. He had been undergoing an awakening process that began right after they had settled everything with the vultures. It just took a while to fully materialize. Even now he'd go through bouts of what he thought of as "crack head purchase dreams," but he was settling down in ways that were beginning to make him feel awkward.

He had turned 33 a couple months back, and for some reason his brain kept harping on the fact that Christ had been 33 when he made his big sacrifice. It seemed to be the last possible youthful age to make a difference in the world. The rest of his birthdays would be milestones along a rapid march down the road toward death. The thought nagged at him. He had to start living.

Redbone had violated their agreement and told the BSS Head Shrinker he'd won the lottery. He figured the guy wasn't allowed to tell anyone, so it was a safe move. He just needed to talk to someone neutral who could help him make sense of it all. The guy didn't believe him at first — not until Redbone showed him a copy of the ticket and explained their plan. Once he'd been convinced that Redbone wasn't delusional, he got strangely excited. It was almost as if he'd never had an interesting patient before. He did help Redbone make some decisions about what he should be doing with his future. He asked the right questions and made Redbone figure out his own answers. It turned out he wasn't a typical city worker — he was actually good at his job.

Redbone had been doing lots of research about cancer charities. He'd narrowed his list of possibilities down to three, and when he talked to the Batts Brothers about it he was surprised to learn that they knew everything there was to know about one of them. It turned out they also had a sister who had suffered from breast cancer at an early age, but theirs wasn't a miracle story like Redbone's. Their sister had died far too young, and they had been channeling their extensive resources into cancer charities ever since. Their main charity of choice was the one Redbone liked the best (based on what he'd read). He'd spent an entire day with Brian Batts planning charitable scholarships for surviving children, all-expense-paid temporary housing for families during the medical-battle times, and helping to take part in setting up a charity therapy system for survivors that had long been a Batts Brothers dream. Brian also had linked him up with their personal charity that funneled millions of dollars into research for cures. Redbone's trust was already set up to make his first of many lasting contributions. He wasn't finished, but his desire to do something to acknowledge his gift was heading in the right direction.

I think I've finally found my meaning. It's only the start, but I already feel like I'm really making a difference...for the first time in my life. I wonder how the rest of the world discovers what they are supposed to do with their lives. Do they ever find out? Would I have ever found out? Winning a huge cash windfall obviously doesn't figure in to people's plans. Who gives a fuck? I know who I am and what I want to do. This is going to be a fabulous life, thought Redbone as they drove silently around 77th Division.

They had ended up down on Hoover Street, heading north from Manchester at 83rd Street. Hoover was two lanes wide north and south, and their shop was stopped at the 83rd limit line for a solid-phased red tri-light in the lane closest to the sidewalk.

On the east sidewalk just north of the intersection was one of the typical Hispanic street-meat vendor carts that were popping up more and more as the demographics of South Central changed. Some sold pupusas, the Salvadoran treat, but most sold tacos and burritos on the cheap. This one had a tower of Al Pastor meat topped with an onion. It was being cooked as it rotated by a homemade flame contraption. Definitely a total and complete health and safety code non-compliant operation.

Redbone glanced to his right and saw that the cart only had two people standing there, which was unusual for a Sunday evening, even with the cold. They normally did break-neck business on Sundays. He could see dark smoke coming off the grill and caught the smell something starting to burn. The cart was on big wheels to make it mobile, and beneath it he could see a pile of blue-and-white rags crumpled on the floor. There was a small Mayan-looking Hispanic female in a white hoodie sweatshirt and peach Capri pants standing at the north end of the cart. She had her arms at her sides and was just a little too close to the only customer, a late twenty something black man. He was talking to her, but it didn't seem like he was ordering food. It looked more like a conversation. She wasn't listening to him. She was staring directly back at Redbone with a weird smile on her face as they pulled away from the light. Something was wrong, but it didn't click.

They had driven about 25 feet when Redbone suddenly shouted, "Stop the fucking car!" and was out the door before Friedman knew what was happening.

CHAPTER 28

THE PRICE

THE MAYAN CHICK HAD PISSED HER PANTS. RATHER, SHE WAS in the process of pissing her pants as Friedman was pulling their shop away northbound from the limit line at 83rd. Redbone could see the spreading wet spot on her crotch as they drove away. His brain was in the process of disregarding that, along with everything else unusual about the taco cart scene, when everything clicked. No crowd on a Sunday. Burning food on the grill. The mound of crumpled blue-and-white rags on the ground behind the cart. The black guy too close to the Mayan chick. Her body language. His body language. Pants pissed. Something bad was happening, and Friedman and Redbone had turned the corner just as the shit was going down. Redbone figured it was probably a robbery, but he had no real idea what they had just stumbled upon. Patrol cops rarely did.

Redbone had his 40-caliber Glock out of its holster the instant he popped out of the shop.

"Show me your fucking hands!" screamed Redbone, as the Mayan chick dove down behind the cart, leaving the young black guy standing solo.

She had told her brother a thousand times. If they ever got robbed, he was just supposed to give up the cash without an argument. And he always had. Until tonight. Something made her brother take a stand. When the black guy walked up and pulled the small chrome gun out of his right front pants pocket, the other customers ran off immediately. The girl just figured they would have to chalk up another Sunday night's earnings as the price of doing business in the ghetto. She *really* didn't care about the money when she got a good look at the robber. She could tell right away there was something wrong with him. He wasn't scared. Usually when they got robbed, the guy doing the crime seemed more scared than they were. This guy was definitely not scared. He looked bored. That made her nervous. Her brother got pissed when he realized what was going on, and he decided he'd had enough. He refused to give the guy the money and told him to fuck off. She was in the process of telling her brother in Spanish that this was definitely not the time to fuck around, when the guy simply shot him in the face. One single shot. She could see the tiny hole the bullet made when it entered his face just below his right eye. And just like that, everything was ruined. Now she was holding her youngest brother's head in her lap as blood flowed out the back of his head all over the white shirt and blue apron he always wore while cooking.

The shooter was dick in the wind. He was paying too much attention to the cops and not enough to his only hope —the small Mexican chick. He thought everything was going to be OK when the light changed and the cops pulled away. He couldn't believe they hadn't jammed him up right away, but they must not have heard the shot when he burned down that smart-assed cook. He would have run, but he didn't even see the black-and-white until it was slowing to a stop for the red light. It was too late. Everyone seemed frozen in time. The cops, the Mexican chick and him. While they were all waiting for the light to change, he was whispering to the Mexican chick that he'd kill her first if she alerted the passenger cop, who was staring right at them. The shooter was so relieved when the black-and-white drove away that he was caught off guard when it stopped abruptly and the passenger popped out, gun in hand. The Mexican chick dove on top of the cook, crying before the guy with the gun could snatch her up as a shield, so he had no choice. He leveled his burner at the cop who was charging him and let fly.

"Gun!" shouted Redbone, as he opened up while heading toward the shooter.

The front sight of Redbone's Glock started dancing wildly before he instinctively slowed his pace and hunkered into a slower, more effective, shooting-on-the-move walk. He heel-toed smoothly, as his right hand held the grip of the gun softly and his left pulled in slightly to tighten his hold. He was doing his best to put his front sight on the shooter's chest as he smoothly pulled his trigger back, but it was tough going with his adrenalin flowing like a river. His training was paying off, though, as he could see round after round strike the shooter in the nine and ten rings.

Redbone didn't even feel the impact of the shooter's 25-caliber bullet, as it flew directly below his Glock and struck him square in the chest. It didn't even make it through his vest, much less his trauma plate, but it was a testament to the luck of the criminal. All criminals are lucky. The shooter was spraying and praying—no sight alignment at all. But he still managed to get off a shot that would have had a devastating effect, in spite of his lack of skill.

He wasn't going down, so Redbone stopped, sighted up and finished him with a failure drill — two more to the chest and one to the head. The last round struck the shooter dead center just above his upper lip, and he collapsed like someone had turned off his light switch. Later it was determined Redbone had delivered seven hits…three were fatal.

Then Redbone heard Friedman scream a warning, and there was nothing.

Friedman had no idea what Redbone was up to. One second they were talking about the future and then next Redbone was out of the car with his pistol blazing. The entire exchange of gunfire took less than five seconds. Friedman never even saw the shooter's gun, and by the time he got the shop into park and made it to the rear quarter panel, Redbone had finished his work.

He was just about to check to make sure Redbone was OK when he saw him. To their left and almost directly across from the passenger door on the east sidewalk of Hoover, Friedman spotted a black guy wearing an orange shirt and a big natural Afro pointing a cut-down tube directly at Redbone. He screamed for Redbone to get down, but he was too late. The shotgun roared, and Redbone collapsed like *his* switch had been turned off. Friedman opened up with his Glock 45 as the gangster turned and ran northbound on the sidewalk. He was trying his best to track him, but he could see the impacts of his rounds striking the buildings adjacent to the sidewalk, first in front of, then behind the fleeing asshole. Friedman ran northbound in the street alongside him and as the Shotgun Gangster made the corner to run eastbound on 82nd Street, he exposed his entire upper torso. Friedman pulled up short and let go three quick ones. He wasn't completely sure but pretty confident he'd hit him at least once. He ran to the corner and could see the asshole make the entrance to the alley on the north side of 82nd just east of Hoover. Friedman knew those alleys all ran east/west and made north/south "T's" on either end, creating a long, flat "H" if viewed from above. He followed him to the entrance and saw him turn east down the alley into the darkness.

Friedman ran back over to where Redbone was lying in the street. He'd seen enough death to know his partner was gone. Redbone had taken the full brunt of the double-aught buck in the left side of his face and neck. The puddle of blood that was spreading from his head was already huge and growing bigger. There was brain matter on his uniform. Friedman looked around and could see faces staring at him from every window of every apartment and house on the street.

He looked back down at the twisted form of his friend and reached down and closed his eyes. He'd never done anything like that before — lots of people died with their eyes open — but he couldn't stand for the last thing Redbone to ever see be a nasty gutter in South Central Los Angeles. Redbone's lungs were spasmodically sucking in air in short gulps, as his dying brain tried to keep him alive. Friedman had seen that many times, but it broke his heart to see his friend…his brother…engaged in a death struggle. While he watched, the gulping stopped and Redbone seemed to be at ease.

"I'm so sorry, Tim," said Friedman softly. "This is my fault…we should have left sooner."

His grief was palpable, but almost instantly it turned to rage. He briefly considered giving Timothy Patrick Obrador the Last Rites of the Catholic Church, but he couldn't remember the prayers from his youth and he knew he didn't have time if he was going to handle his shit. Mourning could wait. There would be a time to mourn. Right now was the time for vengeance. It was time to hunt.

He knew what he had to do. He reached over and grabbed Redbone's 40-cal Glock from his lifeless hand and stuffed it into his left rear pants pocket.

Friedman keyed the mic on his ROVER and said the words that no policeman ever wants to say:

"Officer needs help, eight three and Hoover. Shots fired, officer down. Send an RA. Male. Early 30s. Gunshot wound to the head. Unconscious, not breathing."

Friedman had an agreement with Redbone that most long-standing partners have with each other. If either of them were killed, the job of the surviving partner would be to shoot and kill the person responsible. Not take him into custody, but kill him. Friedman always told his partners that they would never be able to explain to his boys how their dad was dead but the asshole responsible was living out his years as a hero in prison. Even if the asshole got the death penalty, it would take forever for the state to finally carry it out. He would most likely get to plead to life in prison in exchange for the DA not seeking the death penalty anyway. Redbone agreed wholeheartedly. Most cops did. The Department would forgive a lot when a cop-murderer was dispo'd in the field by the dead cop's partner.

Friedman had no choice. He left his friend, dead and unarmed, in the middle of Hoover and 83rd Streets. He knew Redbone would only be alone for a minute, but if he was going to keep his promise, then he needed to hurry. He could hear the RTO asking for additional information and the Airship putting them en route, so he turned down the volume on his ROVER and sprinted northbound Hoover then eastbound into the alley after the Shotgun Gangster.

The alley was dark, and there was no sign of Shotgun. It was a long alley, and Friedman could see a garage light all the way down to where it T'd north/south near Figueroa, so either he was hiding or had broken northbound or southbound through the houses. He was pretty sure he'd tattooed him at least once, so jumping fences would be difficult. It wasn't for sure, but it was Friedman's best guess that he'd hunkered down somewhere in the dark alleyway.

The problem, of course, was that Freidman didn't have the time or resources to conduct a proper search. That meant he'd have to sacrifice his safety to make his best play at keeping his promise to Redbone. He conducted a tactical reload of his Glock to top off his firepower and started running down the alley. He could hear the sirens of the responding units and knew he didn't have much time at all. When they got to Redbone and found him dead and Friedman gone, they'd immediately start setting up a huge perimeter.

The Shotgun Gangster, aka Rayvon Semaj Thomas, aka S-MAC from 74 Hoover Criminals, was in a bad way. He was just supposed to cover his homie, Mad Dog, while he took the money from the taco Mexicans. They'd done it a hundred times before. He'd always known Mad Dog was crazy, but when he dropped the cook with the cops right there, his lunacy had reached new heights. Rayvon had seen the black-and-white coming up

Hoover from Manchester, and he'd tried to get Mad Dog's attention, but he was in his zone. He always got in his zone when he was doing criminal shit.

When Redbone started shooting it out with Mad Dog, Rayvon knew he had no choice. They'd eventually see him hiding behind the bushes and he'd be dead next. Everyone he knew in the hood had a story about 77th Street killing homies. He steeled his nerves and reminded himself that shooting a cop was no different from shooting a gangster. He'd done many drive-bys in his time and had done two walk-up shootings (both confirmed kills) on enemies. He'd never even been questioned by the police about them. It wasn't the shooting part. It was the red cop's partner that worried him. He'd seen him before and knew he wasn't some soft rookie fresh out of the academy. He looked like he had experience and was a lot older than Rayvon. He might be dangerous. In the end, he decided he had no choice. If he could get one of them, the other was unlikely to chase him because he'd be worried about his partner. All he needed to do was to get away into a friend's house. He'd shave his head, take a shower, borrow some clothes, and he'd be golden. But which one should he burn down? That was the million-dollar question.

He'd chosen Redbone because he figured that the devil known was better than the devil unknown. He was *pretty sure* Friedman was something he needed to be worried about, but he was *absolutely sure* he needed to worry about Redbone. He had watched with professional appreciation as Redbone put Mad Dog, a much-feared 74 Hoover Criminal Original Gangster, out to pasture with extreme efficiency in a very one-sided gunfight. It was like watching a movie, but in live, real-time. In his own hood. With one of his road-dogs up for best supporting actor. That cop had balls. Granted, he had superior firepower, lots of training, and the law was on his side. But all that shit didn't equal balls. He had put in work like a gangster and earned instant street cred. Rayvon Semaj Thomas, who thought all white boys were pussies from Orange County, repaid his bravery with grudging respect. He shot Redbone in an effort to affect his escape because he was afraid of him.

But he was in a bad way because Friedman had managed to pop him in the left shoulder just as he almost made it to the safety of the alley. He knew he'd taken a risk and would have to make about 50 feet of open ground without cover, but he had no choice.

He just hadn't counted on Friedman having his wits about him. Two LAPD patrol cops with balls. What were the odds? A gunshot wound changed everything. There was no way he was able to jump fences. He could barely lift his left arm. Now, even if he managed to escape, he'd need to get medical attention. He was pretty sure he killed the red cop because of the way he collapsed when he'd shot him.

That meant a *big time* search would be going on. He'd need to get one of his homies to take him to Las Vegas to get his shoulder treated. He'd have to get that done by tomorrow for sure. It hurt like a motherfucker, and Rayvon could tell it wasn't just a flesh wound. He was bleeding a lot. If it didn't get treated quickly, it would end up killing him.

A bit of quick reasoning and logical gangster deduction told him there was no way he was going to get away. He could hear the sirens coming. He was a full three blocks away from safety. Sure, he had friendlies in this hood, but he wasn't going to be able to get to them with his arm so fucked up. He was leaving a blood trail, too. He'd seen Metro out in the hood with their bloodhounds. Both of the Metro cops who ran those dogs used to work 77th Street Gangs back in the day, and they'd jacked him up many times. He'd talked to one of them about the bloodhounds and knew they could find a little kid by the smell of their socks. Following a blood trail was nothing. That would be easy. Rayvon Semaj Thomas knew he was fucked. He was going back to prison. This time for life. He'd be an old man if he ever got out. That wasn't such a daunting thought for him. For a normal person who had just ruined the rest of his life it would be, but not for Rayvon.

He'd always figured that sooner or later he'd get caught up in some bullshit and end up spending the rest of his life in prison. That was the gangster way. At least now he'd be doing his time with the mantel of respect that killing a cop conferred upon him. You gained instant credibility inside for killing a cop. He'd enjoy many perks that the other inmates would have to earn. It might not be so bad after all. He'd be a celebrity. Even the Mexicans would respect him.

He'd hunkered down in the shadows about three-quarters of the way down the alley. He was leaning up against a short stretch of ancient chain-link fence that some homeowner had put up between his garage and the house next door. Probably in the late '70s to try to stem the rash of thefts that the burgeoning crack-cocaine epidemic was already starting to fire up. He caught his breath while he tried to plan his next move.

Rayvon peeked around the corner of the garage and could see Friedman jogging down the alley toward him. He was sweeping the hidden corners of the alley with his flashlight and gun. Something made Rayvon shiver. This cop had balls…for sure. Either that or he was stupid, but his innate sense told him Friedman wasn't stupid. He was all by himself, and Rayvon could already hear the sirens getting shut down back near Hoover. He wasn't talking into his radio like the cops usually did when they were chasing someone. Friedman wasn't calling for backup — he was looking for the gangster who had just murdered his friend.

He lookin' fo' me an' he don't seem scairt. I'm gonna havta kill this muthafucka, too, thought Rayvon. *Fuck it, cuz. One dead Po-lice is good… two dead Po-lice is better. I'm gonna be a muthafuckin' Hoova legend…*

CHAPTER 29
THE NIGHT SUN

OFFICER RICK NOTHMICH HAD JUST EARNED HIS WINGS AS A tactical flight officer. He'd been trying to get up to Air Support Division for more than two years, but events seemed to conspire against him. He'd worked patrol in 77th Street Division for nearly 10 years and loved every minute of it. He was a transplant from Boston who'd come out to join the LAPD for some excitement and money. East Coast departments didn't pay shit and had been completely emasculated by liberal activists. He went straight to 77th Street as soon as he could because that was where the action was. Being only about 5 foot 7, he compensated by being yoked up from lifting weights, and he held a reputation as a warrior policeman who took no shit. His friends called him "185 lbs. of hate."

Rick had applied to and been accepted for a loan to Air Support as a TFO two years ago. Right before the transfer hit, he'd gotten involved in a "use of force" in the 77th Street Jail that made the command staff panic. He'd been booking an Adam Henry gangster who had tried to head-butt another officer while at the booking window. Rick punched him hard in the face with a closed right fist and rode him all the way to the ground. Then another copper hit the asshole with a TASER and the fight ended. It was all captured on the jail surveillance equipment, of course, but he wasn't really worried. It was a straightforward "use of force." Short and to the point. He'd been involved in many of those over the years. The problems began when Commander Boyle learned the asshole gangster had been handcuffed when the "use of force" occurred. Apparently, a handcuffed suspect didn't pose a threat in Boyle's world. Patrol cops knew better, of course. But to someone who hadn't had his nose broken via head-butt, or his knees taken out by a mule kick from a "safe" handcuffed suspect, the whole video seemed brutal. It actually was brutal, but brutality was sometimes necessary in the world of patrol.

Boyle was going to make him an example for the troops, so Rick found himself assigned to the 77thStreet kit room, handing out car keys and shotguns pending an investigation. His loan to Air Support was cancelled, and he was immersed in the disciplinary process. So egregious was his crime that he was directed to a Board of Rights because upper management didn't feel that a 22-day suspension (the maximum possible punishment that could be given by a captain at a divisional level) was sufficient. Boyle attended multiple roll calls and let everyone know it was un-tremendous to face-punch anyone — much less a handcuffed anyone.

So Rick languished in career no-man's-land for more than a year while the Department afforded him a "speedy" trial. In a strange game of bait and switch, several plea-bargains were offered then withdrawn by the deal brokers from Internal Affairs. The whole debacle was finally set for a Board of Rights hearing. Fortunately for Rick (and unfortunately for Boyle) the Trial Board was chaired by Captain III, who was on the DROP program and about to retire. He didn't want any more promotions from the Department and was free to actually evaluate the facts and come to a logical conclusion. He heard the case, and with knowledge borne of street fighting in the '80s, decided that a handcuffed suspect did, in fact, pose a threat. Rick Nothmich's actions were not only *not* misconduct but within policy and utilized Department-approved tactics. Not guilty on all counts.

That's when the phone started ringing. What passed for loyalty in the LAPD was a strange thing. Ranking officers would consistently stand by and watch a patrol cop get fucked by the system. They'd even call the cop and tell him they were getting fucked, but there was nothing to be done.

They'd tell him to ride things out and hope for the best. Every climber knew better than to run the risk of standing up for a copper before he went to a Board of Rights hearing. If one were to back the wrong horse, it could affect promotion later on. So instead, they waited for the verdict from the board, then backed the winning horse. It was the safest move. No one ever considered the effect of the process on the accused officer. When Rick's "not guilty" verdict came back, his cell started blowing up:

"Hey Rick...Captain Neverworkedthefield here. Heard everything worked out for you at your board. I knew it wasn't going to amount to anything. Had your back the whole time."

"Rick. Lieutenant Onmyknees. Congratulations on the 'not guilty' verdict. If you need anything, let me know. Had your back the whole time."

"Officer Nothmich? It's Sergeant Norisk Officepogue. My sponsor accelerated rapidly, and my head popped out of his ass, so I thought I'd give you a call and offer my congratulations on beating your Board. Those things are the worst...or so I've heard. I had your back the whole time."

Rick didn't give two shits about any of those calls. He was no fool and knew exactly how the Department worked. The only call he was looking forward to was from Air Support telling him his loan had been reinstated. The tactical flight officer was the guy who rode shotgun in the airship. While the command pilot was responsible for flying the craft, the TFO was responsible for basically everything else. He handled the radio, directed the pilot to the locations they were needed and operated the Night Sun (as the huge spotlight was known) among a multitude of other duties. It was a tough job and the washout rate was high, but there was no way he was going to fail. That would mean being sent back to patrol and subjecting himself to the system again. That sort of thing wasn't going to occur if he could help it, and when the call came he was ready.

Although Nothmich and Friedman had never been partners, they'd worked the same watch and had known each other for more than a decade. Nothmich had known Redbone since he arrived at 77th Street morning watch. When he heard Friedman's broadcast, it was like a knife in his heart. He knew right away that Redbone was dead. He could tell by the inflection in Friedman's voice. When he didn't come back up on the radio after multiple tries by the RTO, he also had a good idea what Friedman was up to. Rick knew what he would be doing if some asshole had just dumped his partner. He'd be looking to kill that fucker.

The command pilot knew exactly where 88th and Hoover was, and since they were over the north end of Newton Division when the call had been broadcast, they had only about a one minute ETA. While en route to the scene, Rick's mind was spinning. As they got closer, he turned on the Night Sun and started scanning the area to look for runners, but he didn't see anything unusual. They made the scene and immediately initiated a counter-clockwise orbit, which afforded the TFO the best possible eyes-on advantage. The LAPD Air Ship commonly stays in an orbit while at a scene in case there is a mechanical issue that causes a forced landing. An orbiting helicopter is easier to auto-rotate and gives the pilot more options in an emergency. A hovering helicopter tends to fall like a rock.

There was total confusion for 30 seconds. Nothmich could see Redbone's body as he lay sprawled in the middle of the street. Even from the sky he could see his red hair in the center of a big black puddle. There were three or four officers standing over him, and Rick was trying to raise one of them via the 77th Street base frequency. He didn't recognize the voice that answered, but he could tell that it was a rookie.

He told him Redbone was down and unarmed and Friedman was gone on arrival. He sounded scared. He wanted the airship to set a perimeter, so Rick advised Communications that he wanted a huge containment. He ordered responding Newton Division units to take up positions on the eastside of the perimeter starting from Florence, going west to Hoover and all the way south down the 110 freeway to 79th. He wanted responding units from Southeast Division to take all of Manchester from the 110 Freeway to Vermont Avenue and up the 110 to 79th. He had Southwest units take all of Florence from Hoover to Vermont and then down Vermont to Manchester. As units began to take up positions on the perimeter, he reminded everyone that this was an "officer down" situation. That meant total and complete lockdown. No one outside in the street. No cars in or out. No pedestrian traffic at all. Don't tolerate any movement. Don't take any shit.

The command pilot broadened their orbit to survey the perimeter so Rick could direct responding units to plug any holes. When they were making one of their orbits on the west side of the perimeter, over about 82nd and Vermont, a quick bright flash down toward Figueroa caught Rick's eye. Almost instantly one of the units at 83rd and Hoover broadcast a shot fired to their east. The pilot broke orbit and directed them straight toward where Rick indicated he'd seen the flash.

Breathe. He's here somewhere, thought Friedman. *I can feel it.*

The alley had a semi-new concrete drain running down the middle of it. The drain was almost three feet wide and fairly clean. The alley had also been repaved down each side of the drain within the last year. The city, in its infinite wisdom, had decided to spruce up this particular location rather than fill up the millions of potholes that plagued nearly every street in South Central. Very typical of a failed bureaucracy. It was on a list somewhere, so the alley got paved, and damn the logical use of resources.

While searching up the alley, Friedman's über-light had revealed a fresh blood trail crossing the concrete drain. The blood was so fresh it was still wet. There was a shitload of it, and the drops were huge. The trail disappeared into the blackness of the asphalt, but Friedman knew he'd scored a solid hit.

I got that motherfucker good. Bet I hit his brachial artery. If he's bleeding like that, he's gonna die in about half an hour. Quit fucking looking for him. This is too dangerous. He's still got that shotgun and the advantage. Broadcast your position, and things'll get locked down. Metro can come in and find his body with the dogs. He'll be dead and you'll be alive. Turn around and go back to Hoover.

But something in Friedman's sense of honor told him he had to keep going. He also had to hurry because the airship was going to see him as soon as it narrowed its orbit once the perimeter was set. He couldn't take the chance of breaking his promise to Redbone. What if that fucker lived? The doctors at California Hospital and Harbor UCLA were miracle workers. He'd seen them save guys that would have died for sure 10 years ago. He couldn't run the risk of having to live with failure for the rest of his life.

There were so many dark corners. Both sides of the alley were filled with hiding spots. Friedman was simply doing his best to guess which one appeared better. He'd sweep left to clear a spot, or sweep right as quick as he could, knowing if he guessed wrong he would get blasted in the back with no warning. His heart was thumping with adrenaline and he was scared shitless. Things had slowed down, and his mind was churning with thoughts of cowardice. It's easy to be brave right at the beginning of a dynamic situation when there's no time to think, but once things have moved on a bit the brain begins to act more logically.

Friedman started thinking about his boys. He started thinking about his parents and his brother and sister. What would they think of this vendetta on behalf a dead man? Would they understand what it means to make a deal with your partner? With a man who trusted you with his life? With a man who you trusted to do the same for you? Could they ever understand this type of obligation? Would they understand if it cost him *his* life, too?

Friedman stopped searching. He could hear distant sirens and the thumping of the airship rotors as it circled wide, but the noises seemed far away. It was almost peacefully quiet in the alley. He was three-quarters of the way down it...almost to the north/south "T" down near Fig. He decided to turn back. He'd failed. He was a coward. He had convinced himself that the Shotgun Gangster was hit bad and would die. He was already rationalizing his behavior to himself. No one would ever blame him. He'd done his best to kill the man who had killed his partner. He'd probably be a hero for having made such a difficult shot in the first place. Even if the asshole lived, he'd probably get executed. Only Friedman would know the truth...

What the fuck's he doin'? thought Rayvon Semaj Thomas.

Friedman stood facing east in the middle of the alley. He was directly across from where Rayvon was hiding against the chain-link fence, in the shadows created by the garage and the house next to it. He had the shotgun at the ready and was waiting for him to turn toward or away from him so he could get off a full body shot. But Friedman wasn't turning left or right. He was just standing there. His gun was in his right hand, on the side facing Rayvon, and his flashlight was in his left.

Fuck that shit. I don't have a choice, thought Friedman. *Redbone is dead. I can't change that, but if I don't keep my promise then what am I worth? I'd rather die keeping my word than live the rest of my life knowing I was too afraid to...*

The blast caught him full on his right side and knocked him off his feet. His Glock 45 and flashlight went tumbling through the night air. His right arm, from the elbow to the shoulder, took five of the nine thirty-two caliber pellets from the same double-aught buck load used to kill Redbone. Friedman's bullet-proof vest stopped the outside two of the spread pattern, with the front and rear wrap-around flaps that covered his sides. Two of the pellets penetrated his chest...one in front of and one behind his bicep, just over the top of the sides of his vest. The first punctured his right lung and ricocheted around a bit, devastating everything in its path. The second travelled along the back of one of his superior ribs and lodged in a thoracic vertebra. He spun half way around in the air and landed flat on his back. He'd had the wind knocked out of him, and when he sucked in hard it felt like hot lava burning a path straight through his chest.

Rayvon "S-MAC" Thomas was not a planner. He'd wracked a round into the chamber after he shot Redbone, but it never dawned on him that he wouldn't be able to do it again after he'd been shot. In the end it didn't matter. His left arm was so weak he couldn't keep a hold of the fore grip of the tube, so when he pulled the trigger and blasted Friedman, the recoil kicked the gun clean out of his hands. He could hear Friedman struggling to breathe as he searched the ground of the dark alley for his shotgun. When he finally found it, he picked it up and turned toward Friedman, ready to finish him off. Then everything lit up.

The command pilot steered their ship directly to where Rick said he saw the flash and pulled up in a hover. The Night Sun lit up the alley, and the scene below Rick and the pilot was terrifying. They could see Friedman lying on his back and a black man in an orange shirt standing over him, attempting to work the action on a cut-down shotgun. The gangster stopped working the gun and looked up at the blinding light and the over-whelming thumping of the rotors from the low-flying helicopter. As the pilot and Rick watched, Friedman rolled onto his right side, reached into his back pocket, and came up with a pistol in his left hand. The Shotgun Gangster looked back down at Friedman and saw he'd been had, dead to rights. He let the shotgun slip from his grasp and fall to the ground. He lifted his hands in the air, adopting the posture of surrender.

Rick looked over to the command pilot, a crusty old dog with 30-plus years on, and turned off the Night Sun. The command pilot nodded and took them into their customary counter-clockwise orbit. The dark alley below them lit up with bright staccato muzzle flashes, as Rick broadcast a help call to Friedman's location.

EPILOGUE

FRIEDMAN OPENED HIS EYES AND SCANNED THE ROOM. HE was confused. He had no idea where he was. His whole body hurt, but he couldn't pin down the source of the pain. It was overwhelming. His throat was on fire, and as he moved his tongue around his mouth it felt raw everywhere. Every time he took a breath, it felt as if he was being stabbed in the chest. The air he drew in seemed superheated. His brain finally told him he was in a hospital somewhere, and for a brief moment he hoped it wasn't a county hospital. He didn't want to have a kidney removed by mistake or die of a staph infection.

Then it hit him. He wasn't dead.

He couldn't remember how he ended up in the hospital, but as he lay in the bed organizing his thoughts, little bits and pieces of the story began to come to him. He remembered kneeling down over Redbone and closing his eyes. *He* must be dead.

A wave of grief flooded over him.

He recalled running down a dark alley. He remembered the pain of rolling on his side and freeing a gun from his back pocket. Redbone's gun. The Night Sun and the whoomp, whoomp, whoomp of the helicopter. The look of surprise on that asshole's face when the muzzle flashes lit him up. He remembered riding in an ambulance and the sirens. The bright lights in his eyes, like in the dentist's chair. The pain.

He closed his eyes and tried to remember more, but his thoughts weren't clear. Had his boys been in the room? That would've been impossible. They were in South America. His brain gave him a flash of Father Casey putting oil on his head and praying quietly in his ear. His parents. His brother and sister. He vaguely recalled uniforms in the room. Sergeant Leinen. Captain Yasuke. He could hear the Big Chief saying something. How long had he been in the hospital?

He remembered the ticket.

He lay in bed thinking. He thought about the things he'd done and seen during his years as a police officer with the Los Angeles Police Department. The arrests. The uses-of-force. The foot pursuits. The car chases. The victims. The suspects. The injuries. The death…he'd seen too much death. It was always lurking. The death was always there…never far from a police officer's thoughts and deeds. He was so tired of it all. But he loved it just the same. It was a part of him now.

The 77th Street motto, emblazoned on their challenge coin, suddenly crowded into his thoughts: Impavidus Bellator. *Fearless Warrior.*

He remembered the fear for sure. He wondered if the warrior cops were afraid sometimes. He knew the weak ones were always afraid.

He felt embarrassment because he knew he'd been weak and afraid.

Friedman had no idea what his future held. He didn't know the extent of his injuries. He couldn't tell where or what was hurt. He didn't know how long he'd been in the hospital or when he'd be getting out. He didn't know if his career was over or even if he wanted it to be over. There was total uncertainty.

But he knew one thing for sure…

His life had just begun.

The End